More Praise for

BRIDE

of

NEW

FRANCE

"A meticulously researched, lyrical tale. . . . *Bride of New France* succeeds in bringing history to life. Laure Beauséjour's story adds a great deal to our understanding of the period."

—Monique Polak, *National Post*

"Laure's voice is the backbone of this story and it is a strong one. . . . The setting may be essential for this story but it is in the relationships between characters that readers will feel themselves swept away." —Christa Seeley, *Winnipeg Review*

"Laure never surrenders to despair in Desrochers' grim, yet thoroughly enjoyable tale." —Jo Ann Butler,
Historical Novels Review

"Vivid historical background." —*Kirkus Reviews*

"Fans of historical novels that look for colour and romance will . . . enjoy this novel." —Michel Basilières, *Toronto Star*

"Suzanne Desrochers weaves together history and fiction to dramatize the life of one imagined *fille du roi*, Laure Beausejour. . . . [The] descriptions are vivid and unforgiving; any romantic notions the reader may harbour about pre-revolutionary Paris disappear. . . . Desrochers has given history's silent *filles du roi* a voice."
—Christina Decarie, *Quill and Quire*

BRIDE
of
NEW
FRANCE

BRIDE

of

NEW

FRANCE

SUZANNE
DESROCHERS

W. W. Norton & Company
New York • London

To Rod and our son, Julien

For information about permission to reproduce selections from this book,
write to Permissions, W. W. Norton & Company, Inc.,
500 Fifth Avenue, New York, NY 10110

For information about special discounts for bulk purchases, please contact
W. W. Norton Special Sales at specialsales@wwnorton.com or 800-233-4830

Manufacturing by Courier Westford
Production manager: Julia Druskin

Library of Congress Cataloging-in-Publication Data

Desrochers, Suzanne, 1976–
Bride of New France / Suzanne Desrochers. — 1st American ed.
    p. cm.
ISBN 978-0-393-07337-9 (hardcover)
1. Filles du roi—Fiction. 2. Canada—History—To 1763 (New France)—
Fiction. I. Title.
PR9199.4.D488B75 2012
813'.6—dc23

2012017364

ISBN 978-0-393-34585-8 pbk.

W. W. Norton & Company, Inc.
500 Fifth Avenue, New York, N.Y. 10110
www.wwnorton.com

W. W. Norton & Company Ltd.
Castle House, 75/76 Wells Street, London W1T 3QT

1 2 3 4 5 6 7 8 9 0

*But what shall I tell you of migrations when in this
empty sky the precise ghosts of departed summer birds
still trace old signs.*

Leonard Cohen

"THE SPARROWS," IN *LET US COMPARE MYTHOLOGIES*

Prologue

The sound of hooves on stone reaches the family huddled in the rain. The man, an actor and street performer, is singing, "*Un campagnard bon ménager, trouvant que son cheval faisait trop de dépense, entreprit, quelle extravagance! De l'instruire à ne point manger*"—A good country householder, finding that his horse was costing too much, attempted, what an extravagance!, to teach the beast not to eat. But as the raid draws closer to their hiding spot, the words die in his throat. He pulls his daughter to his chest. He hugs her tightly the way he sometimes does when he teases her, only this time he doesn't let go, doesn't loosen his grip. Instead, he wraps his cloak around her little figure, trying to make her disappear the way the words of his song faded away into the air moments earlier.

The child squirms a little, letting out a whimper as she turns her head to breathe. She is too young to recognize the sour smell of her father's woollen cloak as something unpleasant, disdainful to others. She accepts the scratchy material against her cheek just as easily as she falls asleep when the hollowness of her stomach makes it difficult to stay awake. She does not yet know that this man, who lifts her high above his head with ease, who fills the air around her with melody, cannot protect her from every danger.

The girl's mother, who sits wrapped in a blanket beside them, doesn't sing. The look on her face suggests she has already begun to withdraw from the world. Her cheeks are sunken and dark. The hooves grow nearer and a frightening voice spurs them on. The archers are checking every corner tonight, determined to find even those who normally remain hidden in the alleyways. Three years have passed since the 1656 decree to clean the streets, and there are still too many beggars in Paris. Too many troublesome sights for the young King and his regents.

The woman looks up at her husband, her features angry and old. It is the same way she looks at him when she is forced to prepare the body of a rat over a fire and feed morsels of its flesh into the mouth of her daughter, who doesn't know any better. The hooves finally stop and the family sees the warm breath of the horses in front of them. It has come to this, the mother says to her husband without uttering a word, just as I knew it would.

The questions come quickly when first one, then two more archers reach the family, their horses protesting against the sudden halt. Don't you know the King's rules? There are to be no more beggars on the streets of Paris.

I am not a beggar, sir, I am a performer.

And what has happened to your audience tonight? The archer's gloved hand cuts through the darkness that is all around them save for the glow of his lantern.

They have gone home.

And you should have as well. Very resourceful for a country man to have remained hidden in the city all this time.

The poor man is ordered to stand up. He can no longer hide the little girl. She squirms out of his coat. Noticing the child, the archer dismounts.

The kingdom can use children, even those of beggars. He brings the lantern close to her pale cheek and she blinks against its brightness, turning her head into her father's chest.

The mother stands up. You're right. This man is a beggar. Take him. Leave me with my daughter and I will bring her back to our farm in Picardie. We'll leave first thing in the morning. You won't ever see us in the city again.

The archer, looking at the child, ignores the woman, although one of his companions takes an interest in the youthful voice and the lingering traces of her beauty.

What will you do once we get rid of your husband? the second archer asks. It's very dangerous for a woman to travel alone.

He dismounts and joins his companion beside the father and his daughter. The third archer remains on his horse, but keeps his eye on the man and his little girl.

Don't be afraid, the first archer says to the child, reaching to stroke her hair. The girl begins to cry as if she finally understands what is happening. Her wail cannot be contained and only grows louder as the archer pulls her from her father's chest. One of the horses nickers and paws at the wet stone as the girl is wrenched away. Once he has taken the child, the archer is quick to mount his horse again. The other two struggle to hold back the parents. The girl's screams travel far in the quiet darkness as she is taken away.

The two remaining archers wait until the retreating child's voice and the hooves of the horse become a distant echo, an imagined sound, before they begin the long walk to the edge of Paris to banish the girl's parents.

The smell of her father's body lingers in her nostrils as she travels through the city in the uniformed arms of the strange man. The warmth of her father's chest, the words of his songs, these are the things she tries to hold onto as they ride.

The following morning, she is brought to the women at the Salpêtrière Hospital. Along with the other found children her head is shaved, and she is bathed, deloused, put into a stiff linen dress, and brought to the Enfant-Jésus dormitory. She is asked if she knows how to pray, if she knows who God is. Strange incantations are uttered to her and the other children. She listens as some of the older girls repeat the words in monotone voices. These are nothing like the songs of her father. She tries to recall the lyrics to his songs, the strength of his voice carrying the tune over her head. *Charmé d'une pensée et si rare et si fine, petit à petit il réduit sa bête à jeûner jour et nuit*—Enthralled by such a rare and fine idea, little by little he made his beast fast day and night … It is no use. Those times, retreating further into the past, have turned into the stone walls around her.

Part One

The Salpêtrière was what it had always been: a kind of feminine inferno, a città dolorosa *confining 4000 incurable or mad women. It was a nightmare in the midst of Paris.*

—GEORGES DIDI-HUBERMAN,
INVENTION OF HYSTERIA

1

*T*he commotion in the courtyard below reaches Laure when she steps into the Sainte-Claire dormitory. There is only Mireille lying in the long room of tightly made beds when Laure enters with Madeleine. The two girls have been given special permission by the dormitory governess to sit with their sick friend for a few minutes before returning to their needlework lessons. Laure doesn't really believe that Mireille is ill and refuses to show her any sympathy. She knows that Mireille is just trying to get out of her last month in the workshop. Mireille found out last week that she was going to marry an officer stationed in Canada. He is a young and handsome man and wealthy enough that Mireille will not ever have to return to the Salpêtrière. While Laure has been struggling to learn new *point de France* stitches, Mireille has been feigning sickness, the distant soldier's locket tucked under her pillow. Still, Laure is happy to have an excuse to come up to the empty dormitory. With no officers around, she can talk freely without being hushed or told to start reciting the Pater Noster.

Madeleine rushes past the window toward Mireille's bed at the end of the room. She has brought with her, in the pocket of her dress, an ounce of salted butter that she saved from lunch. She takes out the melting pad and brings it to Mireille's lips.

"Why are you feeding her your lunch? She already gets wine and meat with her pension." Laure can't stand to look at Madeleine fussing over Mireille as if she were a blind kitten in need of milk. How can she be the one getting attention when she already has more than the others? Laure walks to the window and looks down at the dozens of people gathered in the courtyard of the Maison de la Force. They have come today to watch the city's prostitutes being transferred to the Salpêtrière.

The girls of the Sainte-Claire dormitory are forbidden to observe these women. Even mentioning them is punishable. The administrators say that observing the prostitutes will taint the morals of the *Bijoux*. They fear that the years of shaping these carefully selected orphans will be lost by one glance at the ill-reputed women. The Superior herself has told them that their melodic voices singing *Ave Maris Stella* and *Veni Creator* will be spoiled, and that the stitches the *Bijoux*' fingers have been trained to produce in imitation of Venetian lace will unravel in the coarse company of the *filles de mauvaise vie*.

Laure knows she wouldn't be a resident of the Sainte-Claire dormitory at all if it hadn't been for the years she spent being refined in the house of Madame d'Aulnay. Seeing the prostitutes gathered by the archers and the crowd that has come to jeer at them reminds Laure that even the *Bijoux* dormitory of the Salpêtrière, where girls are taught skills, is still a division of the most miserable institution of the kingdom. To those who are not imprisoned within its walls, the Salpêtrière is nothing but a place to lock away the most wretched women of France.

"Madeleine, half of Paris is in the courtyard. We can finally watch the prostitutes being brought in."

Madeleine's gentle voice pauses in her recitation of the Pater. Laure waits, but after a moment the girl restarts the prayer from the beginning. Whereas Laure is considered a *Bijou* because of the swiftness of her fingers and the sharpness of her wit, Madeleine is among the favourites of the hospital because she is gentle and kind. The officers must watch over Laure, but they say that Madeleine sets an example for all the lost souls and fallen women of the hospital. Although the tiny girl is but a sheep herself, the officers try to make her a shepherd. They ask Madeleine to read from the giant prayer books at the front of the dormitory. Her voice emerges as the weak murmuring of a distant angel, and the girls hold their breath so they can hear it better. Laure has known Madeleine, her only friend among the girls of Sainte-Claire, since the day she returned to the Salpêtrière at fourteen years old, following her stay with Madame d'Aulnay.

When Laure was ten, Madame d'Aulnay came to the Enfant-Jésus dormitory in search of a servant girl. The children were accustomed to seeing wealthy women walking between their beds, inspecting the *marchandise*, in hopes of finding a girl who could wash and mend clothes, clean floors and scrub pots. Although Laure was afraid, having heard that some mistresses beat their servants with sticks, still she hoped to be chosen. She wanted to go away with one of these wealthy women, to travel by horse, and to see the city beyond the walls of the hospital.

Madame d'Aulnay, who wore bright *fard* on her cheeks and feathers in her hat, stopped in front of Laure's bed and exclaimed that this was the urchin she wanted. The entire way to her *appartement*, through the filthy and fascinating city,

Madame d'Aulnay prattled on about Laure's pale complexion and black hair and about all the things she would show her about life outside the hospital walls. Laure felt like her chest would burst. Before long, Madame d'Aulnay acquired an *abécédaire* from one of the women in her salon whose children had already grown. Madame d'Aulnay said that Laure would need to learn to read so she could teach her own children one day. Laure had just turned eleven and was not thinking in the least about having children or falling in love. But these two things, finding love and having children, were the central preoccupations of Madame d'Aulnay, although she was not married and was too old to have children. But Laure didn't mind all this talk about husbands and babies so long as it meant she could learn to read the marks, called letters, embroidered on the *abécédaire*.

Laure soon memorized them all. The letters were no different from the patterns she was taught to sew in the dormitory, the butterflies, the flowers, the birds, branches, and leaves. She quickly learned the precise shape of each of them. Before long, Laure had moved on to syllables and was soon sounding out familiar prayers and hymns in Latin.

Laure's most important task in the *appartement* was to serve the women at Madame d'Aulnay's weekly salon. Madame's other servant, Belle, who was mean, and frightened even Madame d'Aulnay, had no desire to interact with the women she referred to as the Wednesday Fools. Laure was slow and clumsy in the kitchen, so she just watched Belle, who was strong and quick, as she prepared syrupy cakes, jams, and butter breads. When the trays were laden with sweets and cut fruits, Laure carried them out to the women.

The guests treated Laure like a doll. They would say that with her complexion, it was unfortunate she was born so low in rank. But isn't it the way, one of the women said, that the girls with the most beautiful faces are always poor and soon ravaged by it while wealthy women, who have the means to afford powders and perfumes, fine clothing and *une vie aisée*, have only mediocre features to begin with. The women even dressed Laure in some of Madame d'Aulnay's dresses and coats, but she always ended up looking like a puppy beneath the heavy materials. Of course not all the Wednesday women approved of this play with a mere servant girl, especially those who had daughters of their own who were not so pretty.

Once Laure had learned to read, Madame d'Aulnay taught her to write, a skill that Laure found much more difficult to learn than reading. Madame d'Aulnay said that mostly it is men who write. Even some poor men, she said, sit on street corners as clerks and write out accounts and letters for those who require their services. Sewing and needlework are much more useful for girls to learn, but Laure was already quicker and knew more patterns than most eleven-year-old servants girls, so Madame felt there was no harm in teaching her to write a few words.

Laure first traced the letters in a box of sand, over and over, until Madame d'Aulnay was satisfied that she was ready to try writing them in ink on paper. Madame d'Aulnay sat Laure in front of her *écritoire* and removed from it the objects she would need for writing: a sheet of thick paper made of linen fibres, a goose feather, a small knife to trim the nib of the pen, a vial of ink, an instrument to scratch out mistakes from the paper, and sand, to dry the ink. Laure first learned to sign her name, and once she mastered this skill, Madame d'Aulnay told her that she could already do more than most women in France.

But these memories of a better, more hopeful time are long past. Laure would probably still be in her salon had Madame d'Aulnay not died three years ago. Being forced to return to the Salpêtrière after her mistress's death had been a cruel fate. Not even being placed in the Sainte-Claire dormitory or meeting Madeleine, her first and only friend in the hospital, could compensate for her loss. For Laure, the years since Madame d'Aulnay's, clothed in the hard grey hospital linen, have passed like a prison sentence.

"Don't tell me you're going to sit over there brooding and miss out on your chance to see this. Why don't you tell Mireille to come and see for herself? She might learn something for her new prince in Canada." Madeleine does not respond. Laure turns back to the window and the scene below.

The Superior has reason to be concerned about the morality of the Sainte-Claire girls. After all, the Salpêtrière houses every sort of woman imaginable in the kingdom. Laure has even heard that there is a woman of the court imprisoned in a special chamber on a *lettre de cachet* from the King. There are also some Protestants, and a few foreign women, from Ireland, Portugal, and Morocco, mixed in with the others. Laure isn't sure of all the hospital's divisions. Only that there are about forty other dormitories. Infants are kept in the *crèche*, slightly older boys and girls are put in separate dormitories. There are also several divisions for girls working at cloth making and bleaching, one for pregnant women, another for nursing women and their children, several for madwomen young and old, a number for women with infirmities—blindness, epilepsy. There are a few dormitories too for old women, and one for husbands and wives over the age of seventy. There are no men in the Salpêtrière between the ages of eleven and seventy, other than the archers and the servant boys.

The people gathered in the courtyard of the Maison de la Force are standing in clusters, exchanging news and gossip.

Their voices are loud and punctuated by laughter. Occasionally, someone will glance back at the entrance to the courtyard, eager for the prostitutes' arrival. Laure can see that the people are dressed in tattered clothing and have the same vulgar tongues as some of the Salpêtrière residents. Sometimes a voice will rise above the others carrying a piece of information. She learns things the officers do not tell the residents. The administrators attempt to keep the divisions of women from mixing. Of course, occasional stories still manage to find their way through the dormitory walls, fragments that are whispered at church service, embellished during the long workdays, and passed along so often that they become legends. There are women that everyone knows even though they have long since gone. The Baudet sisters who seduced the cardinal in his antechamber. Jeanne LaVaux who took over her father's poison trade. Mary, the twelve-year-old Irish girl who had been a prostitute since she was six.

Laure is hungry for these stories. She wants to know all that she can about the hospital that is her home and prison. Below, she hears a man with the voice of a market vendor telling the others that the prostitutes are brought to the Salpêtrière once a month. They are gathered in by street constables and held in a smaller prison on rue Saint-Martin until they are transferred here by cart. The man who screams out this information is quickly surrounded and questioned by others who are eager to learn anything they can about the captured women before they arrive. Clearly, this spectacle provides entertainment for those who cannot afford the price of an opera ticket. For the administrators of the General Hospital, the public humiliation will provide the first of the women's punishment.

Madeleine, still sitting next to Mireille, calls across the room. "You shouldn't watch the prostitutes being brought in."

But Laure doesn't want to pull herself from the window. Especially not to go and listen to Madeleine fuss over Mireille. Laure has learned that prostitutes live together in the city with other women in a house like the Salpêtrière, only much smaller. While the royal authorities celebrate the Salpêtrière, showing it off to the princes and religious authorities of the kingdom, the houses of prostitutes must remain secret. Inside, there are many small rooms, but unlike the Salpêtrière, men are invited into them. Laure imagines the prostitutes dressed in bright layers of clothing, the quality of the fabric depending on which men they service, the degree of their beauty, which house they belong to. In Laure's mind, heavy draperies of velvet and silk separate the girls' rooms one from the other. Their skin smells of perfume, and their hair is curled and worn loose. Just like women at court, they are the queens of their domains.

Laure knows that thinking this way about prostitutes is blasphemous, especially for a *Bijou*.

The crowd below begins to cheer at some sign of the arrival that Laure cannot make out. Two archers appear first in the courtyard, pushing their way through the mass with the tips of their bows. "In the name of His Majesty, make way as we pass." The crowd parts for the archers, but grows tight again as onlookers from the edges close in for a better view. Short seconds later, Laure hears a high-pitched screech, like that of a wounded animal, followed by loud wailing. The sound carries above the voices of the crowd. One man cheers, but otherwise an excited hush takes over.

"Laure, please get away from the window. You're frightening Mireille." Madeleine starts to pray louder in an attempt to drown out the noise.

Laure continues to look down. "What are you praying for? Nothing's happening. They're just screaming like that to try to get rid of the crowd." Laure cannot see the women yet, but it sounds like there are many.

More archers arrive in the square. Like their counterparts, they are clad in bright blue and white with red stockings. The gold buttons of their clean uniforms look impressive in the sunlight. Some of them have been recruited from the best of the male orphans. "Make way, in the name of His Majesty, King Louis XIV, and the director of the Hôpital Général de Paris. Make way at this instant."

The crowd opens up, leaving a circle at the centre for the archers and their sentenced charges. There are about forty women crushed tightly together on the horse-drawn cart. They are standing on straw and are contained by iron bars. Some cover their faces, while others stare out at the crowd. Laure is disappointed to see that the women look so dishevelled. Only a few of the prostitutes have bright tresses and colourful gowns. Most of them have covered their hair in long, dark capes, and some seem to have cuts and bruises on their faces as if they had been beaten.

"They are nothing like what I expected to see. They look like the old beggar women from Les Saints dormitory." Laure cannot imagine what sort of men would pay to spend the night with these women.

Despite the shabbiness of the cartload, the gathered observers whoop and holler, grabbing at the women's dresses through the bars. One of the women spits into the crowd. Before the man she hits can retaliate, two of the archers drag her out of the cart. They restrain her with difficulty as she screams at them.

"You should see this one, Madeleine! Two archers can hardly hold her back." Laure laughs as the woman below hisses at her captors. "The officers are going to have a good time with her."

Once they reach the doors of the Maison de la Force, the rest of the women are herded off the cart and led to the entrance of the building. They are then made to stand in a line against the wall. The hospital physician comes over to them. Two officers hold a blanket in front of each woman while a doctor kneels to examine them. The women suspected of disease are separated from the others. Laure wonders what symptoms make the doctor suspicious as he passes down the line of women.

Madeleine calls across the room. "You shouldn't watch them being brought in. We must be examples for all the women of the hospital."

There are times when Laure believes, like Madeleine does, that they are somehow set apart from the women in the other dormitories. There might indeed be the possibility of a higher plan for the *Bijoux*. The other residents of the Salpêtrière are aware that the girls of Sainte-Claire are the first to receive the *douceurs* of charitable donors, gifts of seasonal fruit or vegetables. They also get the occasional thimbleful of wine in addition to their water rations. But more than just because they receive these coveted treats, the others envy the *Bijoux* because they are being prepared for a future.

Laure isn't interested in some of the other options available for residents of the Salpêtrière. Sometimes the hospital will arrange a match between a *Bijou* and a tradesman, a shoemaker or an innkeeper who braves public opinion to get his bride from the same place where men send for punishment the wives who dishonour them. Laure has heard that some of these pairings end badly. The same man who comes to the hospital with his hat in his hand often takes to drinking and mistreating his wife once he has her to himself. Laure doesn't want to take her chances on a blind match. If she can get hired by a seamstress, she will have plenty of opportunities to meet men shopping for ribbons for their sisters and mothers. She will have the time to get to know their character before deciding to marry one of them.

Some girls from Sainte-Claire eventually get chosen to become officers at the hospital. They are then put in charge of the morning *toilette* of dormitory residents, of dishing out the food rations, and of reading prayers from *L'Imitation de Jésus-Christ* to the residents. Laure has no interest in becoming an officer at the Salpêtrière. She couldn't imagine wearing a morose black dress and bonnet like the Sisters of Charity for the rest of her life, whispering at indignant street girls to pray and sing hymns, to straighten their dresses and comb their hair. Besides, officers get to spend only thirty minutes in the parlour with outside guests, and one day a month in the city, and then only if they are chaperoned. Even the letters the officers write must first be read by the Superior. Madeleine, who dreams of joining the Ursulines but has no dowry to pay them, is at least hoping to become an officer of one of the dormitories. She looks forward to teaching the others how to pray.

While the physician's inspection is going on, another group arrives in the courtyard. Several of the archers approach the newly arrived carriages pulled by dark horses. Laure cannot see who is inside. One of the archers has stuck his head into the first set of curtains and emerges after a few moments with a handful of coins. He brings these to the hospital official overseeing the transfer. Then the brigade of archers assembles around the carriages. One of them uses a trumpet to quiet the crowd and announces that the transfer is now complete and that the assembly must disperse in accordance with the orders of the hospital director and the King. There are a few groans from the crowd, but they begin nonetheless to make their way out of the courtyard.

Once the onlookers have gone, the door to the first carriage opens and the women inside descend. They are older and better dressed than the prostitutes who came on the cart. But Laure assumes by their tight bodices and curled hair that they work in the same business. They must be the ones in charge of the prostitute houses. One of the women pulls out her purse and hands some more coins to the archers, after which the women are quickly taken inside the building.

"Do you remember the cure for the mal de Naples?" Laure asks as she walks toward the back of the dormitory where Madeleine is sitting on the edge of Mireille's cot, wiping her forehead with a cloth. "I guess they'll get a good whipping to start. That seems to be the cure for most things around here."

"Laure, why are you talking about all of this? Mireille isn't feeling well. One of her teeth has fallen out."

Laure is surprised to hear this and to see that there is blood on the cloth Madeleine has been using to wipe Mireille's forehead. She wonders which tooth it is. Laure has lost two of her own teeth since she returned from Madame d'Aulnay's.

"If that's all she's lost, she shouldn't be complaining." Laure is glad to see that Mireille does actually look awful. Maybe she has made herself a little sick with all her pretending and going around with a sour face. After all, if you pretend anything for long enough, it starts to become reality. Mireille looks for sympathy from everyone she can, although it is Madame du

Clos, the needlework instructor, and Madeleine who pity her the most. Just because her father was an officer, she thinks she doesn't belong here and that everyone should feel sorry for her.

"I think the cure is mercury and rhubarb. I guess she won't be coming back to the workshop this afternoon. Good timing when we have all that *point de France* work to finish off. I can barely see my own fingers let alone the needle by the end of the day."

"She would work if she could." Madeleine folds the cloth into a square, covering up the bloodstain, and places it on Mireille's forehead.

"What does she care, now that she has a husband waiting for her in Canada? She doesn't have to worry about finding work in Paris." Ever since Mireille arrived at the Salpêtrière the previous year, Laure hasn't spoken directly to her.

"Laure, where is your sympathy? Mireille needs to get better, to be strong for her journey."

"And what about us?" Laure asks. "Left behind in this place that keeps beggars and diseased women from the street. Why should I feel sorry for *her*, when she is the one getting out?"

Mireille tugs at Madeleine's sleeve when she stands up to go. But Laure takes Mireille's arm and shoves it back onto the bed. She is surprised at how easily the light limb relinquishes its hold.

2

The physician enters the dormitory just after the girls have changed into their nightdresses. Laure recognizes him as the same man who examined the prostitutes earlier in the day. Tonight he is wearing a long gown and gloves, and the Superior trails behind him in her black cloak. The residents' usual nighttime chatter has been silenced by their arrival. The eyes of the girls follow the impressive figures as they cross the room toward Mireille's bed. It is the closest Laure has ever been to the Superior of the General Hospital.

This small woman, dressed in thick layers of black cloth, controls each of their destinies. She commands the hundreds of officers, governesses, and servant girls, reminding them that it is their duty to devote themselves entirely to caring for the residents. But more importantly, the Superior is the only woman who can decide when Laure and all the others will be free to leave the Salpêtrière. Each departure must be signed by her hand. Laure has heard that the Superior's quarters are as grand as those of a lady at the royal court. That she has her own carriage and driver, footmen and servants, a private garden, and a poultry yard.

Laure wonders why the Superior has brought the doctor to the dormitory. She wants to tell them that Mireille's weakness is just for attention, to get out of her last few weeks of needlework before she leaves the hospital for good. But they'll find that out soon enough when the physician examines her. It will serve Mireille right, Laure thinks, to get forced back to work, maybe doing laundry or sweeping the dormitory as punishment for her deception. Laure strains her eyes in the fading light to get a closer look at what is going on in the bed next to hers.

The doctor examines Mireille for a moment, then lifts her fingers up with his gloved hand. Mireille moans as her arm is raised. Laure blinks. It almost looks like Mireille's fingers are bleeding around the nails. The doctor inspects them carefully before placing her hand back on the cover. Removing his glove, he reaches for her mouth and uses his finger to hold up her lip. Whatever the doctor sees there seems to be enough for a diagnosis. Nodding, he turns back to the Superior. His task is complete. The Superior, who looks like a raven in the dimness of the room, passes her swift eyes over Mireille, copying down the bed number. She then gives a quick glance at the rest of the girls, who bow their heads to avoid meeting her gaze. "Next we have to see if anyone needs to be removed from Saint-Jacques." She turns, and her heavy skirt brushes against the floor. The physician follows her out of the room.

Laure is awakened that night by Mireille's voice. Her first instinct is to be annoyed. It is the same disdain she normally feels when Mireille starts to chatter with Madeleine in that quiet, careful tone of hers. But this time the sound coming from her throat isn't quiet or careful. Laure opens her eyes and turns to see that Mireille is sitting up in her cot, wide awake.

"Father, don't be angry … I can't marry you."

Laure looks around the room. Nobody else stirs. Laure hears only the deep breathing of the rows of girls all around them. Did Mireille mean to wake her? The girl really is going too far to get out of working.

"Papa, I'm afraid. There's so much water everywhere." Mireille raises her hands and waves them in front of her, as if the air in the room is choking her. Surely she expects an audience. But none of the other residents seem to hear her. "I don't want to drown before I get married. It hurts so much." Mireille drops her hands and starts to cry. Laure's chest fills with sick warmth. The sound is pathetic, weak as the crying of the hungry and orphaned babies of the *crèche*. Laure walks by the *crèche* as quickly as she can on her way to the workshop each day. She wonders if Mireille's fingers were really bleeding earlier that night. Maybe she has lost another tooth. The stupid girl with all her self-pity has probably hurt herself.

Laure remembers when Mireille Langlois first stepped into the basement sewing workshop, accompanied by Madame du Clos, their instructor. The new girl had entered the room like a cat lowering its paw into the river. Mireille wore white gloves that reached her elbows and clutched against her chest a round purse adorned in metal. Her dress was a pale yellow, trimmed in what looked like real Venetian lace, banned for import to France. Laure presumed that Mireille was the daughter or a widow of some rich benefactor on a tour of the institution.

The girls saw a number of these women each week, though they weren't usually so young and generally wore the same black cape as the Superior, to symbolize their piousness. Also, Mireille didn't smile at the sight of the dark room's crowded tables piled with completed work orders the way the visitors always did. Laure forced herself to look away from the rich girl and resumed cutting the lace pattern she was working on.

Looking right at Laure, Madame du Clos had said with some sternness: "This is Mireille. She will be moving into the Sainte-Claire dormitory."

Laure's eyes widened in surprise, but she remained quiet.

"And Mireille will be starting today on making lace." Madame du Clos asked Laure to make space for Mireille to sit between her and Madeleine on the workbench. The new girl nodded her head in gratitude, smiled at Laure, and placed her hands on her lap. Laure moved aside a few inches and Madeleine squeezed herself into the corner far enough so Mireille could sit down. Shortly afterwards, Madame du Clos came to collect Mireille's fashionable little purse and to present her with her own spool of silk and needles. She asked Laure to give Mireille a pattern to produce.

Madeleine smiled. "You know how to make lace?" There was no rancour in her question.

"Yes, my mother taught me. I made this myself." Mireille lifted her arms to show the cuffs of her sleeves. Laure looked from the corner of her eye to see if the stitch was as good as her own. It was on that first day that Laure decided she would never speak to the new girl who already knew how to make lace.

When they finished for the day and were lining up to leave the workshop, Laure asked Madeleine why she had decided to be so friendly to a girl who would only steal the little chance they had of finding a suitor, or being hired on in a seamstress or tailor's shop in the city. Madeleine responded that she felt no such threat and that Mireille was just a sad girl in need of friendship.

On her first night in the dormitory, Laure was pleased to see the well-born newcomer stripped down to the simple flax nightdress, although she was allowed to keep her head of thick golden curls. The officer, who ignored distinctions of birth and privilege, placed Mireille in a bed with two girls recently arrived by bull cart from Picardie with letters from their local priests. Their skin was grey and they were crawling with bugs. Laure listened with pleasure to the sounds of Mireille crying while her bedmates snored beside her. The girls from Picardie were sent out of Sainte-Claire by the governess the following morning, but Mireille was there to stay.

In the morning, Mireille had looked pale, but she didn't complain and did as she was told all through the long day of work and prayers. She already knew her Ave, Pater, and Credo by heart in Latin and in French and how to read from prayer books. There wasn't much to teach this new *Bijou* as she was better educated than most of the officers. It was only a matter of time before something better came along to remove Mireille from the Salpêtrière. Laure doesn't understand why she can't just finish off her last few weeks in the workshop before she leaves for her officer husband and forget about putting on this sick act for attention.

⚜

In the darkness of the dormitory, Mireille's cries turn into whimpers and she starts to pray. Laure searches for the sounds of Mireille's usual careful Latin beneath the theatrics. But the voice she hears from the other bed belongs to someone else entirely, to a drowning animal. The words that come out are a mix of French and Latin, a confused jumble of prayers. *Sancta Maria mater Dei, ora pro nobis peccatoribus, nunc, et in hora mortis nostrae* ... Laure's ears start ringing. Why doesn't anyone else hear this? She wants to say something to Mireille to make her stop. But she sticks to her resolve not to talk to her. Not to waste her voice on a girl lucky enough to have a rich father who left her a pension but who still has the nerve to complain. Laure wouldn't know what to say to Mireille. She can't even think of something harsh to make her shut up. Laure considers waking Madeleine, who is lying next to her, but she cannot take her eyes from Mireille.

"Hold my hand." She is looking right at Laure now, stretching out fingers that look bloated. "Do something. You're the only one who can." Laure blinks, trying to see through the darkness around her. A prayer wells up in her, asking God to make this stop. She pushes the prayer away and closes her eyes.

When there is finally silence in the bed next to her, Laure cannot get back to sleep. She watches Mireille, a pale shadow slumped back down in sleep, and waits for morning to come. Surely Laure just imagined the desperation of Mireille's pleas, or maybe the girl is more cunning than she thought and put on the despondent show to stir her up. Either way, she will know better in the morning. Daylight will bring some clarity.

3

The massive stone hospital is behind Laure. But what good is it to be free of a prison when it is even more dangerous outside? Especially for a girl walking alone in a work dress grown thin from wear. Madeleine asked Laure this morning why she was risking so much for Mireille, whom she disliked. Laure had assured Madeleine that she wouldn't get caught so long as Madame du Clos in the sewing workshop believed that she was ill in the dormitory. Besides, Laure was tired of listening to the whispered rumours of the other girls in Sainte-Claire and wanted to see for herself that Mireille was well and just looking for a way to get out of the hospital. Laure couldn't let Mireille get away from her work duties that easily. There was also the possibility that Laure was going to the Hôtel-Dieu to quell that other feeling that rose up in her last night. The fear she felt when it occurred to her that maybe Madeleine was right and Mireille was indeed sick.

Disease is not new to the Salpêtrière. Many, especially children, come in with *gale*, ringworm, pustules, and other skin sores. There are women who arrive pregnant and end up dying in childbirth, leaving behind their weak infants. The voices of these babies fill the hallway with ghostly pleas for milk. There was even a small outbreak of the *peste* at the hospital last year. The doctor had come in then wearing a mask with a long nose filled with spices to ward off the contagion. The residents of Sainte-Claire had all been moved to other dorms for two nights. Despite all of this, Laure hadn't expected Mireille to fall ill. After all, she hadn't come in starved from the crop shortages of the countryside, or afflicted with diseases or pregnancy.

The rising sun is spreading pale light along the river path. If she follows this road along the river, she will end up at the Hôtel-Dieu. Up ahead, Laure sees men unloading barrels from boats. They shout to each other about the best way to get the load onto the land. The last of night is being broken by their voices. Laure worries that the men might recognize her grey hospital dress despite her efforts to cover it with the dark shawl. Even if the boatmen don't notice the dress, they might see the direction she is coming from. Unlike the country women who carry in fruit and bread to sell in the city, Laure's arms are empty. They will know that she has escaped from the Salpêtrière. At least she doesn't see anyone from the Police des Pauvres among them. These men have been hired to search the streets for destitute people and take them to the General Hospital.

It was easy enough for Laure to sneak past the servant girls sweeping in the long hallway outside the dormitory this morning. She slipped down the stairs to the central entrance and outside into the Cour Mazarine. Although the sun was just beginning to rise, already a group of men in bright white stockings and velvet coats had gathered around an old man in the courtyard. The men had looked high ranking, and Laure worried they would report her to someone and send her back.

"Good one, Monsieur le Vau," she heard one of them say as she passed. "The windows for the new church are to be nice and high. That should keep them aware of how far they are from the Divine light."

All the men laughed except for the old man. He was looking at Laure. "Yes, how to bring the light of God into a prison."

"And what are you doing later today?" one of the men asked him. "Do you have a little time for a drink? Another great monument to the King is well on its way. You should at least celebrate."

Laure wondered if the old man, upon seeing her, was about to yell for an archer. But he was silent as he continued to stare at her.

Laure was glad that it had only been Luc Aubin guarding the hospital gate. He was one year younger than she, and she had known him when they were both little children in the Enfant-Jésus dormitory. He tried to stop her from leaving that morning. But she had been able to quiet him just as her singing voice had once carried over his boyhood murmurs in the Enfant-Jésus. In the end, he let her through the gates without a permission slip. He accepted Laure's story that girls who knew *point de France* were working for the King and his ministers and so could come and go as they pleased. Laure could see that he hadn't exactly believed her but he was still a few years too young to do anything about his suspicions.

When Laure reaches the place along the river where the men are unloading the boats, someone calls out to her. She can't make out everything he says, only that it is something about her being too young to be covered in black. One of the other men joins in, beckoning her over to them. Laure lowers her head and quickens her pace until they grow quiet behind her.

As she walks along, the sun gets stronger. Her skin stings as the rays touch her cheeks. The unaccustomed brightness makes her eyes water. The river to Laure's right laps the bank, and her heavy hospital clogs slide in the mud as she tries to speed up. She is thinking of the bread she ate for breakfast. How quickly it disappeared from her stomach once she went outside, like dew evaporating under the sun's rays. She won't make it back to the Salpêtrière in time for lunch, and dinner is still twelve hours away. When Laure is in the workshop, she is careful not to move her limbs more than necessary, letting only her fingers guide the needle in and out through the tiny patterns. That way she grows hungry less quickly.

Farther along, an old man watches over two grazing sheep. He nods at Laure as she passes, and goes back to tending his animals. There are guards outside the Jardin du Roi, so Laure falls in next to a family pulling a cart of wood. The crowd has grown thicker here. There are a few men on horseback, and even a black carriage being pulled by two horses. But mostly the road is filled with the slow movement of people carrying goods from the nearby fields to sell in the city. The odour of the animals intermingles with the sweat of their owners and the apples from a young girl's basket.

Laure knows that one day her letter-writing and needlework skills will raise her above these street merchants. She won't have to walk among them, listening to their voices hoarse from calling out the prices of their goods. But for the moment, her spindly legs carry her alongside them. Laure is thinner and shabbier looking than the wives of the more prosperous country merchants, who wear white aprons over their dresses. The coarse material of Laure's grey dress is the same as that used to bury the dead at the hospital. It is a practical consideration to dress the residents of the Salpêtrière in this way considering that last month, eighty women at the hospital died.

Still, Laure sees people walking into the city who look worse than she does. She passes a man bent over crutches holding up his footless leg. A few beggars take their chances with the mangy dogs; they lower themselves to the passersby, hoping to receive a piece of bread. Or to be picked up by the archers and taken to one of the hospitals.

⚜

Laure finally reaches the cathedral next to the Hôtel-Dieu after half an hour of watching it grow nearer. On the *parvis* of the Notre-Dame church, the crowd is thicker and includes a procession of priests. Laure looks up at the towers of Notre-Dame. She wonders if there really are spirits so hungry for human life that frightening creatures had to be carved into the church's stone to fend them off. Notre-Dame rises from the dirt like an ancient amulet for the city, guarding against what evil Laure isn't sure. The *parvis* is exposed to the sun, and dust circles around the people gathered on it. There is desperation in the way they stand, arms extending in jerky movements, as if they are bargaining for goods at a market or awaiting the arrival of a doctor. Some pray standing together in small groups, waiting for their turn to enter the safe haven of the church.

Once past Notre-Dame, Laure realizes that the height and breadth of the Hôtel-Dieu makes the church look like a small appendage. There is nothing particularly notable about the construction of the hospital other than its tremendous size. How will she find Mireille inside? She circles the building, looking at each entrance for a guard with a gentle or lascivious eye, one who is handsome enough to be a little kind, to overlook her shabby dress and to let her inside. Finally she spots a boy not much older than Luc Aubin standing beside one of the doors. He is engrossed in the approach of the white-clad Soeurs hospitalières coming back from washing sheets at the river.

Until last night, Laure had been fully convinced that Mireille Langlois was just playing sick for attention. It was just the sort of thing she would do. Laure spoke to Mireille only through Madeleine and even then as little as possible. In Laure's opinion, Mireille had been fortunate and so didn't need the kind attentions of Madeleine's friendship. Mireille's father had been a distinguished soldier in the King's army, not some street performer reviled by the authorities. Mireille had been lucky enough to enter the *Bijoux* dormitory on her very first day at the Salpêtrière without first having to spend weeks or months in one of the less salubrious rooms.

It had taken Laure years of good behaviour, of memorizing her Latin prayers, of singing hymns in a clear voice, to earn her spot among the handful of the most privileged of the thousands of women of the Salpêtrière. Mireille Langlois had entered Sainte-Claire on her first day simply because she had been taught needlework and prayers in her father's home. How dare she cry herself to sleep as if she'd just been thrown into the worst basement cell of the Maison de la Force? Last year, a girl who did receive such a fate was bitten to death by rats.

Laure slips into the Hôtel-Dieu behind the Hospitalières without a word from the guard. She hopes Luc Aubin will be the one guarding the gate when she returns in the afternoon. Laure has decided she will speak to Mireille today. There is certainly a fair share of things Laure has wanted to say to her since they first met. She hopes that Mireille has actually been a little ill in this frightening place, or that the moaning and fetid odour of the sick will at least have had some effect on the spoiled girl. After all, Madeleine is right: Laure is risking a lot by escaping from the hospital to come here. If she gets caught, she could be put into the Force.

Once in the courtyard of the Hôtel-Dieu, Laure asks one of the young nuns where she might find the patients newly admitted from the General Hospital. She is sent down the hall to a room that is larger than the Sainte-Claire dormitory. In the sickroom, there are three rows of wooden beds covered in white canopies and two aisles to walk between them. Many of the curtains around the beds are closed. Behind the open curtains, Laure sees sick men and women, several to a bed. The air in the room is more putrid than at the Salpêtrière. Along with the general smell of poverty and bodies crowded together, there is the odour of illness—the excretions of sick bodies—and an underlying odour of the astringent medicines used to comfort them. The foul smell of decaying flesh and bodily excrements is clearly prevailing over the attempts of herbs and doctors' concoctions to rid the room of disease. A young novice sweeps the floor near where Laure stands. Nuns dressed in clean habits tend to people crowded into the thirty or so beds. Several carry basins back to the patients. One of the older nuns notices Laure and asks what she is doing.

"I'm here to see Mireille Langlois. She arrived this morning from the Salpêtrière with a fever." Laure lowers her eyes. "I am her sister."

The woman easily recognizes the grey tunic. Her eyes widen a little. "I am not the one who authorizes visitors. You'll have to—"

"I just want to know where she is." If Laure hasn't been able to fool this woman, she'll certainly be sent back, or worse, by her Superior. She looks around the room, trying to spot Mireille. "I can't leave without seeing her first."

"I'm not supposed to do this. I could get in trouble too. What was the name?"

"Mireille Langlois. She is the daughter of an officer. Of course, his fortune has since—"

"I have heard every story you can possibly tell me about fortunes drying up and wounds becoming wet again." The nurse is a thin woman with drawn lips. A deep line runs between her eyebrows. But Laure thinks she spots a hint of tenderness there. She is used to looking in the eyes of older women for traces of sympathy. "My legs are so tired of walking between these beds. I've heard the entire sad story of the kingdom in this room. The solution is always to build another hospital. One for the children, one for the soldiers, another for the old women. Who will be left on the streets when all these new hospitals are full? That's what I want to know." She pushes past Laure and starts walking to a table at the far end of the room. One side of the nurse's hip looks higher than the other. The uneven weight makes her limp as she walks down the aisle. When Laure doesn't follow, the nurse turns back. "Well come on. Who is it you're looking for?"

Laure hurries down the aisle. She gives her Mireille's name again.

The nurse checks in a black registry that covers the top of a desk in the corner of the room. After finding Mireille's name, the nurse walks over to a bed in the second row and pulls back the curtain. An old man pokes his head out at them, surprised by the interruption. The nurse glances back at Laure and closes

the curtain, standing still for a moment. When she turns back
to Laure she is frowning.

Laure looks around the room. How can they keep track of
so many sick people, coming in and out all the time? Mireille
has probably been moved to one of the other beds. She must
be somewhere else in the hospital sitting up, taking some
broth. But Laure's eyes follow the nurse as she heads into the
adjoining room marked with a sign that reads *Salle des morts.*

Laure puts a fistful of her scarf over her nose as they enter.
The smell, even through the scarf, makes her stomach rise to
her throat. On the floor of the windowless room, Laure makes
out the shape of several wooden stretchers. They are covered in
dark cloth embroidered with white crosses.

Laure hears a scream in her head, her ears are ringing from
the sound, but she cannot open her mouth to let it out. No
sound she makes will be strong enough. She is powerless to
shatter windows and crumble stone. She wants to scream loud
enough to reach beyond the Hôtel-Dieu and the towers of the
neighbouring cathedral, along the river to the Salpêtrière and up
into the deaf heavens. Instead Laure stands quietly and watches
the nurse lift the grey cloth to reveal Mireille's pale face.

"Is this the girl you came to see?" The nurse stands up,
straightening her white habit.

Laure's throat constricts. She nods. Laure remembers
Mireille reaching for her in the dormitory last night. She
hadn't been able to speak to her. If she had known Mireille
was going to die, she would have said something. She would
have wakened Madeleine at least to offer her the comfort she
was pleading for. Mireille would have liked to hear Madeleine's
prayers. Laure's mind is racing. How could she not have seen
what Madeleine knew all along, that Mireille was truly sick.

"She was your friend?" the nurse asks.

"My sister." Laure doesn't know why she bothers to keep up the lie, what difference it makes what she tells this old nurse who has seen decades of orphans and widows and soldiers all end up the same way, in this room. Laure crouches down next to the body. Where the cloth had been pulled back, she sees the collar of Mireille's dress. It is the same as the one Laure is wearing. Maybe they are sisters of a sort. How wrong she had been to think that Mireille was the lucky one. The softness and light that Laure had envied is gone. In the dark dampness of the workshop, Mireille's graceful fingers had looked golden, always just a little quicker, a bit more precise than her own. Now, Mireille's yellow hair falls back from her face like dark rope, pulling her down into the stone floor. Her cheeks look like bone.

When Laure stands up, a younger nurse enters the room. The stinking air fills with her words.

"We were sure that girl was going to live. She was talking to us so clearly. She told us that her father, a soldier, would be around to see her in the afternoon."

"Her father is dead," Laure says, wishing this new girl would go away. She should have gotten out of bed last night and listened to Mireille at least. Maybe if she had comforted her, things would have turned out differently. What would she tell Madeleine?

"Then the poor soul became convinced that we had her on water. That she was out at sea! We tried to tell her there was no boat. She must have been thinking about being taken down the Seine from the Salpêtrière."

"She was going to Canada to get married." Laure wonders if the locket is still under Mireille's pillow in the dormitory.

How useless that little piece of jewellery now seems. What will happen to the soldier waiting for her there?

"Canada? Well, it's just as well she died, then." The young nurse looks down at Mireille's body. "Terrible. Just because we don't know what to do with them here doesn't mean they deserve to be sent over there to freeze in the forest." She pulls the cloth back over Mireille's face and says to Laure, "It's best to keep them covered."

Laure hurries past the sick people in their beds and down the long hallway of the Hôtel-Dieu de Paris before reaching the street. The guard at the door calls after her but she doesn't turn around. She can think only of air, that she must breathe in something other than the smell of death. Outside, the business of living goes on. Some people, though poor, even dance in front of the cathedral. It is only a beggar, with a blanket wrapped around his shoulders, who reflects what Laure is feeling. She stares at the old man. Judging by his startled reaction, Laure imagines that nobody has looked at him in days, let alone dropped a coin into his tin cup. He flinches as she comes closer. "What are you waiting for?" she wants to ask him. "Protection? Someone to save you? Things to get better?" He recoils from her angry eyes, shrinking into the dirt. Laure shakes her head and moves on.

The church is old but not as old as the hospital. The carved creatures of centuries past feed on the bodies of the dead. Growing strong on extinguished spirits. *It is ghosts that raised you, ghosts that tend to you. You are nothing but a thief.* Laure's thoughts are filled with rage as she stares at the indifferent magnificence of Notre-Dame. How can the old beggar and the crowd around the cathedral fail to see how terrible it all is in the end? They probably don't know that behind the heavy walls of the building they dance beside there is that awful silent room. That the church they love so much is just an extension of the tired nurse and her rows of sickbeds and offers no consolation at all. Laure is numb to the activity on the *parvis*. She moves quickly past the shouts and market exchanges. The fine wheels of coloured glass high on the cathedral walls absorb the sun, but they reflect back nothing but hard stone.

Laure heads along the Seine, back to the Salpêtrière. She has nowhere else to go. Her clogs and feet and even her legs are covered in the mud from the road. She stops to drink from the river like a horse. The water reaches the bottom of her stomach and makes it ache. Laure isn't afraid of the Superior's wrath, isn't even afraid of being sent to the Maison de la Force. All Laure cares about is her failure to speak to the dying Mireille. Now it is too late. The God of the Salpêtrière, of Notre-Dame, and the Hôtel-Dieu has robbed her of the chance.

4

It is a different guard at the door when Laure returns to the Salpêtrière. Laure doesn't really expect to be shown any mercy. She has underestimated so much: the distance of the walk to the hospital and back on an empty stomach, the mud on the road that has reached even her cheeks and turned her into a bedraggled beggar in the eyes of passersby. Any strength she might have found for pleading her case to Luc Aubin or some other guard dissipated at the sight of the dead *Bijou*.

The guard takes one look at Laure's dirty hospital dress and asks what dormitory she belongs to. When she refuses to answer, he escorts her down a grand hallway of the hospital, high ceilinged and lined with portraits of hospital officials, to the Superior's office. The room is spacious, with bright windows that look out onto an expansive garden. Birds chirp and the air is fresh. The Superior is seated at a high-backed chair, a shrewd princess clad in black robes. The expression on her face is merciless. Laure cannot imagine a thing to say that could possibly soften those eyes. The Superior scans Laure's face and her dishevelled dress as if she is thinking up the best possible punishment for her misdemeanour.

Laure turns as Madame Gage, the dormitory governess, enters the office with her shuffling footsteps. Her big face is filled with compassion, and Laure knows that she will do her best to plead on Laure's behalf. The Superior arches her eyebrows in anticipation of a story she has heard many times before, some pathetic reason why she should bend the hospital's rules to help a poor girl. Madame Gage's eyes remain downcast as she mutters that the *Bijoux* aren't accustomed as the others are to disease. The girl had been out of her mind with grief over Mireille's illness. If only this were true, Laure thinks. The Superior reminds Madame Gage that the Sainte-Claire dormitory is no place for girls who have lost their minds. There are other dormitories for such girls. What sort of skill does this *Bijou* possess besides the ability to charm her way past our guards and out into the streets? Laure feels the anger rise in her chest at the mocking way the Superior calls her a *Bijou*, as if she is in fact a girl of loose morals all because she escaped for one day beyond the walls of this prison for the poor.

When the Superior discovers that Laure belongs to the sewing workshop, she orders Madame Gage to call in Madame du Clos. While they wait for the needlework instructor, the Superior moves to her desk and begins filling in documents without uttering a word to Laure, who remains standing beside the chair Madame Gage vacated. A servant carries in a tray of cakes, which the Superior leaves untouched beside her while she works. Finally Madame du Clos arrives in the office from the basement. The Superior extends a hand to the chair, and Madame du Clos takes a seat although she cannot sit still. Her nervous hands flutter, fixing her bonnet, straightening her skirt, twisting her fingers in her lap as if she is tying knots. Laure can't imagine how Madame du Clos, whose cheeks are flushed red, can possibly help her out. She has brought with her a sample of Laure's *point de France*. It is the finest piece Laure has so far made and is destined to adorn the collar of a noble garment. It is more time consuming than the coarser bobbin lace the less skilled girls work to make, but will not unravel if one of the bars is broken. Only a girl with a fine imagination and the hands of an angel can attempt to create such an elaborate item using only a needle, scissors, and thread. Madame du Clos' voice trembles as she raises the piece to the light. Laure knows that this strip of lace she has been working on since last fall is one of the finest ever produced in Madame du Clos' workshop, but she doesn't understand how it could possibly be useful to show this to the Superior. Using both hands, Madame du Clos passes the lace to the Superior. "It is not good to bring the lace from the basement," Madame du Clos says. "The colour might spoil. I will need to return it soon."

The Superior holds the material up over her head to examine it. She studies the stitches, the swirls of foliage and tiny silk bars linking one flower to another. Her fingers trace over the pattern, as if counting the many parts. Laure watches the Superior's face and detects a flicker of emotion in her eyes as her fingers move across the pattern. She turns to Laure. "Do you know how much this is worth?"

Laure shakes her head.

"It is better for the poor souls that they not know. Better for the craft," Madame du Clos says.

"Well, of course the value of a piece depends on the hands that make it. Also on that woman's reputation." The Superior turns to look out the window at her garden. "Last month nine coaches on the road to Versailles were attacked by criminals. Did you hear about that? Do you know what the thieves were taking the time to steal? An elaborate plot to make away with fifteen headdresses made of lace much like this."

Laure nods. The story of the stolen headdresses had travelled through a church service. The girls had found it funny picturing the men on horseback coming up behind the ladies bound for Paris and plucking their hats from their heads. Laure had laughed at the thought of these foolish women. How could a girl who spends her day in a basement workshop wearing grey flax be expected to feel sympathy for women dressed in fineries riding in coaches?

"Did you know that some of the women who lost those headdresses are now paupers?" The Superior runs her fingers over the months of Laure's work. "If you are a smart girl, with the right reputation, someday someone might give their entire life's fortune, just as those women did, to buy this piece." She hands back the long strip of lace to Madame du Clos and turns to her garden. "I expect that both yourself and Madame Gage of Sainte-Claire will keep a special eye on this girl. It is always the way that those who cause the most trouble also have the greatest talents. We never know how such girls will turn out."

The Superior informs Madame Gage that Laure is not to be given any food tonight. "If I so much as hear that a crumb of bread or a sip of water has passed through her lips, then this runaway will end up in a worse state than when she first came here."

The Superior then addresses Laure. "Women are now advised to turn their backs to the horses when they travel by carriage. So they can see the thieves coming from behind."

It was the *point de France* that spared Laure from being transferred to another dormitory or, even worse, to a basement cell or onto the street to fend for herself. Laure feels a tremble starting in her legs. She isn't sure if it is caused by the Superior's frightening voice or by the hunger that is making her whole body buzz. Or it could be that underlying it all is the horror she feels knowing that Mireille Langlois is really dead. Laure walks back through the hallways to the dormitory on the arm of Madame Gage, who has returned for her, who tells her that it could have been worse. The Superior is not known to be a merciful woman. She is the one after all who condemns girls to the damp dungeon cells. But Laure cannot imagine feeling worse than she does. She can still smell the Hôtel-Dieu on her skin and is relieved that she doesn't have to eat dinner.

When she enters the dormitory, the other Sainte-Claire girls, who are combing their hair and straightening their work dresses for the evening meal, grow quiet. Madeleine rushes to Laure's side and helps her into bed. Before long she is alone in the dormitory, the sound of the girls' heels growing faint as they make their way down the hallway to eat. Laure's knees are shaking as she pulls them up to her chin. How could she have been so wrong about Mireille? How could it be that the most beautiful and fortunate among them is now dead? She cannot quiet the tremors for the rest of the night.

❧

Laure is still in bed in the morning when Madame Gage announces to the dormitory the news of Mireille's death. She does so between the recitation of the *Veni Creator* hymn and the reading of L'Imitation de Jésus-Christ. In a soft voice, Madame

Gage informs the girls that Mireille received all the sacraments including penitence, the final Eucharist, and extreme unction at the Hôtel-Dieu. Some of the girls continue talking, combing their hair, putting on their bonnets, as if she is telling them about work assignments or times for Mass.

A small funeral ceremony will be held in the Salpêtrière chapel after the regular morning Mass. Madame Gage then announces that Madeleine and Laure have been given the morning off from their needlework duties by Madame du Clos to attend the ceremony and to stay afterwards in the dormitory. Laure doubts that the Superior knows about this. An angry murmur rises at the news of this privilege. Madame Gage ignores the dissent and tells the girls to hurry up their *toilette* and to form a line for Mass. The governess then walks over to Madeleine and hands her two lilies for the ceremony. The other girls look with greedy eyes at the flowers as if they are candy or cheese.

Although Laure is weak from going without food, she rises from her bed at the sight of the flowers. When she stands, she feels for a moment as if she will fall to the floor. She steadies her feet and makes her way to the shelf where Madeleine placed the black shawl after Laure left it in a heap at the foot of her bed the day before. Laure also gets her comb from the shelf, but doesn't have the energy to run it through the dark tangles. Instead of tying it under her scarf, she leaves her hair long and loose beneath her bonnet. It is forbidden to do so. The other girls whisper and look at Laure as if she is a country witch, but she doesn't care. Laure's long, knotty hair is a deliberate cloak to keep them out.

Madame Gage smiles when she sees Laure standing by her bed. She hands her a goblet of water mixed with a few drops of wine. Laure takes a sip and gives the cup back to the governess. When Madeleine comes over to help Laure put her hair under the bonnet, she swats her hand away and reaches instead for the flowers she has laid on the bed. Taking one by the stem, she brings it up to her nose. This is not the first funeral that Laure has attended. When Madame d'Aulnay died three years ago, Laure had worn this same cloak over a blue dress that was lent to her by Madame d'Aulnay's cousin. After the funeral, the cousin sent Laure back to the Salpêtrière, saying she no longer needed a servant in the house. How deluded Laure had been to think of herself as the daughter of a wealthy woman. She would never be such a thing.

For Mireille's funeral, Laure has no special dress to wear. This time the funeral Laure is attending feels like her own. She still has no appetite. Seeing Mireille Langlois's dead face at the Hôtel-Dieu has left Laure feeling too light for the world around her.

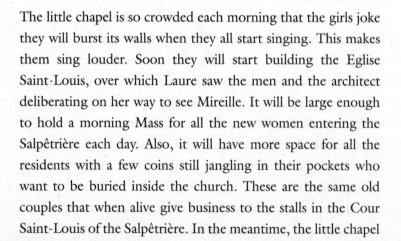

The little chapel is so crowded each morning that the girls joke they will burst its walls when they all start singing. This makes them sing louder. Soon they will start building the Eglise Saint-Louis, over which Laure saw the men and the architect deliberating on her way to see Mireille. It will be large enough to hold a morning Mass for all the new women entering the Salpêtrière each day. Also, it will have more space for all the residents with a few coins still jangling in their pockets who want to be buried inside the church. These are the same old couples that when alive give business to the stalls in the Cour Saint-Louis of the Salpêtrière. In the meantime, the little chapel

Saint-Denis is crowded each morning and reeks of the rotten bodies of the pensioners who have saved enough money to be buried in it. No amount of flowers or incense can cover the smell of the dead.

Laure usually finds going to morning Mass to be the most frightening part of her day. She is glad it takes place at quarter past six in the morning so she can put it behind her for the rest of the day. The only interesting part about going to church is the chance to hear a good story. If she prays at all in the stuffy little building, it is for the ceremony to end so she can follow the other girls of the Sainte-Claire dormitory into the fresh air and sunlight for the short walk to the dormitory before the start of the workday. But today Laure appreciates being trapped in the chapel. The priest's Latin murmurings are a perfect echo for the whisperings of her own mind. When she walks up the aisle, she sees the bodies wrapped in shrouds. There are three of them, but Mireille's is not among them for fear her disease might be contagious, which is ridiculous, Laure thinks, since she died of starvation really. But the hospital administrators are so afraid of the poor residents and their diseases. The day before yesterday there had only been one. Madame Gage stands beside Laure and Madeleine for the Mass.

She knows the story going from ear to ear today is the one of Mireille Langlois' life. *Her father was a prince*, a washing girl says. *It was her mother who couldn't stand to see her. So pretty. Couldn't have her around the house after the father died. She'd never get a second husband. Had to get rid of her.* Usually Laure is glad to hear these exaggerated, invented stories. She would run the rumours around in her head, adding new details, while her fingers repeated hundreds of minuscule stitches in the basement throughout the long workday. But today Laure wants to scream at all the indifferent girls who are hungry for the usual entertainment. Unaware that one day, maybe sooner than they think, it will be their body lying near the altar, covered and silent. What kind of stories will they want to leave behind? Their lies make her sick.

Mireille is being buried along with two other women and a boy. The priest assures the dozen or so people gathered that one of the stinking mounds had died a quiet death, an old death. The best kind. The other woman had died in childbirth. There was no mention made of the baby. Presumably, it had survived and was fighting it out with the tough little bundles known as the *enfants-trouvés*. If a child of the *crèche* lived through its first year, it was because they were able to get the greatest share of the milk of some malnourished mother. For the privilege of having her baby in secret, a nursing woman at the Salpêtrière would be assigned a few orphaned nurselings to feed from her. Some of the milk from the cows kept in the Salpêtrière pasture was also destined for the *crèche*, but it was so diluted with water and flour that only the most determined infants could suck any life out of the mixture.

Several women had been brought up in chains from the Maison de la Force for the funeral, and they wailed without restraint when the final blessing was pronounced over the dead mother. Girls from other dormitories would have been punished for filling the church with such unholy lament. Mourning, like everything else, was best done in silence. But these women had nothing to lose. A few extra lashes, maybe a missed meal, but those things were expected, ordinary for them. Screaming at the loss of a friend is worth the extra punishment. Laure wishes she could join them. The last soul being put to rest is that of a small boy who arrived last week with a cough common to street dwellers. His father stood at the front of the church, his hat in his hand, a country man in shabby clothing. Laure covers her nose with her scarf. If she tries hard enough, she can still smell the lavender of Madame d'Aulnay's perfume on it.

Several weeks ago, before Mireille had fallen sick, the girls had crowded around the trunk given to her by the hospital. It contained all the things that were meant to turn her into a wife in Canada. Laure had never seen so many luxuries gathered together for one young girl. The trunk contained a taffeta kerchief, shoe ribbon, one hundred needles, a comb, white thread, one pair of stockings, one pair of gloves, one pair of scissors, two knives, a thousand pins, one bonnet, four laces, and two silver livres. These things were all provided by the King. Mireille had also packed some additional belongings into the box. These included the yellow gown she had been wearing when she entered the Salpêtrière and the locket she kept under her pillow from the officer of the Carignan-Salières regiment whom she was going to marry. Mireille told them she would also be given a hundred livres as dowry, and a transit paid to Canada aboard a ship. The new coffer carrying her dowry from the King was being kept by Madame du Clos in the workshop until her departure.

Laure had been most jealous of the image of the young soldier in the locket. All the girls had crowded in to look at the tiny likeness. The boy's name was Frédéric, and he was commanding an army of men sent to fight the Savages of Canada. Mireille told the girls that these Savages were so fierce that they actually ate human hearts.

Ask her if they also eat women's hearts. Madeleine repeated Laure's question to Mireille.

Well, usually only those of men, who they think are brave, Mireille answered, but maybe they eat women's hearts as well. Actually, tell Laure that they mostly eat the hearts of priests.

Laure had envied the things Mireille had: the elegant fingers, the fancy dress, the soldier's locket, the refined words and clear singing voice. But Laure would not have wanted to go to Canada. Especially not when she learned about the Savages. Laure knew she had a brave heart. Madame Gage had even said so last night—*fille courageuse*—when she pulled the blanket up to Laure's neck after she had seen the Superior.

Remembering what Mireille had said about the Savages made Laure want to turn to look over her shoulder. At the altar, the priest is praying to send Mireille's spirit out of this prison of starvation and filth, up even past the gargoyles of Notre-Dame, to the clouds. Laure wants to turn around and see if the priest looks brave, if the Savages of Canada would choose to eat his heart.

Finally, the priest goes quiet. Madame Gage is pulling at Laure's sleeve, but her feet remain firm on the chapel floor. The flower in her hand has begun to wilt.

The Salpêtrière's finest example, a girl with a golden life, fingers that moved with confident grace, and a husband waiting across the sea, will be burned as dirty pestilence, her body not good enough for the overflowing cemetery. Laure doesn't want to leave. She doesn't want to know that by now outside the chapel door the sun has risen. She will have more space on her sewing bench. Hers is now the best lace in the workshop.

5

Back in the Sainte-Claire dormitory, Laure is sitting on Mireille's bed. They have already found another girl to occupy her spot. Madame Gage introduced her in the dormitory after the funeral. Her name is Jeanne, and she is tall with a large, homely face and hair already turning grey although she isn't even old. She is considered a *Bijou* because she can read and knows how to embroider. For the time being, while the other girls are at work, Laure is alone in the room with Madeleine, who carries in her arms Mireille's yellow gown. After the funeral, Madame du Clos brought the dress up from the workshop and handed it to Madeleine. The needlework instructor is holding onto the locket of Frédéric until she can give it to a suitable girl bound for Canada to return it to the officer. She also said that the royal gift of the trunk filled with the essentials for Mireille's new life in Canada had been reclaimed by the hospital.

"We shouldn't sit on this bed. It belongs to Jeanne now." Madeleine is standing, her torso hidden behind the bulky dress in her arms.

"I thought you were Mireille's friend," Laure says. "You

sound like the Superior who brings in a new girl before the old one has even been put to rest."

"Are you going to come for the midday meal today?" Madeleine asks, sitting down beside her. Laure doesn't answer, and Madeleine lays the dress down between them. Laure's eyes are drawn to the skirt. The bodice is even more impressive. It is reinforced by strips of whalebone and has short sleeves, and ends in a point over the abdomen area.

"Come on, Laure, you can't keep guarding this bed like a dog. Mireille doesn't care who uses it now." Madeleine takes the skirt onto her lap. "I think this dress would suit you well. I really have no use for it." She lifts the bodice up to Laure's chest.

Laure touches the dress and then pushes it away. "When will I ever need to wear this? Besides, I'm too thin now to look good in a gown." Laure can feel the bones of her shoulders if she brings them up to her ears. It doesn't help that she hasn't even been eating the usual meagre portions for the past two days. She slumps forward and rests her head on her palms.

"In the sewing shop. You'll need it when you get hired. Just like you always talk about."

Laure feels like it was years ago that she dreamed of finding employment and eventually a rich suitor through the Halles garment industry. The image of Mireille reaching for her with bleeding fingers and the smell of the Hôtel-Dieu and the chapel have shut out her thoughts of being a seamstress.

"What about you? Madame du Clos gave the dress to you." Laure knows that Madeleine is the favourite of Madame du Clos. She is everyone's favourite.

"That's only because it fits me." Laure raises her eyebrows, as they both know that isn't true. Madeleine shrugs. "If I need a dress someday, I'm sure it will be there for me. This one's for you. When you get your apprenticeship, you'll be able to start earning money right away. You won't have to pay off the debt for your dress." Laure knows that dresses such as the one in Madeleine's hands, a requisite to a seamstress position, often take years to pay off. But she cannot bring herself to feel enthusiastic at Madeleine's generous offer.

"They want us to pretend that we're different from the prostitutes just because we are called *Bijoux*. Do you think the people standing out there cheering like it was a public execution know that somewhere in a corner of this place a handful of girls know how to make *point de France* as well as they do in Venice or Alençon?"

"It doesn't matter what they think." Madeleine smiles and reaches for Laure.

Feeling Madeleine's hand on her shoulder, Laure shakes it off. "Don't you understand? We have been removed from *out there*. Those people gather outside our window for their monthly entertainment. To women like the Superior who come from their fine chambers, we provide a chance to be charitable." For once Laure actually believes her own words.

"Yes, Laure, there is no doubt that some women and men involved in charitable work are not motivated by their hearts, but what is the use of dwelling on that? Think of Madame du Clos and Madame Gage and how much they try to help the girls under their care. We are fortunate, Laure, to be here in this dormitory. With the working girls, learning skills."

"But when will we use these skills? When we're dead? When they've killed us with their watery broth and morsels of bread?"

"We'll get less if we complain. Come on. Let's put your dress away. I actually don't eat much, Laure. In fact, I find the portions to be too large at times. You can have my butter tomorrow and my beans on Friday. Then you'll fit this dress."

Laure watches as Madeleine, who has the body of a child, carefully folds the bulky dress. She notices that Madeleine's hands are shaking. She has frightened her by saying that they are no different than prostitutes. Laure wishes she could say something to reassure her. Something about being a seamstress next year, about meeting a Duke in the shop and being happy as his wife with children and fine clothes and a carriage. But now Laure doesn't believe these things are possible. Not with Mireille Langlois dead. What hope could there possibly be for a naive and pious child, and herself the daughter of a street singer?

Laure agrees to return to the sewing workshop under the condition that Madame du Clos helps her to compose a letter to the King. Laure has decided that frightening Madeleine with her bitter thoughts on their situation is of no use. She has to do something more. Madame du Clos tells Laure that she doubts the King will read the letter. He has many things to worry about in the kingdom, such as expanding his rule into the Spanish Netherlands, destroying the churches of Protestants, and building new ships. Nonetheless, Madame du Clos agrees to let Laure write the letter.

The needlework instructor isn't authorized to teach reading and writing, as she is neither a *maîtresse* nor an officer at the hospital. She cannot even read very well. She says it is because her eyes hurt too much at the end of the day, but Laure doubts that she could ever read. In fact, when Madame du Clos discovered that Laure knew how to read and write, she asked her to help out with her account books.

Laure looks forward to this task at the end of every Wednesday. The other girls are jealous that Laure gets to leave her needlework thirty minutes before the end of the day to retreat into the back room of the workshop. The small room is even darker than the main work area, and the air inside smells of ink and paper. The account books are on a shelf at the back of the room. Laure has to stand on a stool and use both hands to pull the heavy books down from the shelf. They contain the records of the workshop since 1663. Each book details the production of that year: the sewing, knitting, embroidering, and lacemaking of the girls in the workshop. How many tablecloths and napkins, handkerchiefs, socks, and sheets are produced and embroidered by the handful of girls who work there.

Letters written by hospital administrators about the workshop are kept in a separate book. Laure knows she isn't supposed to read these letters. But on the days that she finishes up early with the accounts, she hurries to take them down. Laure has a hard time deciphering the handwriting and can't understand all the words the writers use. Most of them are about the prices of supplies for the workshop. But there was one letter written by a man named Jean-Baptiste Colbert, one of the King's ministers, that complained to the Superior about the quality of the girls' needlework.

Laure was angry when she first read the words of this man. But now she will use his very complaints to address her concerns to the King. Laure will explain why the embroidery and lace of the hospital basement cannot compete with the work of other women in the kingdom. Madame du Clos has told Laure that there are thousands of women living in the Salpêtrière, and more entering each day. Maybe the King doesn't realize how thinly the food and water rations are stretched across the population. Laure knows there is no use complaining to the Superior. She will only talk about the girls' moral character and say that they should pray more.

Laure works on the letter to the King for two weeks. When the bells signalling the end of the workday ring throughout the hospital, she hurries to the back room of the workshop and writes one or two careful sentences that she has been rehearsing in her head all day. Then she makes her way back alone through the dark basement hallway, feeling the cold wall as she goes and listening for the sound of the other girls up ahead. She hurries up the two long flights of stairs, past the babies of the *crèche*, to the Sainte-Claire dormitory in time to catch up with the others for the evening meal.

When the letter is finished, Madame du Clos promises to seal it with her red wax and stamp. But Laure first wants to read what she has written to Madeleine. Laure hasn't told Madeleine about the letter. She wants to surprise her now that it is finished. Madeleine is kneeling at her cot when Laure rushes into the dormitory with the completed letter tucked under her sleeve. Since Mireille's death, Madeleine has been receiving special privileges of her own from Madame Gage. The governess has granted her permission to pray in the quiet of the dormitory while the other girls wait in the adjoining room for the arrival of the dinner cauldron.

"I've written a letter. To the King," Laure whispers. "I'll read it to you."

Madeleine turns to Laure, her eyes glazed. "To the King?"

"I think once he reads it, once he realizes our state, we will start eating food like the dinners I saw at Madame d'Aulnay's place. Pheasants and partridges, candied fruits, wine." Laure can still smell these dishes three years later as if she had just taken them heavy from the oven.

Madeleine crosses herself and kisses her fingers. She gets up from her knees and turns to sit on the floor beside Laure with her back against the cot. She listens as Laure reads the letter in a whisper, after first showing her the look of the black lines on the thick paper of Madame du Clos' account book.

March 1669, from the Salpêtrière, the Women's Division of the Hôpital Général de Paris

Mes salutations le Grand Roi,

This humble letter comes to Your Majesty from a girl enclosed in the Salpêtrière, the women's division of the General Hospital. I am living here, with all sorts of cripples, sick, and madwomen, some of whom are violent and disorderly as well. I thought it was my duty to inform you of the true conditions of the hospital. I hope you will accept what I have to say despite my lowly birth and humble stature.

I should first tell you how, at seventeen years old, I still find myself here. I lived for several years with Madame d'Aulnay of rue de la Chapelle. There I was taught to prepare lavish dinners, to sew, and to read. My former mistress was a widow and childless and very kind. In her home, I was treated almost like a daughter. This was after first having spent several

years in the Petit Enfant-Jésus dormitory of the
Salpêtrière. But Madame d'Aulnay, who was an old
woman, died three years ago. As I was her daughter in
appearances only, I did not reap any benefits from her
passing. I was brought back to the Salpêtrière where I
now find myself among the Bijoux of the Sainte-Claire
dormitory. As the months pass, I ask myself: Will I
be so lucky as to find another benefactor? I am only
seventeen, but already I have learned that the older a
woman gets, the fewer choices she has.

Still, I try to remain hopeful. I have received at the
hospital, along with a number of other young girls,
lessons in needlepoint. I excel at this skill and stand
to be apprenticed to one of the city's seamstresses. If I
work hard enough, and also use my skills at reading
and writing, I might one day have my own workshop.

However, I must bring something to your attention.
I understand that Your Majesty is very busy with wars
to fight and other concerns. But I know that tending
to this matter that affects the many girls and women
residing at the Salpêtrière will be of utmost concern
to you. Our food rations here are insufficient. For an
entire day, we are given only a pint of broth and five
quarterons of bread. Several times each week, peas and
salted butter are added to the broth. How can we fulfill
our respective duties on so little?

One of the girls in the dormitory, Mireille Langlois,
died of scurvy this spring. Her father had been an
officer in the war with Spain. I have since been given
one of her gowns, though of course it is not as fine
as those you are accustomed to seeing at court. The

dress, under better circumstances, that is when I am consuming some meat and a bit of cheese along with my bread and broth, would bring out the onyx brilliance of my eyes and hair. As it stands, my eyes and hair have grown dull and the dress too loose.

I am certain that this woeful circumstance is an oversight, preoccupied as His Most Christian Majesty must be with matters of great import throughout the vast Kingdom. Your Royal attention to the matter of our rations can quickly remedy our abject circumstance.

> Yours in humble service,
> Laure Beauséjour

Please accept from me a ribbon cut from the gown and a lock of my hair.

6

Madame du Clos agrees to help Laure get the letter to the King. The instructor likes to repeat that she would do anything in this world to help her girls. Unlike most of the officers of the Salpêtrière, Madame du Clos has been hired on contract for her knowledge of lacemaking. She has no particular interest in remaining employed for life at the hospital like most of the officers and *maîtresses*, and so cares less about its rigid rules. She lives with her widowed sister in the city and does not rely on her wages for survival.

Madame du Clos has promised that she will bring Laure to the seamstress district of Paris on Friday to deliver the letter. She says she knows just the messenger to give it to. But first she wants Laure to be fitted for Mireille's dress so she can wear it on the day that they meet this messenger. Madame du Clos says the letter will have a better chance of reaching the King if Laure wears the dress. Laure detests when Madame du Clos calls her a "poor soul" and pats her on the back, but this time she lets the foolish instructor talk this way.

Laure has been excited to put away her lace at the end of each day to work on the dress. Fortunately, she is the same height as Mireille was, so the length of the dress was fine, but the bodice had to be drawn in a little as Mireille had been well fed, therefore a little plump, when she entered the hospital. Madame du Clos also encouraged Laure to make a few changes to the dress to suit current fashions. Now that the alterations are complete, she is less excited about trying it on. She wants nothing more than to put on this gown and to look as elegant as Mireille did when she first entered the workshop wearing it. But Laure is afraid it won't fit her right even after all the adjustments, that she will look like a foolish pauper playing dress-up in the clothes of a princess. She must also admit that she is a little frightened to put on a garment that is above her social status. She was a child when Madame d'Aulnay would place silk hats on her head, long gloves, fans, all of which were far too big for her. Although the women of Madame's salon disapproved even then of dressing a poor girl in finery, it had been no more harmful than outfitting a toy doll in the Queen's fashions.

Laure lifts the box containing the gown from beneath the sewing table and follows Madame du Clos, who has two gold ribbons streaming behind her, into the back room. The needlework instructor holds the dress away from her weak eyes. "Not a bad job considering we only had muslin and fake gems to work with."

"It looks like a gown for the royal court." Laure has already slipped off her work dress.

"Not quite, poor soul. Court dresses are made of taffeta and decorated with precious gems. They cost ten times what this dress is worth."

Laure cannot imagine a dress ten times more exquisite than this one. Madame du Clos has given her a small amount of silver thread to sew into the bodice and some ruby and turquoise beads for the trim. She had also suggested to Laure that the bodice cut be lowered. Not so much that Laure will be mistaken for one of those despicable women that sell themselves for coins on the street, but enough to give a hint of her soft chest. She has also given Laure a leather string for tightening the whalebone corset, and the two ribbons for her hair.

Madame tightens the corset with one swift yank. Laure feels her ribs squeezing against her lungs. She exhales and cannot draw in a new breath. Any fat Laure has on her bones has been squeezed up to her chest. She raises her hands. Panic rises in her throat.

"You can't breathe?" Madame du Clos laughs. "Breathing is for peasant girls tending their sheep in the countryside. You are choosing another life." Madame du Clos' voice renews Laure's hope in the future. In the dark basement of the hospital that was once an old munitions factory, where madwomen of all ages can be heard wailing upstairs and starvation rations are carefully accounted for at mealtimes, Madame du Clos dishes out kind words. "In elegant circles, women do not breathe. They steal breath from those around them. Now suck in your stomach and lift your chest."

"Even if I only—" Laure's breath is cut off again as Madame tightens the corset further. How would she be able to work as a seamstress all day in such a constricted garment?

"Yes, no matter, you will be a charming lady. It isn't so bad once you get used to it. Besides"—her chubby face breaks into a smile—"you must suffer to be beautiful. Now suck in your stomach and lift your chest."

When Laure finally emerges from the back room, her cheeks are flushed from the effort of changing into the dress. Madame has lent her a sparkling red necklace to wear for the day. Laure strains her eyes to look past her chin at the jewels resting on her pale chest.

"Look at those ribbons in your hair," Madame du Clos says, and Laure reaches to touch the silky material. "Many women dressed in far more elaborate and expensive gowns could only hope to look as lovely as you do." Madame du Clos pushes Laure's back until she is standing in the workshop in front of the other girls. Laure can tell by their eyes that Madame du Clos wasn't exaggerating.

While the instructor is describing to the girls the adjustments that were made to Laure's dress, a man enters the workshop. The girls freeze, and Madame du Clos turns to him and bows. "Bonsoir, Monsieur le Directeur." It is the director of the entire General Hospital, including the men's division. He comes by the workshop every few months to check on the progress of their production. Normally, the girls are at their stations and working in total silence when he comes through. This is a surprise visit.

"Bonsoir Madame, mesdemoiselles." His words are polite, but he doesn't remove his hat as he surveys the disarray of the workshop and the girls standing around Laure. He belongs to the Compagnie du Saint-Sacrement. The Superior said to the girls one day that the members of the Compagnie are good men who are trying to build Jerusalem in the middle of Babylon. Laure asked Madeleine what that meant, since she knows more biblical quotes and references than Laure because she had been with the Sulpiciens before she ended up at the Salpêtrière, but she just said that it meant the men of the Saint-Sacrement were trying to make the Salpêtrière a better place. Nobody knows very much about the Compagnie, as it is a secret gathering of religious men.

"You have a client with you …?" The director sounds confused. There aren't normally customers in the Salpêtrière workshops. "It looks like you're turning this room into a real commercial enterprise. I hope you fit in plenty of prayers for these girls." His wooden soles reverberate on the floor as he walks by each of the work stations.

Madame du Clos nods her lowered head.

"Some men," the director continues, "think that commerce is the ultimate purpose of existence. They'll use any hands they can, even those of the poor, to fuel their greed." The director has his arms crossed over his chest and is walking past the table filled with the girls' completed work. "There isn't much I can do to oppose this kind of thinking." He then walks up to Laure, examining her dress. His eyes stop on her chest. When he gets beside her, he whispers into her ear: "Cover that breast that I am not to see. By such things are souls injured, and guilty thoughts made to enter the mind." Then he says to her aloud, "Mademoiselle, what do you think of these young women? They aren't exactly cultivated, but they do work very hard."

Laure blushes. She glances quickly at Madame du Clos, whose eyes are wide with fear. Laure does her best to suck in a little air.

"Yes, they work … like angels." She feels her cheeks burning.

"*Très bien*, Mademoiselle. The King will be happy that his aims are being realized." The director doesn't return Laure's smile, but turns instead to Madame du Clos.

"Madame, *excusez-moi*, but next time you might want to keep Divine values in mind when you fashion your dresses." He glances again at Laure and turns to go.

After he has gone, Laure breaks into laughter. "Did the hospital director really think that I was a Parisian lady?" she asks.

"Yes, thank God for us all that he did." Madame du Clos is trembling, but manages a smile as she quickly helps Laure out of the gown and back into her work dress.

In the morning, Madame du Clos gives Madeleine instructions to look after the workshop. She then sets off with Laure and the letter for the seamstress area of the city. Their destination is on rue Saint-Honoré, in the new fashion district near the Place des Victoires. According to Madame du Clos, their only hope of getting Laure's letter to the King is to bring it to the shop of the Tailleur Brissault.

For sustenance on their journey through the city, Madame du Clos has brought with her some bread and meat, which she carries in a fashionable purse. Both women have on their best dresses—in Laure's case it is the only one she possesses—and bonnets to protect against the sun. The archer at the hospital's gate lets them by with a flourish of his arm. On this walk, Laure receives envious stares from the peasants along the Seine path. She keeps her head raised high and pretends that she cannot see them looking at her. She holds up the skirt of her dress to guard against the mud of the streets and is both relieved and impressed when Madame du Clos offers a man with a donkey cart a few sous to carry them to the Pont-Neuf. From there, Madame du Clos chooses to walk only the paved streets, and even then they keep to the elevated centre of the road to avoid the sludge from the ditches on either side.

"Is this Tailleur Brissault some sort of duke or prince?" Laure asks as they near the shop. "What is his connection to the King's court?"

"No, he is a tailor. Not even a good one." Laure looks at Madame du Clos, who goes on. "Even the cut of his suits is mediocre. But he provides something noblemen have a hard time finding at the Palace … poor girls."

"But there are poor girls all over, on every street corner." What a ridiculous notion that anyone should find a shortage of poor women in Paris. There are all types, tall, short, pious, crass. On their journey to the tailor's shop, they must have passed three dozen destitute girls.

"Yes, but the noblemen prefer the ones that Brissault selects and cleans up for them. He calls them his sewing assistants. But their skills have nothing to do with sewing." Laure is unsure why Madame du Clos is bringing her to this man who sounds despicable.

Tailleur Brissault is there when they enter the shop, crouched at the haunches of a nobleman. Both men turn to look at the women entering through the door. Laure can see the tailor's eyes straining to make them out. Judging by what Madame du Clos just told her, Brissault is probably trying to assess them. Laure guesses that Madame du Clos is in her forties although she has never dared to ask her age. She is short and heavy, with soft features and gentle eyes, like a kind grandmother. She does not look at all like the sort of woman who would be a sewing assistant to this Brissault, but her dress is made of calico, a good material, even though the cut is more outmoded than the one Laure is wearing.

"Tailleur Brissault, how do you do today?" Madame du Clos' voice is stern. She remains standing near the door.

"What brings a fine lady such as you to my shop? Come on in so I can get a better look." Laure can tell the latter part of his comment is addressed to her even though he speaks to her instructor. She wonders why Madame du Clos had her dress up to see this ugly man. He is like an enormous cat, even to his rounded midriff.

His shop is easily three times the size of the workshop at the Salpêtrière. Brissault's shelves and tables are overflowing with bright silks, plush velvets, and cottons. His hangers are filled with finished men's suits, as well as women's whalebone stays and dress skirts. These are all items that seamstresses are forbidden to make. Many of the scraps from the tailor shops get resold in the riverside markets to women like Madame du Clos so they can make hats, purses, and hair ribbons.

In Brissault's shop, five or six apprentice tailors work cross-legged on the table. None of them glanced up when the women entered. They must be accustomed to the arrival of high-ranked people and so do not find the women to be interesting. Laure recognizes Gamy, the pin merchant, and he tips his hat to Madame du Clos when he sees her. Gamy is seated near the door waiting for Brissault to finish up with the Duke.

The Duke is wearing a powdered wig, breeches, and an embroidered velvet jacket. He is more magnificent than the archers in their uniforms. Laure wonders if this intimidating man is really seeking a pair of pants from Brissault's shop.

Madame du Clos wastes no more time with formalities.

"I have with me a letter for the King written by this young lady."

"What sort of letter? Not a petition on behalf of the seamstresses, I hope. The King is quite satisfied with the way clothing is being produced." Brissault rises with a loud intake of breath. "There we are, Monsieur le Duc. I think that does it."

The nobleman's two guards step forward. They draw back again when the Duke waves his hand at them.

"No, nothing like that. I am not here to interfere with your … business." Madame du Clos says the last word as if she is spitting something rotten from her mouth.

Brissault smiles. "You know that even the King asks the police for detailed descriptions of the city's prostitutes when they are arrested. He then pores over these reports in between his official duties. If the King himself seeks this sort of entertainment"—Brissault laughs—"then my shop is guaranteed a good and prosperous business, built on the simplest of precepts. No need for fancy cuts."

The Duke clears his throat. "A letter for the King, you say? From this lovely young lady?"

Laure looks away as his eyes meet hers.

"I suppose only the King himself is good enough for her. But you do know, Mademoiselle, that His Majesty has many important affairs to tend to."

Brissault chuckles. "And quite a few young ladies to look after as well."

The Duke gives the tailor an irritated look. "I am on my way to the court tonight, Madame. Maybe I can be your messenger."

"It is a letter of flattery. It is sure to put His Majesty in a good mood." Madame du Clos holds out the letter. Laure doesn't like the way the Duke's eyes have remained on her even while he speaks to Madame du Clos. She wishes she wasn't wearing this dress, that they hadn't lowered the neckline. She wants to protest that it isn't that kind of letter. It is about something important. She wants to tell these men that not all poor girls are prostitutes. She wishes Madeleine were here.

"I suppose it can't hurt to pass it on. As long as I have your assurance that its contents will please His Majesty."

"Oh, yes, in a trifling way, of course. The girl is barely seventeen and has her head in the royal clouds. She can do nothing but speak of the powerful spell she swoons under each time she imagines her letter being read by the King."

"I—" Laure feels betrayed. She wants Madame du Clos to stop telling these lies about her letter.

"But His Majesty has been known to abhor flattery by his ... inferiors." The Duke raises his eyebrow and smiles at Laure. He extends his hand for the letter.

"I am certain that even the King can tolerate a few innocent pleasantries from a sweet young girl," Madame du Clos says as she relinquishes it to him.

"As long as she isn't too innocent." The Duke smiles, tucking the letter into his velvet pocket.

Madame du Clos bows and puts her hand on Laure's back, steering her out of the shop with hurried feet.

Laure is shaking. She wants to tear the restrictive dress off her body and replace it with the coarse fabric of the hospital dress. It is this gown that is slowing her down, keeping her from getting away from Brissault and the Duke and their filthy eyes.

Madame du Clos takes her by the shoulders. "I'm sorry, Laure, you poor soul."

"Why did you let them think I had written that kind of letter to the King?"

"If I had told them what the contents really were, they would have thrown it out just as quickly as we gave it to them. Now it might stand some chance of getting where you want it to go. Besides, don't worry too much about what men like Brissault and that Duke think of you. They have only one way of looking at women."

When Laure returns to the Salpêtrière, she changes into her grey dress. Some of the girls have heard about her letter and want to know if she succeeded. If there will be something more for them to eat for dinner. Laure tells them she is tired and doesn't want to discuss her trip. Now that she is out of the dress, at least she can breathe again. But she still feels constricted remembering the eyes of the Duke and the fat tailor on her body. Her thoughts return to the prostitutes she saw in the courtyard last month. All the girls in their shabby dresses crammed together like squealing pigs and the madams following behind in their covered carriages. Laure wonders if that Duke, or some of the other men at court, went to see these women before they were brought in to the Salpêtrière.

Laure is called up to the office of the Superior and Madame du Clos is asked to accompany her. The instructor talks about the sewing work of this or that girl the whole time they walk through the dark hallways up from the workshop toward the light of the Superior's office. It only serves to make Laure more nervous. She tries to quiet her breath by concentrating on the sound of their shoes against the floor.

When they enter the office, the Superior is sitting with her back to them. Without turning to face them, she rises to her feet. Although the Superior is short and even thinner than Laure, the sight of her dark-clad frame rising from the chair fills Laure with terror.

When the Superior finally turns to them, she is smiling. It is the cruellest smile Laure has ever seen.

"It seems that no matter what we do to help the poor women of the hospital, there are some who refuse to be pleased." She pauses, as if she is thinking hard.

"It was only a harmless gesture." Madame du Clos has already begun to make matters worse.

The Superior does not respond. Instead she continues to stare at Laure. "Do you remember the place you came from before you entered the Salpêtrière?"

"I was in the home of Madame d'Aulnay." Laure's voice comes out weak like that of a very young girl.

"No. Before that. Where do you come from?" There is a slight tremor in the Superior's lip.

"I was with my father and my mother."

"You were picked up from the street, cold, dirty, and wet, like a starving rat. The very sort of creature that disappears one night and nobody notices is gone."

Laure's face fills with blood.

"What do you think would have happened to you if our archers hadn't saved you when you were a child? What fate would have befallen you if you hadn't been taken in, cleaned up, nourished, and taught to pray?"

"You know how children are," Madame du Clos says. "They have all sorts of ideas—"

"We are not here, paid from His Royal Highness' coffer, to entertain the whims of every wretch with a deluded mind."

The Superior takes several steps toward her desk. She picks up a package.

"Since you seem to have so many talents and much knowledge of the outside world, why don't you tell me what you know of the place they call Canada."

Laure glances sideways at Madame du Clos, who shrugs. What does any of this have to do with Canada? That was where Mireille was going to marry an officer. Laure tries to remember everything she can about this place. "I know only that Canada is far across the sea and that the Savages there eat the hearts of priests." She thinks back to Mireille lying dead at the Hôtel-Dieu and what the nurse said. "And that it is better to die than to go there."

The Superior raises an eyebrow and lets out a caustic laugh. "Yes, that is quite a good description of the place, wouldn't you say?" She looks at Madame du Clos, who has taken a handkerchief from her sleeve and is dabbing her eyes with it.

The Superior then looks down at the package she is carrying and hands two letters to Laure. Laure recognizes Madame du Clos' stamp and the workshop paper. It is the letter she wrote to the King. The other letter must be his response. "You can read this yourself, I suppose."

Laure is disappointed to see that the response is not from

the King at all. Rather, it was written by his minister, Jean-Baptiste Colbert, the same man who complained about the quality of the girls' needlework. It reads:

Parlement de Paris, 1669

Nos chers et bien aimés directeurs et administrateurs de l'hopital général de nostre bonne ville de Paris,
 The King sends his regards and is pleased with the great expansion plans underway at the Hôpital Général. It is particularly wonderful to have Messieurs le Vau and le Brun, architects to the King, replacing the Saint-Denis chapel with a magnificent church. We remain convinced that the founding of the General Hospital, the largest in all of Europe, is one of the great endeavours of our time.
 The young female residents of the Salpêtrière must understand that the hospital provides an excellent opportunity to receive training. They must know that beyond the doors of the Salpêtrière in the alleys of Paris lies a far worse fate for them. I was disappointed to hear your report that the workshops are not producing well. I am sure you will find some way to encourage the women to be more industrious. It is important that we seize the opportunity in textiles. I hope that you will help us to surpass the Venetian production of lace with our new point de France. It has been making a sensation at the French court and is sure to do so abroad as well.
 On the subject of industry, I would like to promote commerce in our colonies, particularly in Canada.

However, because our colonists have been embroiled in wars with the Iroquois there, we have been unable to freely acquire the riches of that place.

There is a vast abundance of furs and wood for ship construction in that country. The main problem is that we do not have a settled population in Canada. There are few women in the colony other than some nuns. But it is not in the best interest of France, which has continental struggles to contend with, to empty its own land of people to fill a colony.

However, the project we agreed upon several years ago of sending to Canada a number of orphans and widows from the hospital has proven successful. The Intendant, Jean Talon, has reported to me that in recent years there have been considerably more marriages and births in Canada.

To this end, I would like to send another one hundred women from the Salpêtrière to Canada this spring. I leave it to your discretion to choose those who would be best suited for this new adventure, provided that they are not too unpleasant to look at.

Jean-Baptiste Colbert
Minister to the King

Laure is confused. There is no mention whatsoever in his response of her letter, and yet they must have read it, for it has ended up back at the Salpêtrière, in the hands of the Superior.

"You are a clever one, so you must have figured out that we have chosen you to be among the girls sent from this hospital to Canada this summer." The Superior smiles, and there is a look of deep satisfaction in her eyes.

Madame du Clos gasps and clutches for her chest as if the Superior's words have brought on some sort of fit. Laure feels as if the weight of the entire Salpêtrière building has just descended upon her body. She cannot go to Canada. Her life is here, at the hospital for now, and later she will be a seamstress. What will become of her if she is sent across the sea to a place worse than death, more frightening than hell itself? What about Madeleine? How can Laure leave her behind? The King is a cruel, cruel man. Laure fills with hot rage, but it is of no use. The most powerful person Laure has on her side is Madame du Clos, and she is blubbering apologies and tears like a child. She is powerless to prevent the Superior from doing whatever she pleases.

⚜

In the days before her departure, Laure thinks about what it means to be going to Canada, how she will not become a seamstress in the Halles, and what a terrible outcome that is. Madame du Clos, who finally stopped crying at the news, tries to reassure her by saying that in New France, as Canada is also called, there are no women begging for their living on the street. In fact, there are hardly any women there at all, so Laure will have her choice of husbands and will live like a gentlewoman.

Laure is seventeen and doesn't want a husband yet, even if it were an officer like Mireille's, so this is of little comfort to her. She asks Madame du Clos if she can be a seamstress in New France. Surely the women there will want to dress well for all these men. Madame du Clos says that maybe Laure will be able to do that. The instructor pulls up the stool and takes down a heavy ream of blue cloth from high on the workshop shelf and cuts enough material from it to make a new dress. It is her parting gift to her most skilled *Bijou*. That night, Laure holds the material in her arms when she sleeps.

7

$\mathcal{L}$aure has found it hard to work on her lace piece and the other sewing tasks assigned to her ever since she found out she was being sent to Canada. The careful attention she pays to her stitches and the pride she takes in completing the pieces have lost their meaning. There is no reputation to build for a career as a Parisian seamstress, no reason to work hard any more. Madame du Clos has permitted Laure, her best set of fingers, to languish behind the others.

Back in the dormitory after their day of work, Madame Gage leads them through the Miserere mei Deus, their usual nighttime prayer. When she has finished, she turns to Laure and asks her to be the one to recite the act of contrition to the group.

"This is the last time you will recite it for us." The governess turns to the others and says, "Laure Beauséjour will be leaving on a ship for Canada next week."

There is a gasp in the room from those who haven't yet heard the rumour. In whispers, they ask what Laure has done to merit such a brutal punishment. Only girls from la Force or Pitié or the worst dormitories would be so condemned. The word they use to describe her departure is *banishment*.

How wrong Laure had been to ever envy Mireille for having a husband in this terrifying place.

Laure waits for Madame Gage to correct the girls, to say something positive about the place she is going to. The governess could tell the other girls that Laure will soon be married, that she will live in her own house and have a seamstress shop across the sea in New France. But the governess only tells the girls to be quiet and looks at Laure to see if she has heard them denouncing her lot.

Laure swallows hard to begin the recitation: "*Mon Dieu, j'ai un extrême regret de vous avoir offensé, parce que vous êtes infiniment bon, infiniment aimable, et que le péché vous déplaît ...*" It does feel as if she has greatly sinned. Why else would she be so unfortunate as to be among the women from viler dormitories being sent to Canada?

There is silence in the room when Laure finishes the prayer. She lowers her head and waits for Madame Gage to leave for the night. If only she could tell the other girls of Sainte-Claire that going to Canada is not so bad. After all, Mireille Langlois was supposed to go there. But everyone at the Salpêtrière knows that it is better to spend some days in solitary confinement in the basement cells, or even to die of scurvy within the confines of the hospital, than to be banished to Canada or the French Islands. For banishment across the sea is just like death, in that no woman has ever returned to the hospital to tell of her adventures there.

But Laure is wiser and knows more than these ignorant girls who have seen nothing of the world. There are people who call Canada the New World and who have posed their greatest dreams in the direction of that place. Could Laure not be one of these women as well? Probably not, as she has not heard of seamstresses or women in elegant gowns finding much of anything in Canada. But another idea comes to her. Suddenly, Canada may not be as bad as she had thought.

Laure can sense as the girls change from their day dresses into their nightgowns that they want to talk amongst themselves about her departure to Canada. She catches some of them looking at her and growing quiet when her eyes meet theirs. Madeleine hands Laure her nightgown and kneels beside the bed for her prayers.

That night, as they lie side by side on the cot, Madeleine takes Laure's hand and tells her not to pay any attention to the girls. They do not know a thing about the outside world, she says. Nevertheless, Laure can feel Madeleine's hand trembling a little.

It is usually during these brief moments, when all the work duties and prayers of the day have been completed and the girls lie exhausted in their cots, that Laure talks to Madeleine about the future she dreams of for them. Their future, if it is to be any good at all, will take place beyond the hospital's courtyard, when they have been released from the Salpêtrière. Usually, Laure talks about how the two of them will become the best seamstresses in all of Paris and how they will have their own lace-production workshop with their very own apprentice girls and become as famous as the women of Alençon. After they have produced the finest, most expensive royal lace for some years, men from the court will come to seek their hands in marriage. With their new fortunes, they will then be able to afford silks and satins for their creations. Although after meeting the Duke in Tailleur Brissault's workshop, Laure no longer mentions the part about the marriages. Besides, Madeleine has often told Laure that she never wants to get married.

After Laure recounts each plan for their future, Madeleine replies in the same way. "That sounds like a wonderful life, Laure. If it is meant to be, God will grant us what we need."

Laure can't think of any reason why God wouldn't want them to become renowned seamstresses. She really wishes that Madeleine could muster a little more enthusiasm about their futures. Instead she seems only to be interested in praying and in the banal routine of their paltry existence at the hospital. Perhaps it is because Madeleine has always lived under the strict rules of an institution and has not seen that it is possible to live another life, one that is not controlled each moment by religious superiors.

Still, Laure cannot imagine waking each day in the meagre light and fetid stench of the dormitory room without seeing the gentle face of her dearest friend. Leaving Madeleine is the hardest part of being banished to Canada by the Superior. Much of Laure's thoughts in the past weeks have been preoccupied with how to get Madeleine to accompany her. She knows that somehow the trip, the banishment, will be less agonizing if her friend is with her. Tonight, while she was reciting the act of contrition to the others, it came to Laure how she would get Madeleine to come. She has decided to tell Madeleine the one story she knows about Canada.

Laure waits until most of the girls have stopped whispering and there is the sound in the dormitory of deep breaths. She then tells Madeleine that she has a very important story she would like to share with her, that it is a story written by a Queen. She heard it when she was a servant in Madame d'Aulnay's house. Madeleine expresses the same peaceful indifference each time Laure mentions her years with Madame d'Aulnay. She feels no envy toward Laure for the enchanting life she had as a young

girl living with a wealthy woman in the city while Madeleine
was a poor inhabitant of a Sulpicien monastery in Aunis.

"What an exciting life you have already lived, Laure. Tell me
about this Queen and her stories," Madeleine says, accustomed
to these late-night interruptions to her prayers and sleep.

Laure tells Madeleine that the story was from a book written
by a French Queen, Marguerite de Navarre. One of Madame
d'Aulnay's afternoon visitors brought over the book, and the
women sat together reading the stories. "Madame d'Aulnay said
that the Queen of Navarre had been too clever for a woman. A
monk who lived during her time thought that the Queen should
be thrown into a sack and dropped into the Seine for writing
such stories, but that never happened, because the Queen was
too well loved." Laure can feel her cheeks start to burn as she
lays the foundation for what she really wants to express to her
friend. Will Madeleine who is always so kind and gentle grow
angry for once at being asked to go to Canada? Does she love
Laure enough to make such a tremendous sacrifice?

"The story the Queen wrote was about a young woman
named Marguerite who travelled to Canada. The Marguerite
in the Queen's story went to Canada a long time ago, before
there were any towns or soldiers in that place. There weren't
any other women from France living there yet."

"It must have been even more frightening in those times,"
Madeleine says.

"Yes, there were no houses, no churches, only the Savages
and the jungle. She travelled with the adventurer Jacques
Cartier, who was seeking gold and a way to China. But you will
see, she was a very brave woman."

Laure pauses as she hears footsteps in the hallway outside
the dormitory. It is probably Madame Gage or one of the

officers coming to check that the girls are sleeping. In the distance, from another dormitory, Laure can make out the faint sound of a woman screaming. If one stops to listen, the muffled cries of the mad and infirm women of the other dormitories can be heard at intervals throughout the night as well as during the day.

"The Marguerite in the story had been a real woman who travelled with her husband on a ship to Canada. Not like the girls they are sending from here that don't yet have husbands."

Madeleine interrupts Laure to say that she never wants to get married like the girl Marguerite.

"The husband isn't really the point of the story, except to show that women can be faithful both to men and to God."

Madeleine nods and goes on listening.

"So this Marguerite follows her husband, who was an artisan, probably a shoe cobbler because Madame du Clos has told me that this is a necessary trade in new lands where people must first do much walking in order to finally settle somewhere. So Marguerite follows her husband the shoe cobbler onto a ship. Onboard the ship, the husband gets into trouble, for it is the nature of men to get into trouble when they travel to foreign places."

Madeleine asks Laure what kind of trouble the husband gets into.

Laure says she isn't sure exactly except that the cobbler had betrayed his master in some way that involved the native Savages. "I cannot imagine what sort of betrayal except it would surely have been bad to trust those people as they do not speak French nor are they Catholic."

"Are the Savages of Canada Protestants? In La Rochelle, there are many Protestants," Madeleine says.

"The Savages of Canada are not even Protestants but something far worse, closer to country witches with incantations and potions of mysterious poisons," Laure explains. "The captain of the ship, Roberval, discovered the cobbler's betrayal of his master and decided to hang him. But his wife, Marguerite, pleaded instead that her husband be allowed to live and that the two of them be dropped from the ship onto an uninhabited island of Canada."

"It is natural that a woman should try to keep her husband from hanging, even though he has been disloyal," Madeleine says.

Laure then tells Madeleine that the wife asked the captain, before he dropped them on the island, to give them only the subsistence they would need: some wine, bread, maybe some seeds for the next growing season, and the Bible. Her husband also wanted to take his arquebus with him.

"But what would she do with a Bible if there was no priest there to read it for her?" Madeleine asks.

"This woman could read the Bible on her own," Laure says. "And so the couple was dropped, by the Sieur de Roberval, onto the island in Canada. They set about right away to build some sort of a hut in the jungle."

"But I thought Canada is a cold place and not a jungle," Madeleine says.

"The Queen didn't know that when she wrote the story, as she had never been to Canada herself. When the lions and other beasts come for the couple, they fight them off, the man with his arquebus and the woman with her stones. They even kill a few of the creatures to eat. At night by the light of their fire, the woman reads the Bible to her husband. But he grows weaker on their diet of meat and on the putrid water of Canada. He eventually bloats up and dies. Marguerite buries him as best she can, but the wretched island beasts dig up his body. They drag it past her in their fierce mouths trying to shake her faith now that she is alone, but for the comfort of her Bible.

"But Marguerite persevered with her prayers and songs in exaltation of God. She fed her body meagre portions of whatever roots and fruits she found on the island, and her spirit drank in the results of her prayers. In the spring a ship came for her. She was brought back to France and introduced to the Queen."

Laure takes Madeleine's hand in hers. "The girl in the story is like you. She was brave and loyal and believed above all else that God would look after the couple in their time of need."

By the time Laure finishes telling Madeleine the story, there is only silence around them in the hospital. The madwomen have been calmed for the night, the officers and governesses retired to their rooms. A few minutes later, when Laure thinks that she is the only one left awake in the room, Madeleine takes her hand and whispers in her ear.

"I will join you in your banishment. Tomorrow, let's talk to Madame du Clos and Madame Gage to see if I can come with you to Canada."

8

$\mathcal{T}$he sixty or so girls leaving Paris for Canada hear Mass in the chapel of the Salpêtrière at three o'clock on the morning of their departure. Laure and Madeleine are the only girls leaving from the Sainte-Claire dormitory. Madame Gage came to get them from their bed and whispered for them to follow her out to the main hallway where the other girls were gathered. Dozens of others have been recruited from the less reputable dormitories. None of the women look much older than thirty, although most seem older than Laure and Madeleine. Some of their faces are meek and dull as if they are still asleep, while others are filled with the wide-eyed rage of the slightly mad. Laure and Madeleine try to avoid meeting their eyes. All share a fear of the tremendous journey that lies ahead.

At four o'clock, following the Mass, the women trudge in silence along the same river path Laure took to get to the Hôtel-Dieu. A brigade of archers, some on horseback, follows them, making the journey feel like a prison escort. Just south of the Bièvre Bridge, they meet up with about thirty more girls from la Pitié. The governesses from the Salpêtrière who have accompanied them have given them strict orders to stay away from these *filles de mauvaise vie*. A few of the Pitié girls are weeping, but most stand waiting with stoic faces and don't look very different from the Salpêtrière convoy, although these women are all chained together at the waist like prostitutes.

It takes a long time for the men to prepare the barge on the Seine that will take the girls down the river to Rouen and beyond to the port at Le Havre, where they will board the ship to Canada. There is much shouting and shifting of supplies as they work to secure the load. The whole time the men scramble from the pier to the boat, heaving food for their journey and their marriage coffers onto the barge. The girls are ordered to remain quiet.

Laure wonders why they are leaving so early in the morning, why there is so much secrecy behind their departure, and why nobody wants to speak to them about the trip to Canada. The officers from the Salpêtrière and from la Pitié, many of whom Laure has not seen before, say they don't know anything about crossing the seas, about living in Canada—that it is men and foreigners who do these things. One of the girls in the line, with a vicious face and scraggly hair, says that they have been given something worse than a death sentence. An archer orders her to be quiet.

Over an hour passes before the girls can finally board. It is May and still quite cold before the sun rises, especially when rain begins to fall in a cold mist over them. As they step onto the barge, the officers of the Salpêtrière lead them in singing *Veni Creator*. The boat has been divided into two sections by hay piled high, and covered in canvas: one side is for the girls from the Salpêtrière and the other for those from la Pitié. Their coffers have been placed at the centre of the boat.

Once Madeleine had agreed to come to Canada with Laure, they went to Madame du Clos and asked her to convince Madame Gage and the Superior that both girls should go. Madame du Clos assured the women that there were other seamstresses who could perform as well in her workshop as the two departing girls and that the productivity the hospital director demanded would not suffer because two of the best girls were leaving. Madame du Clos pretended that Madeleine was also an ill-behaved girl, that she and Laure were both more trouble than they were worth, and that she was glad to see them go. Madame Gage knew that this was not true, that Madeleine was an exemplary girl and that Madame du Clos was fond of both of them, but she remained quiet. Still, the Superior had argued against sending Madeleine, saying she didn't want to see one of the best girls they had in a hospital of useless wretches sent off to Canada. The purpose of their agreement with the King, after all, was to send the worst possible women from the hospital to Canada. In the end it was Madeleine who had convinced the Superior, by vowing she would cause trouble in the dormitory if she were left behind. The Superior had called Madeleine a fool for throwing away her life to please a troublemaker like Laure and had agreed that Canada was the best place for both of them.

The convoy makes its way down the Seine throughout the morning and well into the afternoon. When night falls, the girls strain by the light of the archers' torches to make out the shore of the country they are leaving behind. They pass towns and villages along the way: Poissy, Mantes-la-Jolie, Louviers, and Elbeuf. The archers complain that they should stop and spend the night in one of these towns, but the officers insist that no money has been allotted for such a purpose. They travel for the better part of two days down the wending river and are exhausted when they reach Rouen.

A priest welcomes them to shore and they spend the night in the monastery. In the morning, another dozen or so girls from Normandie are waiting to join them. These girls have been recruited by the priests from poor farms. They are dressed in their best country clothes, although Laure would prefer to be wearing her hospital day dress rather than one of their bonnets and sagging dresses. Laure overhears the priest tell one of these hardy girls, who stares with disdain at the hospital girls, that the sea crossing will rid them of their city filth.

They arrive in Le Havre, where they are to board the ship, later that afternoon. The city itself is small and less impressive than Rouen. But Laure catches her first glimpse of the sea beyond the swampy shore. By now there are only a few archers still with them and a new woman, Madame Bourdon, who is from Canada and met them in Rouen. She will accompany them throughout the ship's crossing. It strikes Laure that she will never see Madame du Clos, Madame Gage, or any of the other women of the Salpêtrière again. Her past is behind her; there is no turning back. Who will be waiting for her in New France, and will they be kind? Who will ring the bells at mealtime, for prayers, and when it is time to go to sleep?

An angry mob of twenty or thirty people waits for the girls when they moor. They are poor men and women, farmers and sailors carrying the instruments of their trade as weapons. As their boat pulls into port, the archers shout into the air for the crowd to back up. Women and men scream that they will not allow their daughters to be banished to a frozen land of misery or to meet their death at sea. That Canada is no place for women and that the King had better hang his criminals rather than send them across the sea to Canada.

Along with the chilly wind and the strength of the foaming waves crashing against the port town, this brutish group of protestors only serves to frighten the girls. There is much excitement at the port as the ships returned from distant, mostly warmer, seas are unloaded of riches: coffee, sugar, cotton, tobacco, and spices. Already this merchandise is being bargained for and sold for dispersal down the very river Laure has just left behind. Laure has never felt smaller or more alone in all her life. Madeleine has been praying her rosary for most of the journey and conversing with some of the other girls from the hospital, who talk mostly of the contents of their coffers, the ribbons and fabric they have brought with them. Madeleine is so kind to all of them, listening to their plans for marriage and a better life in Canada. Laure wishes Madeleine would stop talking to these girls.

Beyond, at some distance into the sea, is the ship they will board for Canada. Laure doesn't know if it is the cold misty air or terror at what lies ahead that makes her shiver. The boat, although one of the largest of its type, looks fragile, almost ridiculous, against the immense backdrop of the ocean. Laure has heard that early summer is the best time to undertake this journey to New France. Attempted too early or too late, their vessel would be shattered on rocks along the coast before they even reached the cruel centre of the North Atlantic.

9

Since the passengers bound for Canada boarded the *Saint-Jean-Baptiste* almost three weeks ago, the vessel has not moved out of the Bay of the Seine. The sailors worry that the lack of wind is an inauspicious sign that the journey to Canada will be a long one. Throughout the late spring days, Laure has been standing with the other passengers on deck looking back across the calm water to the shore. It is too far to swim back, to scream across to the tiny bodies moving on the land, but too close to feel that they have really left France behind.

Beside them, also waiting for the winds to pick up, is another ship, the *Amitié*. Laure has heard much talk on the deck about this other ship. The *Amitié* is bound for the sugar plantations of Saint-Domingue and carries in its hold three hundred *nègres* recently acquired from the Dahomey coast in Africa. The slave ship is larger than the *Saint-Jean-Baptiste*. Normally, Laure only sees the sailors and patrolling soldiers of the *Amitié*, but today there are commands being shouted out and weapons raised. The *nègres* from below deck will be brought up for air.

One of the soldiers on the *Amitié* yells across to a sailor on their ship that it is time to have a little dance. The men in charge of sailing the *Saint-Jean-Baptiste* have spent the past few days grumbling at the sight of the *Amitié*. Laure heard one of them say that there is no money in bringing nuns and priests and a few starving women to Canada, that it costs more to feed them on the journey than they get paid to carry them across.

According to the crew of the *Saint-Jean-Baptiste*, the trade of *nègres* to the Islands is the way for a seaman to make money. One particularly spindly sailor bragged about how he once had to fit a *nègre* the size of a horse with an iron mask to keep him from the sugar cane onboard the ship. Laure could not imagine this sailor with wrists as thin as her own doing anything of the sort. Today this sailor and the others are quiet as they wait with the other passengers for a glimpse of the *Amitié*'s cargo.

After some time, three male slaves, two adults and a child, are brought up on the deck of the *Amitié*. One of the sailors, a fat and bearded man, bends to unbind their legs, but he keeps their hands shackled in iron. A dozen or so soldiers and sailors make a circle around the two adult *nègres* and the *négrillon*. The two large slaves raise their shackled hands to cover their faces as the men around them jeer. But the *négrillon*, unlike the other two, stands with his back straight and his head cocked. When the French men scream out orders for the dance to begin, the *négrillon*, like the other two, moves his recently freed legs, bending them at the knee and raising each of them in slow motion. But the eyes of the *négrillon* remained fixed on the French men, his head moving to look from one sailor to the other. The sailor in charge of the stick raises it when the boy looks at him. The *négrillon* moves his legs faster but doesn't avert his eyes from the sailor. After a few minutes, the three slaves are returned below deck and three more are brought up.

The passengers of the *Saint-Jean-Baptiste* are cheering at the entertainment. But when Laure turns around, she sees that Madeleine has already gone below. Madame Bourdon, the woman who has been assigned to escort the girls to Canada, comes to Laure and leads her by the elbow toward the hold.

"Do you think that *négrillon* was the child of one of those big men?" Laure asks Madeleine.

"I don't know what father and mother he had before he was put on that ship. But all he has looking out for him now is the *bon Dieu*." Madeleine is lying on the grey blanket issued to each passenger. The wool of the blankets has been chewed at by the rats of previous journeys, and they smell of stale vomit. Madeleine has not been well since the afternoon, so she has the dirty blanket raised to her chin. Madame Bourdon says that Madeleine probably got too much sun on deck. "Laure, why do you spend your time thinking about the fate of prostitutes and *négrillons*? Only God can understand these things."

Laure looks at Madeleine's tiny face. Her eyes are wide and sad. She has to pray day and night to have the courage that comes easily for Laure.

She reaches for Madeleine's fingers and squeezes them. Laure then closes her eyes and offers two prayers: one for the little slave who has only God to care for him now and the other for her best friend.

The passengers are gathered in the hold at dusk for their dinner. The cook's helpers, each carrying an end of the iron cauldron, descend below. One of the Jesuit priests comes out from behind his chamber curtain and heads upstairs for the captain's table. The captain has his apartment and deck that looks out over the water. A few members of the nobility and the clergy, each with their own compartment below deck separated by a curtain from the public area, go up each night to dine with the captain. In the hold, along with the three hundred or so passengers, are the ship's livestock. The animals are separated from the passengers by the boards of their pen, but the dirty straw makes its way through the cracks into the general filth of the ship's bottom, and the smell of the animals permeates the air. A few of the sheep, cattle, and chickens are destined for the colony, but most are to be eaten during the crossing. But the animals are not intended for the indentured servants, ordinary soldiers, and women from the General Hospital. One calf was already killed for the first feast in the captain's chamber. The passengers grumble that they hope the notables will be quick about eating the animals, as they are tired of sleeping with the smells and bleating of a stable.

Between the passenger hold, or the Sainte-Barbe as it is called, and the captain's quarters is the *entrepont*. This is where the mail for the colony is kept, including letters from the King to the Intendant and the Governor. These bags are weighed down with cannonballs and are to be thrown overboard if their ship is accosted. In addition, there are religious supplies for the orders of New France, bolts of cloth, wooden furniture, dishes, tools, books, paper, spices, flour, oil, and wine, as well as the passengers' rations for the journey: sea biscuits and lard in barrels, beans, dried cod and herring, olive oil, butter, mustard,

vinegar, water, and cider for when the fresh water supply runs
out or becomes too putrid to drink. If the passengers wanted
additional supplies for the journey, they were responsible for
packing them in their luggage. The girls from the Salpêtrière
have nothing more with them.

The younger Jesuit emerges from behind his curtain also, but
instead of joining his superior, he makes his way to the stern
to eat with the soldiers and indentured servants in the hold.
One of the men says to him, "Come and join us, Père, for our
humble meal. You'll do well with the Savages, getting your
practice on the mush. Best to start training now at leaving the
luxuries behind."

The passengers are seated on the floor planks according to
region and kinship. The soldiers and the three-year men, hired
to clear the land in the colony, sit at the stern; the girls from the
Salpêtrière and the other *filles à marier* from Normandie sit in
the bow with the ship's cannons. Between the single men and
women are the four married couples and their children.

Once seated with the men, the young priest glances over
at the women. His eyes rest on Madeleine. Laure recognizes
the expression on his face. It is the same way that the hospital
director and the Duke looked at Laure back in Paris. Only
there is nothing sneering about the priest's gaze, only a gentle
curiosity and a hint of sadness. Laure hopes that one day a man
will look at her that way. But the young priest's efforts are lost
on her pious friend. Madeleine's eyes are closed. She is already
deep within her soul thanking God for the cold contents of the
cook's bucket. Laure thinks that her gratitude to God should

be a direct reflection of the quality of his gift. She cannot bring herself to be grateful for the sludge that is as grey as the filthy blankets they cover themselves with.

The *faux-sauniers* prisoners, those convicted of selling salt, have spread their fleas to some of the soldiers and three-year men. But generally, the petty criminals are so pitiful with their worm-eaten skin and gaunt faces that they are tolerated by the others. They were brought onboard while the *Saint-Jean-Baptiste* awaited favourable weather. The prisoners had been shackled together after spending several days waiting for the ship on the Île de Ré, where they had been brought to prevent them from escaping. The captain had ordered these men untied as soon as the soldiers responsible for them had departed for shore. In the first week, a collection hat was passed among the male passengers, and some new clothing was purchased for the prisoners from the supplies bound for Canada. The outfits the prisoners were wearing were so tattered and moth eaten as to be barely holding together on their bodies.

The *filles à marier* are forbidden by Madame Bourdon to walk beyond a certain point in the low-ceilinged hold, to keep them away from these prisoners and the hardier men also bound for Canada. But there are no walls to keep the girls from hearing the men's conversations. It is certainly a more interesting dormitory than the Salpêtrière, although more crowded. Madame Bourdon has tried to allot a separate section of the hold for the *filles de bonne naissance* who are bound for Neuville, the place where she lives with her husband. These women, mostly from Normandie, have significant dowries and are intended for marriage to more prominent men than the rest of the scraggly orphans. But Laure has heard the complaints of these women who are disappointed to learn from Madame

Bourdon that their future husbands are illiterate seigneurial tenants. The women are also upset at their treatment onboard the ship. Mostly they do not like being so close to the hospital girls.

The cook's boys ladle out the stew first to the hired men, then to the decent country families, one scoop from the bucket into each bowl. The men groan when they see that they will be having the same grey mass from breakfast. "Can't you even heat it up?" one of the men asks, but the cook's boy replies that there are to be no fires lit outside the captain's quarters on this journey. The men protest that there is obviously no wind to worry about since they haven't moved in weeks. Those who have extra sprinklings reach into their sacks for them: a pinch of salt, a swallow of brandy, a slice of fresh apple.

Laure is so hungry tonight that even the smell of the cook's sea biscuits mixed with cold fish broth has her salivating. As the boys drop the mounds on their plates, one of the girls from la Pitié laments the portion size. The others go quiet at her impudence, and Laure wonders what will happen to this girl who hasn't learned how to hold her tongue. Complaining aloud about the meal at the Salpêtrière would have meant losing dinner for the night. But Madame Bourdon ignores the girl's comment, leading them instead into an extended grace for the contents of their bowls. Laure looks around at the girls, wondering if any of the others have noticed. This Madame Bourdon, a rich wife from the colony, dresses and speaks like the officers at the Salpêtrière, but she cannot send anyone to the Maison de la Force or really punish them at all. Although they are crowded into a hold that is smaller than any of the dormitories of the hospital, Laure suddenly feels that there is a vast expanse around her. She doesn't mind so much that she has no delicacies to add to her dinner plate. She spoons the monotonous mush into her mouth, savouring the cool thickness of it, because mixed in somewhere with the dry biscuits and fishy stench of her meal is the taste of freedom.

When they hear the drum roll, the men hurry to wipe and put away their empty bowls and to pack up the flasks and jars of luxurious extras, hurrying for the ladder to the deck. Even the mothers reach for their children, hoisting them on their hips and grabbing them by the hand. The ship is finally moving. After three weeks of waiting, they are heading out to sea. Madame Bourdon raises her hand, indicating for the girls to remain seated and to finish their prayers despite the commotion. But when a cannon is fired from the deck, reverberating against the walls of the wooden hold, the girls grab their skirts and scramble to follow the others up the ladder.

It is easy to see that the ship is no longer still. The commotion alone would be enough to give it away. The sailors raise the sails on the masts, struggling against the wind to secure them. Laure can also feel the waves under the ship as they ride over them. She isn't sure if she should join the three girls huddled together and wailing that they want to turn back, they are too afraid to go, or if she should rush forward to the bow of the ship where some men are hurtling their voices forward into the sea as if Canada will appear before them at any moment. They will be crossing the North Atlantic, the roughest seas, into the

New World. First they will pass the *îles anglaises* de Scilly, the southwest of Great Britain, then Ireland and into the freezing northern waters. This trajectory has been discussed daily by the men while they waited for the winds to pick up.

The disorder and confusion caused by the ship's movement is resolved when the Jesuit priests, seconded by a Soeur hospitalière bound for the Hôtel-Dieu in Québec, and Madame Bourdon call for prayers. The group recites the Ave Maris Stella and the Domine Salvum fac regem, followed by the cry of "Vive le Roi!" The ship as if propelled by their prayers surges even faster into the open water. Laure is quiet, her hand sweaty as Madeleine reaches for it. Madeleine says, "Don't worry. We're leaving France behind, but God is still with us."

Laure looks around her on the ship. The sailors are the only ones who seem ready for the journey. While the passengers pray, they go about their business tugging ropes, raising sails, checking that the ship's weight is balanced. Behind the ship, the land quickly becomes so small that by the time they finish the prayers, it is nothing more than a grey set of hills. The passengers start asking the sailors the same questions about the journey that they asked three weeks ago. The men shout out the answers between tasks: Yes, there will be wine in Canada! And a church for each settlement with more priests than you'll want to see! A fortune to be made? I'm afraid you got on the wrong ship, my man. In Canada, there are forests and men as savage as the beasts they hunt. The whole country is frozen solid for the better part of the year. But I wouldn't know all of that for sure, since I have never set foot in the place. Each time I have seen the shore of Canada, I have decided that crossing back across the perilous sea is better than taking my chances on its hospitality.

The three girls are still crying, but have taken off their scarves and are waving them above their heads, their tiny fluttering voices joining in for the cries of "Vive le Roi." Laure stands watching the coast recede, fading like the end of a dream. Then she turns, walking the distance across the deck to face the ocean ahead.

She tries to imagine how far they have to go across the sea to reach Canada. Six weeks if they catch favourable winds, two months or more if they do not. Laure had hoped that during the uneventful three weeks that they stood immobile gazing at the shore something would make them turn back, unable to leave after all. That they would disembark and make the return journey by straw-covered cart back through the towns and villages of northern France and up the river on the barge back into Paris. That she would be made to return to the dormitory, to the routine of prayers and paltry meals and the long days in the sewing workshop. There is no hope of that now.

One of the sailors, a young man whose beard is as red as his wind-burnt face, sees Laure looking at the wooden carving of the woman at the ship's prow. "That's Amphitrite," he says. "She's the one that will get us across to the other side. But you can't trust her mood from one day to the next, especially as this ship has so many women on it. I don't know whether I'm already in a mariner's heaven, or if I should ask the captain to bring me back to shore and forget about my wages for the next half year at sea. If there's one thing a sailor knows it's that nothing good ever comes of a ship with women onboard."

It is night and the waves beneath them continue to grow

stronger. The sailors are concerned about any possible signs of trouble. That must be why there are so many rules to be observed, such as no rabbits onboard because it is feared they will chew through sail cords. Even in speech, the passengers have been warned that rabbits must be referred to as the long-eared animals and not by name. Nobody is to whistle on the ship, as one indentured servant quickly found out when he received a sturdy sailor's fist to the gut. "The winds will come soon enough," the sailor had told him.

The goddess at the ship's prow is bare-breasted and armless. Her chest juts out over the open water, although Laure can see only the curls of her hair and shoulder blades from where she is standing. Below the waist, the sculpture takes on the scaly form of a fish. The lamps on deck make her golden skin luminescent. It is easy to believe that she really is guiding the ship into the powerful black waves.

Behind her, Laure hears a passenger asking about the weather. "I cannot tell any better than you by looking at these waves what kind of storm this is. But when a man who has crossed the sea eleven times tells you to get below deck, you had better listen and not stand around asking questions about the size of waves." The sailor then makes his way over to the Jesuit priest and two nuns, huddled in prayer.

Their mumblings are being swallowed up by the wind. Each new wave seems larger than the last, and the water far below churns with white foam.

Laure looks again at the figure on the prow, cutting her way through the sea spray with her chest outstretched. The lamp on deck goes out and Laure feels her hair being whipped around her neck by the wind and water. Someone grabs her arm and thrusts her toward the hatch. She is one of the last passengers to go below deck. In the Sainte-Barbe the Salpêtrière girls are already lying prostrate, clinging to the slimy floorboards when she stumbles over to them.

As the storm deepens, the animals begin to groan and kick. Laure imagines that their stomachs must also be rolling with the rough weather. But when the rocking becomes so frantic that it seems the ship will split in two, the animals, like the passengers, grow quiet. Each living creature is concentrating on keeping itself fixed to one spot on the floor and the contents of its stomach intact. The silence is broken only by the occasional scream as the ship is struck by a particularly strong wave. Laure hears Madeleine beside her make a monstrous retching noise before they are both covered in a spray of vomit. A steady murmur of prayers in French and Latin is maintained in the Sainte-Barbe.

Just as quickly as the storm came on, it passes. Girls who were ill a few minutes before are now sitting up, still pale but bright eyed. They look surprised that they no longer have to hug the damp planks of the ship, uttering prayers of salvation. Rosaries and talismans have been stuffed back inside skirt pockets and trousers. Only the evidence of the churning storm surrounds the passengers: the contents of an overturned latrine bucket, vomit, and bits of uneaten sea biscuits. Otherwise all is calm, and the sea's only movement is a gentle quavering like a mother idly rocking a baby's cradle. Madeleine is the only one who did not sit up when the waters grew calm. She is shivering and rolling back and forth as if the storm had not stopped at all.

Laure hears a click as the hold's latch is unlocked. A young man descends the spiral steps. "Come up and breathe some air," he says, and a few of the male passengers, lying with their belongings on the floor, let out feeble cheers. "We're planning a dance. The sky is clear. Stars are out. After surviving such a storm, we have reason to celebrate."

The young sailor doesn't seem to have been affected at all by the storm. It is as if he missed it altogether. A few of the sturdier men scramble up and crawl toward the staircase. In their haste, they trip over other passengers and the bags of salt and plates of stones added as weight to balance the heavy cannons on deck. The young officer raises his lantern and turns it toward the women in the ship's bow. The girls from la Pitié and the Salpêtrière, along with those they picked up in Normandie, are sprawled across the floorboards like an abandoned doll collection. Before the storm, the sailors had frightened the girls with stories of pirates and corsairs and what they would do if they came upon this ship filled with women in addition to the usual spoils. They tell the women that the many bays along the shores of Canada are the perfect hiding place for these dangerous men.

A few of the girls smile weakly at the men. Madame Bourdon has finally fallen asleep. While the storm raged, she had led the terrified girls through every Catholic prayer she knew; her voice had risen a degree with each new assault. Madeleine whispers that she will be fine and that Laure should take this chance to get some air, so she crawls among the girls and their blankets and grabs hold of the ladder. She goes up the levels, past the storage area being guarded by the *maître-valet*.

⚜

The air is chilly, but so fresh that Laure opens her mouth to swallow it. She can no longer see the land behind them, nor can she make out the familiar shape of the *Amitié* beside them.

The *Saint-Jean-Baptiste* is surrounded on all sides by open water. They are alone at sea. The sailors are scrambling around the deck, assessing the damage done by the winds. They are ordering the carpenters to nail down the planks that came loose in the storm. Some of the men set about sewing up a tear in one of the sails, while others work at pumping out the water.

One of the passengers has brought a violin on deck. The music starts quietly, a single warbling string, bringing the passengers back to life. Laure sees that it is mostly men who have come up from below, with the exception of a few wives looking out into the night with their husbands' coats around their shoulders.

Laure hugs her chest, looking up at the sky. A man approaches her. It is the red-bearded *quartier-marin* who talked to her about the sculpture. The *quartiers-marin* stand guard in four-hour shifts over the ship's operations, but must remain in their uniforms at all times, even while they are at rest, in case an emergency should arise. He extends his arm to her, but Laure hesitates to take it. She has never held the arm of a man. Madame Bourdon and the Jesuit priests have worked ceaselessly for the past few weeks to keep the single women separated from the men. They have been more successful with controlling the girls, who are generally accustomed to obeying orders at the hospital. The men have been harder to keep from gambling at their card games and from drinking from their supplies of *eau-de-vie*.

"That was quite the storm. It must have scared you." He has a strange accent.

Laure shrugs. She wonders what makes this little fox of a man think he can speak to her.

"So are you going to Canada to find a husband?" He smiles, and Laure sees the gaps between his teeth.

Laure looks beyond the *quartier-marin* at the tall masts. She nods.

"And what sort of husband are you looking for?"

"I don't know the slightest thing about husbands," she replies, turning away from him to look out over the water.

He laughs. "Neither do I."

Laure turns to look at him. "Have you seen Canada yet?"

"I have. Well, some of the coast, anyway. I haven't been on the fur trade, though. Some of the men say it's a profitable venture."

Laure shrugs again. "It seems to me like the best way for a man to earn a fortune is in sugar. At least that is what they say in Paris." In fact, Laure heard this only yesterday while the soldiers were making the *nègres* dance and the men of the *Saint-Jean-Baptiste* were wishing they had the mettle to transport the slaves.

"Yes, and it's a finer climate in the Islands too. But there are more black slaves than French men there. I think it's better to make a smaller fortune killing beasts of the forest than trying to run a sugar plantation with slaves." He narrows his eyes as if thinking deeply about these two prospects. They both sound equally reprehensible to Laure. She really doesn't see much in these men. They couldn't make a decent living for themselves in Paris or in their countryside towns and so have set off to conquer new places with their same meagre talents.

"You might find that Canada lacks in a few of the comforts you're accustomed to."

"I am not accustomed to very many comforts." Laure has been wearing the same simple hospital dress since they have been on the ship. Because they are sharing the quarters with the men, Madame Bourdon has forbidden the girls from changing their clothing. They will do so only before they arrive in Québec.

He is gazing at her with playful eyes. "A tough one, are you? Good, then, shall we dance?"

Laure, not wanting to show her nervousness, takes his arm this time and lets him lead her to the centre of the deck. The tap of the dancers' shoes against the soggy wood makes a hollow rhythmic sound. A few men whistle and cheer when they see the sailor with Laure on his arm. The violin takes on a more energetic tune. The ship is between storms and all those who have the strength do not hesitate to dance. A few of the more reckless men jump overboard for a night swim. Their nervous companions hold lanterns out over the water and prepare to reel them in should the winds suddenly pick up.

The whole time the *quartier-marin* spins her across the damp boards, Laure looks up at the sky. The stars are so numerous they almost hum. Laure feels far away from everything: Paris, the hospital, Mireille, her father, the country she is going to. The sailor holds his hand over her head as she twirls. Her dress snakes around her hips. *Look, it's Amphitrite come to life*, someone says. A new man, older and stronger, takes Laure's hand from the young sailor. *Delphinus has brought her back. She will marry Poseidon after all.* Laure feels like she will come crashing to the ground or spin right over the side of the ship. Everyone has stopped dancing and is watching her as she is twirled from one man to another.

Laure steps down the stairs and back into the stinking hold. Upstairs the men found a barrel of *eau-de-vie*. Once they started drinking, they began thrusting themselves without restraint onto the few women on the deck. A fight even broke out between the husband of one of the women and a loud-mouthed sailor. Laure had stopped dancing by then.

While they were on deck, a sailor had gone below with a pail to splash water on the soiled boards. He had come back up saying the worst of the storm had been washed away, that they were now ready for the next onslaught. But Laure doesn't find the air in the hold any fresher. A single lantern burns at the stairwell, but otherwise the cramped space is dark. She does her best to avoid stepping on the fingers and outstretched limbs of the sleeping bodies, feeling her way through the families. When she gets near the place where her friend is lying, Laure sees that someone is crouched next to Madeleine. It is a man speaking in a soft whisper. Laure leans her back against the hull and tries to strain her ears. Madame Bourdon and most of the other girls are asleep.

Laure dozes, sitting propped against the hull. Her body is still tingling in the places where the men's hands had been: on her shoulders, the middle of her back, her hands. Her legs are still filled with the violin's tune. She can discern some of the words the man whispers to Madeleine. He is praying in Latin. It is the young Jesuit priest. Madeleine's suitor is restrained, his voice reassuring. He intersperses his prayers with conversation. His words aren't spoiled by too much drink and wandering hands. The words Laure makes out are: confessor, passion, relinquish, rapture, union. The priest doesn't even know he is in love. They likely think their exchange has nothing to do with the world of men and women, of dancing. But they must know that they would still both be punished for being together, a priest and a young woman, alone among the sleeping passengers.

Laure hugs her arms around her chest. She wishes she could be like Madeleine, satisfied by prayers, trusting the words of priests and women like Madame Bourdon and the Superior. Or at least like the other girls who do not hold their rosaries with Madeleine's intensity, but who already dream of the lives they will live in Canada. They are turning themselves into colony wives even now while they sleep on the sea. Laure is something different, a goddess from Antiquity, a serpent woman who doesn't know where her body ends and the waves begin.

10

Madeleine is sick for most of the journey across the sea. After spending eighteen days with the others, Laure and Madeleine are permitted to occupy a special room beside the Sainte-Barbe, reserved for dignitaries or the sick. Laure is relieved that she doesn't have to sit listening to the other girls any more. They try all day to get the attention of the three-year men, combing out their matted hair and applying perfume to the stench of their bodies. The other topic of their conversations is the life they will soon be living in New France. Several of the women have sisters or cousins already living in Québec, and so the others listen to them recount what they know about the place. They will all be married to soldiers and fur-trading men when they disembark. Laure tries to reassure Madeleine that her fate will be different and that she won't be forced to marry when they land. In truth, Laure doesn't know how either of them will avoid being married to one of the colony's men. It is clear to everyone on the ship, including the priests and nuns, that the dozens of young women being transported in the Sainte-Barbe are destined to be the wives of the men established in the colony. Laure has heard Madame

Bourdon speaking with a priest and telling him that getting married and having children is the only way that these men can be kept off the ships returning to France. Laure thinks Canada must be quite an awful place if these men are all so eager to leave it. She doesn't bother trying to remember the names of the women in the hold. Many of them are called Marie and Jeanne, and Madeleine knows most of them. They enquire after *la petite sainte souffrante*, as they refer to Madeleine, who rarely gets up from her place on the floor of the Sainte-Barbe.

The *quartier-marin* has set Madeleine up in the sick hold, away from the others, behind one of the curtains where the priests and other notables have been sleeping throughout the journey. The cot and blanket inside are cleaner and there is a shelf for placing a prayer book or writing paper. Now that they have moved behind the curtain, Laure does not have the conversations of the other women to distract her, and she grows more worried about Madeleine. Each night when Laure emerges from behind the curtain for dinner, the young Jesuit priest comes to enquire about Madeleine's health. There isn't much for Laure to report. She tells him that her friend has energy for prayers and is eating a little, although she is still not strong enough to join the others.

One day, while Laure is sitting reading aloud from a prayer book, Madeleine interrupts her. "Laure, do you remember when we first met?"

Of course Laure remembers, even though several years have passed since that time. It was on one of her first days in the Sainte-Claire dormitory, after Madame d'Aulnay had died, and Laure had been standing at a window watching the Seine River flow past the Salpêtrière. She had thought at the time that girls must look out from this same hospital window to the river below and imagine leaping out. Some because they wanted to return to a lover they had left behind who lived free somewhere. There must have been a few girls, Laure had thought at the time, who wanted to jump into the Seine simply to drown. Laure had been such a girl when she re-entered the Salpêtrière two days after the funeral of her beloved mistress.

She had been puzzled by the small, pale child with the soft, sweet voice who insisted on standing beside her at the window while she entertained her morbid thoughts. Madeleine hadn't said very much but had listened to Laure tell her about the wonderful life she had just lost. She had responded that our lives were like rivers flowing to all sorts of destinations. Although Laure found herself back in the dreadful women's hospital, Madeleine had given her hope for the future, even if she could not imagine what that would be. Even then it was impossible to remain angry for long around Madeleine.

Laure wonders why Madeleine wants to reminisce on the ship about their childhood in the hospital. It isn't like Madeleine to discuss the past or the future. She prefers always to focus on her present moment, which usually involves saying a prayer or spending her time talking to those around her. When she was feeling better, Madeleine was the one who offered small favours to the others in the dormitory, bits of her food, sewing advice to new girls. But Madeleine is determined today to control their conversation. She says that for a long time she has kept an important story from Laure, from everyone in fact, and that she now feels the need to tell it. Laure is surprised at Madeleine's emphatic voice. It seems impossible to imagine that her docile friend has been harbouring some secret.

Madeleine gains a little energy as she begins to speak, and tries to lift herself onto her elbow. She tells Laure that it is the story of her origins, that she actually remembers her life before she entered the monastery.

"It doesn't take long for the regular customers of En passant, the La Rochelle tavern, to hear that a young girl is growing up right above them. At the time I am ten years old, and they have noticed me rushing in the early afternoon down to the pier, although none of these sailors have ever seen me upstairs in the room when they pay their nighttime visits to my mother."

Laure's eyes widen when she hears that Madeleine's mother had been a port prostitute, but with her usual peaceful smile, Madeleine pats Laure's hand, insisting that she remain silent for the telling.

"One night, a man named Ti-Jean decides to find out about me, a young girl living with the old prostitute. Ti-Jean was a sailor aboard the ships that collect slaves from Africa for work in the French Islands. He is strong enough to outfit the *nègres* in metal masks and is the least favourite customer of my mother's and of the other women who sell their services to the seamen.

"Beneath the table where Maman hides me, I tremble on the nights Ti-Jean's heavy legs mount the stairs to our room. He speaks harshly to Maman, calling her an ugly old whore, no good for anything but giving sailors a bad night.

"'So, I hear you've got a little girl that will be running her old mother out of business before too long,' he says on the night he comes to find me.

"'I don't have anything of the sort,' Maman replies.

"'I never would have thought it, homely as you are. But I've heard the rumour and now I'd like to see for myself.'

"'What's all this you're talking about? I sure know you don't come up here to chat.' Maman's voice is moving toward the bed at the other end of the room, trying to draw him away from where I am hiding.

"'No, I come up here when every last wench on the port has her legs raised and there's nowhere else to turn.'

"I then hear the rustle of my mother's skirts as she tries again to entice Ti-Jean away from my hiding place.

"'First show me this daughter of yours so I can decide if either of you are worth my while.' Then I hear his heavy boots pace across the length of the little room. He is looking for me. When his feet are just inches from where I am hiding, crouched under the tiny table, he lets out a laugh. 'Well, she must already be well trained, hiding under here getting pleasure from all that goes on in her mother's dirty bed.'

"I gasp as Ti-Jean raises the cloth that covers the table. This piece of cloth has been my silent protector, the thin barrier that has kept my mother's employment from fully reaching me. If I plug my ears with my fingers and imagine a daylight scene, the sun on the ocean, the market filled with precious goods, then I can almost forget what my mother is doing with the men in her bed. But when Ti-Jean rips the cloth away, for the first time I am no longer safe.

"Maman is at his side, pulling at his broad shoulders and screaming to get him to turn away from me. But it is of no use, as he is so big and strong and Maman is a woman not much bigger than me.

"'So this is the little woman that's been getting so much attention from the sailors.' His laugh is mocking and he crouches down so that the enormous stout knees are in line with my eyes.

"'Leave her alone! She's only a child!' Maman screams at him.

"Then I feel my legs slide across the hard floor as he pulls me upright onto my feet.

"'You are much better looking than your mother,' Ti-Jean says. I can smell the sour thickness of his breath. 'Nice little face.' His rough hand caresses my cheek and passes over my lips. I want so badly to bite him but I fear that doing so will make things worse. He entwines his fingers in my hair and pulls my head back. His other hand reaches for my neck and I do nothing to stop him. 'Just like a kitten being separated from her mother,' he says to me.

"His lips and unshaven face are sliding across my neck while his hand remains tangled in my hair. He is pulling my body up to his chest and I feel my feet leave the ground.

"'You taste sweet. I think I'm going to get a bit more of this.' His breath has grown a little ragged as he reaches under the nightdress I'm wearing and up along my back. 'Stay away from me, you old whore,' he says to Maman, who is still at his back, and he kicks her hard. I remember thinking that the worst part of it all was that Maman was there through it all, wailing as if I were being killed.

"It took two days for Maman and me to walk to the Sulpiciens monastery in Aunis. We pass beggars, mostly maimed soldiers, along the way and are offered rides several times by men in various types of carts and carriages. Each time, Maman refuses their offers.

"As we walk, she tells me the story of Mary of Egypt, the patron saint of prostitutes. 'Each morning I have prayed to this saint, and it is her voice that told me to take you to the Sulpiciens,' Maman says. Maman tells me that when Mary of Egypt was twelve years old, she ran away from her home, although her family was rich. For seventeen years she lived in the city of Alexandria as a prostitute and a dancer. She then travelled to Jerusalem to search for material gain among the pilgrims gathered there. When she tried to enter the Church of the Holy Sepulchre for the celebration, she was repelled by the Holy Spirit and could not enter the door. She then prayed to an icon of the Virgin Mary and repented for her sinful life. It was only after she had done this that she was able to enter the church.

"'My dear daughter,' Maman says to me, 'please pray to Mary of Egypt every day so that you will not ever have to be a prostitute as she was and as I am. For how much better to be pure in body and spirit, untainted by the filth of this world, when you leave it.'

"But I could still feel the bruises on my body from Ti-Jean and thought it was too late. I was already as tainted as Maman and as Mary of Egypt."

Laure cannot imagine a girl more innocent and devoid of sin than Madeleine.

"By the time we reach the doorstep of the monastery, we are parched and dusty from our journey. Maman speaks immediately to the priest who answers the door and attempts to shut it upon seeing us there. 'I ask nothing of you. I know that I am a condemned sinner in the eyes of this holy place. If you can provide me with a little water and whatever food you normally reserve for the animals, I will be on my way.'

"My mother's blotchy face meets his severe eyes, and he nods.

"'This child I am offering you is the finest of all my worldly possessions.'

"Since the wars, the priest tells them, he has had a number of beggars each day come to his door with stories of their sad plights. The monastery is generally a place where the sons and daughters of wealthy families come to study, with generous dowries, for religious vocations, he tells us. He looks at me, studying my face for some sign of my worthiness, my value. I hope that he turns me away so I can stay with Maman. I have told her that we don't have to return to La Rochelle and to that room, but she tells me that she has no skills and knows no other way to survive.

"'Father, if you turn us away, this innocent young child will have no choice but to join me in my wretched profession. You cannot possibly allow that to happen.'

"'Does she have any skills?' he asks.

"'She is fine at needlepoint,' Maman says, pulling me tightly against her. 'And can read from prayer books.'

"The priest raises an eyebrow.

"'Somewhat,' she adds.

"'Well, she does look healthy enough, and young enough to learn. Can you speak, at least?' He addresses himself to me and I nod in response.

"Maman doesn't give the priest another chance to turn me away. She takes a few steps back and pushes me toward him. 'This will be a better life for you, child. You won't have to worry about men like Ti-Jean, or any man at all,' she whispers to me.

"'But I can't read the Bible, Maman, nor can I do needlepoint, or anything at all such as you have told the priest,' I whisper as he turns to enter the monastery, leaving us for a moment on the step. I have done nothing with my young life so far other than hide under the table at night and shop for discounts in the market for our evening meal during the day.

"'You will learn. Those are all much better things than I can teach you.'

"The priest comes back with some water and hard bread and cheese. He breaks some off for me and gives the rest to Maman for her return journey.

"'Thank you, Father. I am so grateful. My life is one of sin, of the worst possible kind, but knowing that I have spared my child from the same fate is reward enough to keep me happy for the rest of my days.' Maman packs the supplies into the sack at her side, then turns to me and says, 'I have tried my best to protect you from the ugliness of this world. I hope you will remember that and nothing else about your mother.'

"Those were her final words to me before she undertook the long journey back to La Rochelle. I have not seen her since that day."

⚜

Laure emerges from behind the curtain of the ship's sickroom that night and tells the priest, who is always eager to hear news of her health, that Madeleine is doing a little better. He asks if he can see her for a brief moment, but Laure tells him that this is not a good night for visiting with her friend. Afterwards, Laure lies awake on the ship floor, rocking with the gentle waves, thinking about Madeleine's story. How little she had known about her best friend. So many times Laure had thought that Madeleine would not be so kind and soft-spoken to everyone if she had encountered misfortune. But could it be that her devotion and simple, gentle heart were formed out of the suffering of her childhood?

Part Two

En aucun endroit, apparaissaient de hauts et prodigieux glaçons nageant et flottant, élevés de trente et quarante brasses, gros et larges comme si vous joigniez plusieurs châteaux ensemble, et comme [...] si l'église Notre-Dame-de-Paris avec une partie de son île, maisons et palais, allaient flottant dessus l'eau.

[All around appeared tall and prodigious icebergs swimming and floating, as high as thirty or forty fathoms, as large and wide as if you had joined together several castles, and ... as if the Notre-Dame-de-Paris church with a part of its island, homes and palaces, were floating on the water.]

—PIERRE BIARD,
RELATIONS DES JÉSUITES, 1611

11

*T*he men bring fresh water from the iceberg back to the ship. The passengers of the *Saint-Jean-Baptiste* have been surviving for weeks on cider after the fresh barrels of water from France became too viscous and filled with larvae to drink. Some of those who had crossed to Canada before knew to lower rowboats into the frigid sea to obtain clean water from the frozen island. The other passengers on deck held their breath as the men descended into the churning sea below and began to row toward the icy hills around them. The icebergs are the nearest thing to land that the passengers have seen in over two months, so Laure can understand the men's desire to go to them, to be in the presence of something solid. She is grateful for their feat when the men return triumphant with their barrels and she gets to feel, along with the other passengers, the pure icy shards descend into her throat and her stomach. The men say that this water is better for the spirit than the finest brandy, that it is worth the dangers at sea just to taste it. The place they have finally reached is called Terre-Neuve.

But this Terre-Neuve is not what Laure expected. There are no fishermen, no Savages, and no city to behold. The New

World the sailors and some of the indentured servants are cheering for appears to be nothing more than a mountain of ice in the sea. But for the moment, tasting fresh water is reason enough to rejoice, even if the country itself is the loneliest place Laure has ever seen.

After two months at sea, the sailors that lead the vessel have hollow cheeks and dark-bearded faces. Some of the duties of crew members who perished during the journey have been taken over by male passengers. At first Laure attempted to keep track of those who died, trying to determine which man or woman had been thrown into the sea and was no longer among them. But after a dozen or so passengers and crew had perished, and they all grew weakened on their dwindling rations, Laure began to stay below deck, ignoring the sound of the funerary trumpet. It has been a hard crossing, and they are looking for any reason to celebrate.

A sailor opens the hatch to the Sainte-Barbe and Laure descends, balancing the bowl of fresh water in her hand. The sick passengers moan as the light from above reaches them. They are the ones who have not yet succumbed to the stomach illness that killed twelve passengers in three days, including three of the crew. The sailors blamed the disease on the vermin of the *faux-sauniers* prisoners. The insects they brought onboard had so multiplied in the hold that each passenger who came on deck first danced about in the light trying to rid their body of bugs.

Laure calls up to the sailor to close the hatch once she is beside Madeleine. She waits a moment for her eyes to adjust to the darkness of the hold. Her skin begins to itch in response. "We have arrived in Canada," Laure says. She reaches to touch Madeleine's arm.

The ship's surgeon hasn't been able to diagnose Madeleine. At the start of the journey he had attributed her illness to seasickness, but unlike the other passengers afflicted by the same malady, Madeleine didn't gain her footing as the weeks wore on. Other than bites from the fleas and ticks that have afflicted all the passengers of the *Saint-Jean-Baptiste*, Madeleine has no sores or pustules on her skin. There is no visible sign of her illness besides the thinness of her body. All the surgeon can say is that Madeleine has been weakened by the journey. He predicts that she will be fine if she can make it to Québec. He says that the sea doesn't agree with everybody and that sometimes the only cure for it is dry land. But now that Laure has seen the frozen, desolate place they have been sailing toward, she is less convinced of its curative powers.

Laure can hardly blame Madeleine for giving up on the ship's food. The Salpêtrière rations had been a sumptuous feast compared to what they have been eating for the past two months. Since leaving Le Havre, the passengers of the *Saint-Jean-Baptiste* have been living on sea biscuits from barrels. These are the usual staple of the sailors' diet and are so hard that the men crush them with the butts of their muskets so the women can eat them. The biscuits are mixed with a little salted lard and peas to make the cold stew they are served each evening. According to the sailors, this batch of crackers is a good one. They have been well baked and dried, so they don't have any weevils in them, which is fortunate since their journey has been plagued by insects of every other sort. But the seamen are so accustomed to the insidious worms that they nonetheless tap the crackers on their bowls before biting into one. Their sea fare is washed down with cider. The jam, like the meat, is reserved for the captain's table.

Madeleine takes the bowl of fresh water from Laure in her frail fingers and sips from it. "What does Canada look like?" she asks.

Laure helps Madeleine to steady the bowl. "Like a frozen heaven," she responds. The chill from the icebergs they pass can even be felt below deck. There isn't a dry spot left onboard the ship. The sea spray and damp air have penetrated their clothing and bedding so that they have long since given up on being warm. Laure doesn't tell Madeleine that Canada is white and silent and as vast as the sea they have just spent two months crossing. She doesn't express her fear that although the bright mountains of ice do look like a heaven of sorts, she doubts there are any angels in this heaven.

The hold opens and the red-haired *quartier-marin* descends. He is Laure's first suitor, although he has no intention of going to Canada and has instead urged Laure to run off with him to the Islands. "Come up, you don't want to miss the baptism," he says to Laure.

"What baptism?" she asks. The only baby on the ship was born three weeks ago and buried at sea the following day in a sack with its mother, weighed down by stones. Maybe they had discovered another Protestant onboard and were converting them to the Roman Catholic faith before they reached Québec, where that religion was not tolerated.

"This is a sailor's baptism. Not many women have the opportunity to be baptized by a sailor."

Even though the sea air covers the body in a cold salty mist that burns the skin, the deck is the happiest place on the ship. This is mainly because the passengers can shake the insects from their clothes in the light and fill their lungs with fresh air. If the hold is the hell of the ship, then the deck is certainly a sort of paradise. It is where, on calm, sunny days, men—sailors and passengers alike—throw their fishing lines into the ocean. They spend hours waiting for signs of life in the water below. When they tire of fishing, they play cards, read, and have contests of strength climbing the masts.

On the day that they catch their first glimpse of Canada, Madame Bourdon permits the girls to stay on deck so long as they are absolutely silent. But neither the religious women nor the Jesuit priests can control the riotous energy that has taken hold of the sailors on this day. Nets are being cast into the cold water and schools of cod fish in all sizes are being dumped on the deck, silvery glints of life being turned to red by the men's pocket knives. The captain gives special permission for the smaller fish to be thrown alive onto the ship's one cooking fire. Before long, the smell of the roasting cod overtakes the sea salt in the air. Two of the sailors, under the supervision of Madame Bourdon and Laure, have even carried Madeleine up for the occasion. In the light of day, Madeleine's face is as grey as her blanket, but Laure hopes that the sun will revive her. Laure accepts the fillet one of the sailors brings to her, and she breaks off little pieces to eat. She tries to entice Madeleine with some of the soft meat, but receives only a slight shake of her head and a gentle smile in response.

The sailors set out to obtain the list of the passengers arriving for the first time in Canada. It is time to baptize them. The men cheer. Madame Bourdon tries to escort the girls back down into the Sainte-Barbe, but two sailors guard the door.

"You wouldn't keep good Christian girls from their baptism, would you?" they taunt her.

The monstrous creature the men have been awaiting finally appears from out of the captain's quarters. He is made up of several men who are beneath a fur patchwork coat of various colours. His face is covered in a wooden mask of Savage origin, and around his neck hang feathers, arrows, knives, and other instruments of hunting and war. The girls scream as the creature makes his lumbering way across the deck. The men shout out his name as he passes: le Bonhomme Terre-Neuve! The creature finally pauses before a throne made of barrels tied together with rope. Beside him is another barrel, filled with water from the sea. He climbs up onto his throne and turns to the officiating crew member who stands behind a pulpit with a gavel in his hand. He has beside him the book of the ship's maps.

The assistant to this ceremony raps the gavel several times against the wooden pulpit. The sound is a hollow thud, dampened by the sea journey, but silence ensues among the passengers nonetheless. "We will now baptize each man, woman, and child who is seeing the New World for the first time." The passengers cheer even louder.

Madame Bourdon has rushed to the Jesuit priests standing near Laure to ask them to grant the girls immunity from the sea ritual. One of the priests shakes his head and agrees with Madame Bourdon that it is a disgusting practice and one that is blasphemous as well. But, he says, so long as they are aboard their stinking vessel, they are at the mercy of these pagan brutes. There really isn't much to be done to stop them.

"Take comfort, Madame, in the souls we have saved throughout the journey. Do not worry about the ones who live without fear of God."

The saved souls he refers to are the men and women, several of them lunatics to begin with, who began the journey in panicky fear and have since taken to filling their days with ecstatic prayers that keep the passengers awake all through the night. Some of the men threaten to throw these redeemed souls to their watery graves.

The bucket is refilled with freezing sea water each time a man is dunked into it, splashing the contents onto the deck. When the men are all finished, the officiating sailor turns to the women.

"We have had the good fortune, although mariners' lore would tell us otherwise, to have with us on this ship more women than men, a rare honour for a sailor." The men roar. "We think we have treated you well, dear ladies, have we not? We have protected you from pirates and corsairs, fed you a feast of the senses each day, kept you sheltered from storm and sun, and brought you here all the way to the New World."

The men laugh. There is sympathy in some of their eyes. Many had said throughout the journey how incredible it was that women were weathering the brutal conditions of the ship alongside the men.

"Now we will let the Bonhomme himself choose one girl to be baptized, to represent all the others among you. Who will the lucky lady be?"

The girls grab hold of each other, cowering near the floor. Laure is a bit distracted from all of this because she is still trying to get Madeleine to eat some of the cod. The Bonhomme Terre-Neuve slowly lowers himself from his barrel throne and begins his lumbering tour of the deck. He stops before each girl, cocking his head, to inspect them one by one. Some scream and grab hold of each other in terror as the masked face leans in toward them. Laure wonders which sailors are beneath the disguise.

When the Bonhomme reaches Laure, he takes a step back and crosses his arms over his chest. The men who are watching begin to roar. "Choose the dancing goddess!" Throughout the journey Laure has not been able to shake her reputation among the men who saw her dance on the night after the storm. The Bonhomme extends a curled finger to her, but although her heart starts to pound a little faster, she isn't really afraid of these foolish men.

The red-headed *quartier-marin* holds out the book of maps for Laure to swear on. "Normally, we have the men swear that they will stay away from the other sailors' wives once we reach land." A raucous cheer rises from the men. "But I guess for you, our dancing Amphitrite, we need to keep you away from the sailors themselves."

The men laugh, stomping their feet on the planks of the deck. "Let's ask her to dance for us again."

Bonhomme Terre-Neuve oversees the baptism from his barrel throne. He stretches out his hand for a coin offering, seeing that Laure has none, and when the crowd is worked up into a riotous fit, a sailor pulls the plank from beneath where she sits. She hears Madame Bourdon scream just before her body hits the cold water in the barrel. Almost immediately Laure feels herself being yanked out of the barrel by the sailors.

Madame Bourdon has rushed up with a cloth to wrap around her dripping dress. "The horror and indecency of it. To do this to a woman," she says.

Laure's teeth are chattering from the freezing water, but she grins at the *quartier-marin*. To Madame Bourdon she says, "Canada is obviously no place for women."

12

As the ship enters more deeply into the New World, at last the snowy icebergs give way to land—rocks and thick forests—but still Laure sees no sign of a town or city. They have been at sea for over two months and it is now July. They sail for days up the river, which is so wide it makes the Seine look like a country stream. Still, it is reassuring to see land again, even if it is far in the distance on either side of the ship. The first port where the *Saint-Jean-Baptiste* anchors at is called Tadoussac. At first Laure thinks this place, with no more than twenty or thirty distressed inhabitants, is Québec, and she is relieved to learn that it is not. Tadoussac is a rudimentary port where a river called Saguenay meets the Saint Lawrence. It is here that Laure learns of the Iroquois. It is all the men on shore can talk about. The Iroquois are a tribe feared by the French and by other Savages. They attack by surprise in the forest, scalp their victims, and torture even the women and children they capture. The Iroquois are terrifying to look at, with dark, glistening bodies, shaved heads, and painted faces.

There are only men living at Tadoussac, and they look even more crazed than the sailors and men of their ship. Their hair is long and streaked by the sun, their skin dark, and their bodies thin. There is little comfort or much in the way of a welcome to be found in this place. The men come onboard, their wide eyes searching like wild animals for nourishment and comfort. A few stay on to travel with the passengers to Québec, but most of the men take a few victuals and return to their encampment. The ship doesn't stop long at Tadoussac, as it is often the site of Iroquois attacks, and the women do not go ashore. A few men disembark to restock their food supplies and to tell the news from France, but they too are eager to get back on the ship, which is a more civilized and orderly place than Tadoussac.

It is only in recent years that ships have begun venturing farther down the Saint Lawrence toward Québec. The river narrows after Tadoussac, and the islands and rocks increase, which can lead to shipwrecks. They pass Cap-Tourmente and Île d'Orléans. Laure makes out a few wooden shacks and what seem to be storage sheds on the north shore.

As they near Québec, the passengers come on deck to get a better look. Québec is at least a town by the looks of things, if not the bustling city centre Laure and the others had been expecting. But there is something strange, almost unnatural, about the sudden appearance of Québec from the wilderness. The town is high above the river, and dense forest rises from the shore to meet it. One of the priests points out to them the landmarks of the settlement: the steeples of the parish church, the Jesuit College, the Ursuline chapel, and the Hôtel-Dieu. On the eastern tip of the cape is the Château Saint-Louis. Houses have been built around the religious and royal edifices, and there are two windmills on the rocky point of the settlement. There are some other buildings on a narrow strip of land beneath the Cap, in the Basse-Ville. There seem to be some small shops on this strip of land. But even here, Laure can see, behind a cover of trees, the ominous outline of Savage huts. She wonders if this place is any safer than Tadoussac. Her heart feels sick to think of the dangers of this new life.

The ship's men fire a cannon into the air as the *Saint-Jean-Baptiste* approaches the settlement on the hill. Their ship has been badly used by the months at sea. The sails are ragged and worn by the weather they encountered on their journey. The torn bits wave like fragments of flags. The wood of the hull is soaked through and rotting in places.

The passengers look even worse than the ship. The men are dark skinned, their hair and beards long and knotted. Their arms are thin and taut with sinewy muscles. Even the girls who spent the calm days at the start of the trip combing their hair and wondering about the men they would marry in Canada are now pale faced and greasy. According to Madame Bourdon's orders, none of the women have washed more than their faces and hands and have not changed even their undergarments since boarding the ship; their open quarters in the Sainte-Barbe would not enable them to do so with decency. As a result, even the girls who started out young and pretty two months ago now look and smell worse than any vagrant madwoman of the Salpêtrière. Laure knows she must appear the same way, although the journey has done nothing to make Madeleine look as vile as these women. Her illness has simply shrunken her a little and made her seem more like a child than ever. Her eyes rarely open, but there is a small smile on her lips.

The sound of the cannon travels across the water, a lonely reverberation. The fort is surrounded by a stone wall, although there doesn't seem to be any sign of the war it signifies. Soldiers in military jackets patrol the edges of the settlement. The whole town isn't much bigger than the grounds of the Salpêtrière. Laure had expected a city the size of Paris in the New World, not a military outpost. When the ship anchors, there is a mad scramble from the shore to row out to unload the ship's cargo. Several soldiers with guns guard the proceedings. First, men from the shore come onboard with rustic wooden stretchers to carry off the passengers who are too sick to walk to the Hôtel-Dieu. Madeleine is among those they carry away, along with a young nun recruited to work at the Hôtel-Dieu. Afterwards the passengers disembark.

Then a swarm of bedraggled soldiers wearing brown *justaucorps* and blue stockings barrage the captain and the crew with questions about the date of the ship's return to France. The winds on the way back to France are favourable. It would take half the time for the return journey. Laure can see, even though Madame Bourdon and the priests try to push the girls past them, that these men are desperate to leave the colony. The men are held back from boarding by the ship's guards, and some fighting ensues.

Madame Bourdon orders the girls to stay together on the shore. There is no objection to her command, as many of the girls collapse to the ground and cannot stand back up from where they have fallen. Laure's legs tremble as she tries to remain standing. She sits in the dirt as the river and the town spin around her. The sailors tell the girls they will soon get their land legs.

Once they are able to stand, Madame Bourdon leads the girls away from the port. They pass a group of cheering men, who seem to find it amusing that these thin women have crossed the sea. Behind them, two indentured servants pull a cart with the women's coffers over the rough and steep path. A few men from the ship, looking as sick and pathetic as the women, followed by some land reinforcements, protect them from behind.

Madame Bourdon takes the girls up to the Ursulines congregation, the greatest construction in Québec. It is made of grey stone and reminds Laure of the Salpêtrière, only the girls of the Ursulines must pay a dowry to enter and wear black habits. It is a cloistered order, and so they don't see anyone in the courtyard as they approach. When they reach the entrance to the convent, Madame Bourdon makes the girls wait outside.

A small Savage girl answers Madame Bourdon's knock and comes outside to keep the French girls company. She looks to be about six or seven years old. When they ask her, she tells them in a small, careful voice that her name is Marie des Neiges. Her dark hair is neatly braided on either side of her head. She is dressed in a clean white dress and clasps her hands in front of her, as if she is preparing to receive her first Communion. She sneaks glances at the stinking mess of women arrived from France, but remains quiet.

Madame Bourdon is inside for a long time, and when she emerges, she gestures for the girls to follow her, away from the congregation building. The little Savage, Marie des Neiges, bows slightly as they turn to go and says, "*Que Dieu vous bénisse*" before closing the door behind her.

"Won't we be staying here?" one of the girls asks Madame Bourdon.

"Of course not. This is where the Mère Marie lives. I just had to report to her that we had arrived. I also had to tell her how badly some of you behaved during the journey."

Judging by her haughtiness, Laure wonders if Madame Bourdon hadn't also expected that the girls would be staying at the congregation. The whole journey, Madame Bourdon had spoken of Marie de l'Incarnation, a living saint. This woman, the Superior of the Ursulines congregation, had left behind her young son in France and now devoted herself to saving the souls of Savages in Canada.

"Mère Marie has more important things to do than spend her time with a group of *filles à marier*. She has come here to bring God to people who want to receive Him."

People like that Savage girl, Laure thinks. She wonders if behind that stone building that looks so much like the Salpêtrière there are hundreds of Savage girls in dormitories dressed as neatly and speaking as gently as the little girl they just saw.

"You have had every opportunity in France through the holy teachings of so many to become decent women. And you do nothing but give me a hard time, dancing, drinking brandy with sailors, exposing your undergarments to men on the ship!" She looks at Laure when she speaks.

Laure wishes Madeleine were with them so she could meet these holy Savages, who are more pious than French girls.

Instead of staying at the Congrégation des Ursulines, the *filles à marier* are brought to an auberge. Madame Bourdon tells them it is run by a *femme sage*, Madame Rouillard. She has been in the colony for twenty years, back when it had been run by a company that cared only about furs and not one bit about settlement and women. Madame Rouillard will travel with the girls being sent farther up the river to the place called Ville-Marie. Her brother has an inn there, and her services as a midwife will be needed in the new settlement over the next few years when the *filles à marier* begin having children.

❧

The auberge is a large wooden building in the Lower Town. The inside is made of the same wood as the exterior, including the hard seats and tables the girls are invited to sit at. The smell of brandy and roasting meat makes Laure's stomach grumble. The men turn to stare as they enter. Madame Rouillard tells them to leave to make way for the girls. She says, "This is no monastery, but for tonight we'll do our best to bring decency to the place."

The men bow and chuckle, taking their leave of the women. Madame Bourdon remains tight lipped the whole time Madame Rouillard speaks.

Madame Rouillard wears a stained apron over a thick country dress. She is a tough-looking woman with a deep voice, but her throat is full of words about the colony that Laure is eager to hear. She prepares the first meal the girls will eat in New France and talks the whole time that she works.

"The people here are the refuse of the old country for sure, but each with very different ambitions. Most don't want to be here at all, like those men who try to fight their way back onto any ship they can once their three-year contracts are over," she says. "Now they've come up with the idea—and it's about time—that in order to build a new country, you need women as well as soldiers and fur traders. So they've gathered you girls out of every poorhouse in Paris, you'll forgive me for saying so, to be married to whatever men they can drag out of these forests."

Madame Bourdon sighs and shakes her head, but there is no stopping Madame Rouillard from expressing her opinion. "Even the officials don't want to be here. They fulfill their contracts and dream of growing old with a big garden in Paris far from this rough country. Get me some more butter!" she yells out to a slow-moving man of nineteen or twenty. Laure figures that this is Madame Rouillard's son. "The craziest of all, though, are the priests and nuns who come here to convert the Savages." She laughs, her bosom shaking, as she stirs the butter into the pot.

The innkeeper laughs even harder when Laure asks her if there are hundreds of Savage girls in Marie de l'Incarnation's congregation.

"Now that is the biggest farce of this whole colony. Thinking that a few French priests and nuns are going to change the minds of these people. All the Savages want from the French is access to goods and will do any praying and singing required to ensure this. But after they get what they want in trade? They're running around in the forest just like they've always done."

One of the girls asks what Madame Rouillard is cooking.

"Corn mush and squirrel stew. Don't think you'll be eating a thing here that you recognize. Bloody mosquitoes"—she smacks the ample flesh of her arm—"which, by the way, if the food doesn't get you, these things will make sure that you go out of your mind. Oh, it's not all bad, though." She sets down the pot of stew and hands out the bowls. "That's all I have. We've never had this many of you arrive all at once, so you'll have to share. I expect you're used to doing that anyway."

Some of the girls, the younger ones, have tears welling in their eyes.

"If you can forget about that place you came from, which I expect you'll want to if the things I've heard about that hospital are true—"

"But we aren't all from there—"

"Even worse if you're from some starved-out farming town. If any of you are moving on to Ville-Marie with me, you will be fortunate. It's the garden of the New World. In the winter there is so much snow on the ground that nothing beneath freezes." She laughs. "Imagine that. Of course, the Savages are worse there than they are here."

Laure has already been told that she is being moved on to Ville-Marie along with any other girls that don't get chosen to marry men at Québec.

Madame Rouillard shakes her head when the girls start grumbling against her insults to their home countries.

"It's better to start thinking this way as soon as you can. Remembering Old France as if it had been providing you with a king's banquet every night will just make you miserable here. You remember where you came from, what might have happened to you if you'd stayed, and then maybe this forest and these mosquitoes and winters that will shock the heart out of your chest won't seem quite so bad."

Laure wants to tell this old innkeeper with the strange accent that back in Old France she would first have been a seamstress in Paris and then the wife of a duke. But she wonders for the first time how true that is. Why would her lot end up so much better than that of all the other poor girls of the city? She might very well have been the mistress of a nobleman, staying by his money for a while in a small apartment so he could visit her in secret when he pleased, but what about when she became older? If she were lucky, some consumptive disease would have claimed her before she turned thirty. Otherwise she might have re-entered the Salpêtrière in some poorer dormitory, after first doing her time in the brothels she had once thought so romantic, where the masters were numerous and the pay just enough to stay alive. But there is no point thinking of these possibilities since her fate will now be played out in this crude new country where much, including social conventions, seems to have been abandoned at sea.

This Madame Rouillard, fat off beer and squirrel meat, has made a life for herself here. Laure looks around at the newly arrived girls and sees some of them laughing at the woman's stories. Just as the *sage femme* counsels, they are eager to shed their old life for this one. To forget who they were and begin again as innkeepers, wives of forest fur seekers. They shovel the strange greasy food into their plain faces and are content.

"Come on, eat up, you'll be dead by December if you try to be a fussy cat in this country." The woman pushes Laure's bowl closer to her. Laure shakes her head and lets the woman next to her finish it off.

They spend the night in the inn. It is the first time Laure sleeps on solid ground since leaving Paris over two months ago. She dreams of the ship's rocking and also of Iroquois attacks. In her dreams, the Iroquois all look like the Bonhomme Terre-Neuve. When they open their mouths, fangs appear and they roar like beasts. Their enormous bodies are covered in the hair of the women they have scalped.

By the time they leave Québec for Ville-Marie the following week, a number of the women from France are already married and will be staying in Québec or nearby settlements. Madame Bourdon has chosen Laure to go on to Ville-Marie because, unlike some of the other girls, she doesn't have any family at Québec, nor does she have any immediate marriage prospects. She is among the youngest of the women, who are between the ages of fifteen and thirty-six. Laure also knows that their guardian is eager to be rid of her. She agrees without a fuss to move on to Ville-Marie on the condition that Madeleine can come with her. Madeleine has regained a little of her strength under the care of the Soeurs hospitalières at Québec, although they feel she isn't ready to leave. Laure cannot imagine travelling farther up the river into the forest country by herself. Madeleine says she is willing to travel with Laure, and so they release the sick girl from the Hôtel-Dieu.

The remaining women, twenty or thirty from what Laure can see, will be taken in canoes and distributed in the settlements between Québec and Ville-Marie to men seeking wives. The women from France, who have spent the past few months crammed together in the Sainte-Barbe of the ship and before that in dormitories of the Paris General Hospital, are now being dispersed one by one into a land that is much larger than all of Old France and covered in dense forest. The only comfort the girls can hope for in this frightening territory is a gentle husband, although from what Laure has seen so far of the rough men at Québec, there is little chance of that. There are too few women in New France, only one for every ten men, so it seems. At least this means there is some choice in what husband to marry. Several women travelling with them to settlements farther up the river will be marrying for a second time. Their first marriages were annulled, except for one, who is already a widow, although she doesn't look much older than Laure.

At Québec; the *filles de bonne naissance* were matched with the officers they'd been destined for to begin lives as the choice couples of the town. But the men who came to the auberge in Québec, seeking wives from among the homely country girls and the pale hospital *citadines*, had not been in the company of French women for a year or two. They had been working at the two principal occupations of the colony: fighting off the Iroquois and hunting animals for their fur. Marrying one of these men meant being taken away from the safety of Québec into the woods, where the men had been allotted their plots of land in payment for their services to the King. Laure hopes that the men are less feral farther up the river at this new settlement, Ville-Marie. Stories abound of the holiness of the town, which was established by members of the Compagnie du Saint-Sacrement, the same secret society to which the director of the General Hospital had belonged.

Their convoy will travel in three canoes, which the men first load with heavy supplies of salt, oil, lard, *eau-de-vie*, guns, and iron tools. Six Savages accompany them, five men and one woman, to help communicate in case they encounter others along the way and to help them navigate the river. There are also two Jesuit priests eager to get back to their missions near Ville-Marie and ten fur-trading men along with the twenty or so women from France. One of the Jesuit priests is the young man who had taken such an interest in Madeleine. He is travelling with an older Jesuit who has been in New France for several decades. The old man will take the young priest to live with him in a mission near Ville-Marie, where the young priest will help him to care for the souls of the Algonquins and to translate Christian prayers into their language. This man remembers the Huron mission at Sainte-Marie before they had retreated from the Iroquois. Of course the stories the priests had written in those years of conversions and torture are famous throughout all of Old France. The young Jesuit leans in to hear the older priest speak of these times. Laure wonders if this young priest is brave enough to have his heart eaten by Savages, or his body filled with poisonous arrows, or his flesh baptized in boiling water. His face is so young and his words are soft and careful.

For the trip, Madame Rouillard has dressed like a Savage man. She has on leather leggings and a hat, and she carries a rifle. She says this is how she dresses when she travels from cabin to cabin to deliver babies. She knows most of the men and talks easily with them.

The canoes are made by the Savages from the bark of the birch tree and are low in the water. These boats are swift, but they must be carefully loaded to evenly distribute the weight, as they easily tip over. After the supplies have been arranged on the canoes, the French men get onboard, and finally it is the turn of the women. Laure crouches down as she has seen the others do, and sits in the centre of her seat. The slightest movement rocks the little vessel. Madeleine does her best to stay sitting in front of Laure, but ends up slumping forward. The Savages are the last to board and don't seem to have the same trouble standing in the boat that Laure did.

"Doesn't look like that sick one will make much of a wife."

Laure turns back to the man who has spoken these words. He is some sort of fur trader, his skin already wizened by the harsh conditions of his trade, although he looks young enough.

His grin freezes when he sees the anger in Laure's eyes.

"You need to be tough to make a life in the forest." He looks at Laure's hair, carefully combed after her stay in Québec and adorned with the ribbons from Madame du Clos. "I don't know why they send us girls from Paris. You will be lucky if your new husband has a house for you. What we need are country girls." He turns back and smacks the thigh of one of the girls from Aunis who is seated behind him. "There aren't any princes waiting for you in Ville-Marie."

"That is clear." Laure turns back and takes Madeleine by the shoulders to steady her weight. Laure has determined that there isn't much respect for rank here in New France. The forests are too vast to keep track of the fur traders, soldiers, settlers, Jesuits, Récollets, Sulpiciens, Catholic converts, innkeepers, cobblers, carpenters, seigneurs, explorers, officers, Savages working as interpreters, and the Governor and the Intendant who try to watch over the whole venture in the name of the King. Because most of these men only stay a short while in the colony before returning to France, there seems to be less concern for respecting superiors. There also seems to be little protection for women from foul-mouthed men like this fur trader. Even more than at Québec, Laure feels the separation from the hospital and its daily regimen. There is nobody here to tell the girls where to sit, whom to speak to, when to be silent, when it is time to pray, to eat, to comb their hair, to change their clothing, to sleep. There is nobody to follow, only an eclectic cavalcade from Old France travelling toward converts, husbands, and fur riches. Madame Rouillard hums a song as the canoes set off up the river.

There seems to be no end to the river. Each hour brings into view more stones, forests, insects, and birds, but no sign of civilization. When the sun starts to fade on the first night, the mosquitoes become thick, encircling their canoe, feeding on the exposed faces and hands of the passengers. Some of the girls begin to cry at the infestation. The midwife turns back to face the tearful girls, some of whom are begging to turn the canoes back. "You will soon learn that you are not alone. You're carrying in you the seeds of the families you will have. Before long, this will be your only home. There is no sense looking back."

Laure wishes Madame Rouillard's words could bring her some comfort the way it does to the others who cheer up. But she cannot even imagine any of it: marrying one of these men, having children, living in the forest. Surely she will escape this fate.

When the men see the clearing with two cabins and some tents, they tell the Savages to pull onto the shore. They have reached Trois-Rivières. This is where several of the women, including the Belgian Marie and Jeanne-Léonarde, will be married. It is disconcerting for Laure to see the places where the women are being left: Neuville, Grondines, Batiscan. They are little more than clearings in the woods with a handful of inhabitants. Many tears are shed at each stop and the women's faces register shock and terror when the canoes set off without them up the river.

Trois-Rivières is a little bigger than some of the other settlements, but it looks more like Tadoussac than Québec, an encampment surrounded by a palisade. They are silent and quick as they disembark from the canoes onto the sandy shore. Two soldiers and the Savage men will sleep in tents near the canoes to guard the provisions. The others, including the women, are brought into the village. The paths around the wooden shacks are devoid of people. Here too the inhabitants fear Iroquois attacks. The women are ushered into one of the huts.

The family in the first cabin refuses to have any of the women from France stay with them because they have three daughters of marriageable age. They say that these women from Paris with their dowries from the King will ensure that their own daughters remain single.

But the second cabin, occupied by a man, his new wife, and their infant child agrees to accept a small payment in return for having some of the girls stay with them. One of the daughters from the first cabin, who is about twelve years old, comes to see the women from France. She wants to know all about Paris and the fashions of the capital. She sits next to Laure and listens with amazed eyes at the rhythm of Laure's voice as she tells her about the fine materials and the horses and carriages of the wealthy. When the girl's father comes to the door to get his daughter, Laure removes one of her hair ribbons and gives it to her. "Keep this for your wedding," she says, and the child is so pleased about the gift that she runs to show her father.

It is very hot in the one-room cabin that night with ten people lying together on the floor. Still, it is nice to be sheltered and to feel protected by the palisade surrounding Trois-Rivières and by the men standing guard outside. Laure has grown accustomed on their journey to falling asleep despite the chirping of crickets and birds.

Laure and the others travel for days in this way. Each time they reach a set of rapids in the river, they must disembark on the shore and walk through the forest to get past them. The men hoist the canoes and the supplies over the sharp rocks and through the brush. Madeleine, who has not yet regained her strength, is carried on a makeshift stretcher over slippery stones and back into the canoe.

❦

Ville-Marie is the last settlement before the forest completely takes over. Beyond there are lakes and other Savage tribes. Only crazy men with contracts to the King seek their riches beyond the French settlements, ever hungry for new sources of fur. Ville-Marie is also the newest French town, with only a few hundred residents, and the one most likely to be attacked by the Iroquois. Much of the conversation Laure has heard on their journey up the river and even on the ship and at the hospital has been about these particular Savages. They are the ones who for decades have been fighting the French. Even the other Savages fear the Iroquois, who are numerous and allied with the English in the colonies to the south.

The old Jesuit travelling with them lost a portion of his ear when he was captured by the Iroquois a few years ago. But he says he is fortunate, as most do not escape but instead meet brutal deaths once caught by these people. Laure imagines these Iroquois to be larger than ordinary men, at least five heads taller than any French soldier. They are said to move through the forests like silent and cunning beasts. If you encounter an Iroquois warrior on a forest path, there is no chance of surviving the meeting. As terrified as she is, a part of

Laure wishes to catch a glimpse of one of these men through the forest.

Madame Rouillard says the Iroquois are no different than any other men. They just happen to be the enemy, that's all, and enemies are always turned into monsters. As for the Jesuit priests, she thinks they would have been better off staying in Old France studying medicine or law or becoming teachers the way God had intended. In her opinion, coming across the sea to a new land altogether and expecting the people to embrace their Christian ways was the most foolish notion she had ever heard.

"This might well be blasphemous," Madame Rouillard said, "but one thing I have learned after years of trudging through brush and swamp and ice to get from one place to another to bring a new baby into this country is that some other spirit watches over this place. The God we bring from France is just as lost as we are on the winter trails of this country."

Still, Laure thinks that the young Jesuit's pale face is magnificent, much better to look at than those of the fur traders.

By the third day, Laure can whisper the names of many of the trees they pass: cedar, poplar, maple, oak. She learns to study the swirls of the river water for signs of upcoming rapids. The French men also tell the women of their fur-trading exploits across the land, how far they have gone to the west and to the north. Even the Jesuit priests take the opportunity to boast a little about their experiences converting the Savages to the Catholic faith. Since they set off, the Savage men on the canoes, with dark, greased arms and long hair, have been urging them to be silent for their safety, reminding the French men of the threat of the Iroquois. Laure thinks that the sound of French words is beginning to irritate them. The Savages don't speak to the women, only to the fur traders, and in their own language. They don't speak much at all, and when they do it is always in hushed voices and must be translated for the others by the French interpreter.

As they journey on, when all there is to say about the sameness of the new country has been said, the passengers fall into a sort of trance. Laure watches the forms of the trees dip out into the water and the bright sun in the clearings. The only sound is of the heavy paddles skimming through the water. Laure is covered in insect bites and thirsty from the heat. Her muscles ache from sitting in the canoe and on the ground and from walking over the rough terrain. Her stomach burns from eating meat grilled almost to ash over the open fire. The Savages that guide them look pleased that the group is finally quiet.

After a few days it becomes obvious that moving ever farther into this new world is weakening Madeleine. Her eyes have grown dull and she is no longer aware of those around her. She doesn't seem to recognize Laure at first when she speaks to her, and a vacant look inhabits her eyes most of the time. Laure hopes that Madeleine's face is only swollen because of the burning sun, the insect bites, the thirst and hunger that afflicts all of them, and that somehow, despite these rough conditions, she is getting better. Just before they left Québec, a physician had looked at Madeleine and said that the fresh air might improve her condition. The Soeur hospitalière caring for Madeleine had denied his claim and told Laure that the risk to her friend's health in attempting such a journey was a great one.

The fresh air doesn't make any of the travellers feel better because its curative effects are coupled with cold water that splashes onto them over the sides of the canoe so that they feel wet all the time. The air is also filled with thick swarms of blackflies that the Savages urge the rowers to avoid. These insects are worse than the mosquitoes, as they tear off a piece of flesh when they bite. Laure's neck and scalp are a mess of bites, but she refuses to cover herself in the bear grease that the Jesuit priests and the Savages have put on their skin. The prayers the priests utter to the group are spoken from glistening faces. They look more like sorcerers than priests. Seeing Madeleine so weak, Laure wishes she could order the canoes to turn around, to begin to undo the journey up the river.

After a week of travel, they finally approach Ville-Marie. It is a smaller settlement than Québec, but larger than the other encampments they have passed along the way up the river. It is clearly the fur-trading centre of the colony, the gateway into the fur-rich lands and waterways beyond. They have heard enough stories and encountered enough canoes laden with pelts to support the claim. Its newness and dangerous challenges, along with the opportunity for greater fur wealth, attracts the boldest of the adventurers of New France. The courage of these crazed men surrounds Ville-Marie with a joyful energy. Laure finds herself forgetting the future for a brief moment.

Laure sees a gathering of people awaiting them on the shore. Even from a distance, she can discern that they are mostly men. She can't tell what rank or sort of men they are. They wear their military jackets from France over baggy breeches. Some of them have long hair with bits of animal pelts and bright Savage weaves around their waists. Several more distinguished soldiers with muskets stand with a priest to greet them. Laure jumps when one of these soldiers fires a pistol in the air. They mustn't have any cannons to welcome them with. Like at Québec, there are a few religious women and some Savage girls waiting for them as well. It is the most interesting settlement Laure has seen since Québec, and for this she is relieved.

The men on the shore rush toward them, waving their arms and cheering. Laure doesn't know what they are so excited about. Forest life must be even more terrible than she expected if their dirty cortège receives such an eager welcome. If their pathetic group was seen travelling down the Seine to Paris, they would be apprehended and thrown straight into prison. But it is difficult here to dress in fine clothing and to remain clean and untouched by the woods.

Laure only hopes that there is a physician somewhere in this settlement. Someone who can revive Madeleine. Even the loud calls from the shore have not awakened her. "We have arrived," Laure says, leaning in close to her friend's ear. Despite Laure's vigilant guard, there are still welts on Madeleine's neck from the insects. "We don't have to travel any further. For the rest of our lives, we are free to stay here." As she utters this statement, Laure is thankful that Madeleine's eyes remain closed.

13

Laure cannot imagine what the rest of their lives will be. Truly, it is better that Madeleine isn't awake to see this. Behind the crowd gathered at the shore, Laure can make out a few cabins on the hill beyond. There are a dozen or so, constructed of rough wood. The dwellings that belong to the Savages are off to the side of the settlement and made of bark. Smoke rises from the cooking fires.

"Welcome to Ville-Marie, ladies. As you can see, your arrival was greatly anticipated." The captain of their journey smiles, relaxed in the new environment. He has reached the place he calls home.

A few canoes piled high with animal pelts sit moored on the shore. At the sight of these, the old Jesuit priest sitting in front of Laure grows agitated. "What's the point of working to convert Savage souls when there are so many greedy fur traders waiting to corrupt them?"

"Welcome, Father, to the new world of commerce. King's orders," says the young man who had commented on Madeleine's frailty at the start of their journey. He slaps the priest's dark-robed back and clambers out of the canoe. His breeches are rolled up to his knees as he hurries through the water to the shore.

The priest yells after him, but the young man quickly blends in with the other fur traders on shore. "And now women for them too. What an unholy mess is being constructed here. These men do nothing but drink and fight. What kind of example does this set for our converts?"

If Madeleine were stronger, Laure would gladly board a ship back to France. But there are no ships in Ville-Marie. Laure swallows hard and thinks that at least it isn't cold in Canada like the officers at the Salpêtrière said it would be, or like the icebergs they saw at Terre-Neuve seemed to indicate. In fact, the air in Ville-Marie is thick and the sun so hot that Laure feels as if she is standing in front of a bread oven. She wonders if perhaps the boat has veered off course and landed in the French Islands instead.

The captain of their group just laughs at her suggestion. "Women have such a misguided sense of direction. This heat you're feeling is just the summer season in Canada. Don't worry, you'll have plenty of winter weather soon."

Laure wonders what else she has heard about Canada that is untrue.

The only women to greet the new arrivals are a group of religious sisters. Two young Savage girls hover near one of the old women. The girls have on matching dresses, not unlike the one Laure wore for years at the Salpêtrière. The Savage girls have their hair in neat braids like Marie des Neiges at Québec. These must be some of the converts the priest was talking about. Laure stands a little to get a better look at the girls, which sets the canoe rocking. The men on the shore call out to Laure as she falls back onto her seat. She doesn't want to appear eager for their attention.

She is thirsty and can feel the film of sweat on her face. Her nose and cheeks have been burned by the sun despite the bonnet. She wipes her forehead with the back of her hand. Her dress is heavy and wet at the hem of her skirt from the water in the bottom of the canoe. A man with rolled-up sleeves and the arms of a blacksmith is wading through the water toward her. Other men follow behind him to help the women get out of the canoes and onto the shore. Laure tells the big man to take Madeleine first. She has to repeat herself for him to understand. There are so many different dialects of French in the colony, those from Normandie, from Picardie and other parts of the kingdom. She cannot tell which this man speaks, only that he is hard to understand. Finally, he lifts Madeleine, still wrapped in the blanket, and carries her to shore. Another man comes for Laure, and before she can protest, she is clinging to his thick neck as he lifts her out of the canoe. Her skirt drags through the water.

"Didn't they feed you in France? You're as light as a fox. Won't make much of a worker over here. And believe me, there's nothing to do here except work. Cut trees, hunt animals, bake bread. What twenty men used to do in France, one man has to do for himself here." He sets Laure upright on the shore and walks away.

Laure stands teetering for a moment before dropping to her knees. She looks down at the new earth, her head hanging between her arms, and waits for the ground to stop moving.

She hears another man say: "What did they send us? These are the weakest ones yet. It'll take more to revive them than the work they'll do in a lifetime."

The few military officers and officials of the colony stand to one side, observing the commotion of the canoes' arrival. Once everyone is on the shore, they begin to unload the supplies. The men seem more interested in these goods than they are in the group of huddled women sent by royal authority to be their wives. They unload the heavy things the men had unpacked each evening and repacked in the morning: iron axe heads for trading with the Savages, guns and munitions for defence against the Iroquois, salt, wheat flour, and burlap bundles of cloth. And of course the girls' coffers. Soldiers with muskets slung across their chests guard the unloading of the supplies.

After some time, Laure concentrates on standing again. The people and the trees around her seem to be moving toward her. Before she can collapse a second time, two religious women are at her side. They speak in a dialect from the northwest of France as well, but Laure understands most of what they are saying. She asks the women where Madeleine has been taken and tells them that she wants to go to her friend.

"You can see her after the welcome ceremony. The people of Ville-Marie have been waiting all year for your arrival." The woman's voice is kind enough.

Laure doesn't care about the people of Ville-Marie. She just wants to know where they have taken Madeleine. But the nuns lead Laure by the elbows toward the group. Now that she is on the shore, Laure can see that most of the men are older than she is, scorched by the sun and thick with the dirt of years spent in the forest. They are the worst-looking peasants she has ever seen, only they have been bolstered by the fresh air and plentiful food of the New World. The language they speak sounds like the snarl of fighting dogs. She doesn't want to think which of them is meant to be her husband.

Once the final stores have been removed from the canoes, a man in a black hat trimmed with white feathers addresses the crowd. He is Jean Talon, the Intendant of the colony. He is surrounded by well-outfitted soldiers. Laure strains to make out his voice above the mutterings of the crowd. First he praises the men who defended Ville-Marie over the winter and the spring. They are the Carignan-Salières regiment of soldiers. Since the men's arrival, he says, the Iroquois have been retreating from the settlement. These soldiers have been given plots of forest land by the King to keep them in the colony at the end of their contracts. Laure and the other women have been brought from France especially to marry these soldiers turned farmers.

The Intendant then says that men of New France who refuse to marry the newly arrived women will have their hunting and fishing privileges revoked. He says that the settlers must show the authorities that they are worthy to enjoy the privileges of titled men.

A groan rises from the crowd: "How can we marry these women? They can hardly stand up. Look at them, not a single bosom or hip between all of them, and they're expected to produce children. You haven't brought us helpmates. You've given us another burden."

"You can't expect to behave like animals, fornicating in the trees with any Savage woman you come across, and still continue to receive the hunting and fishing privileges of royal men." The official's voice booms across the assembly, sending an echo of his words into the woods. Laure studies the blackness of the trees, wondering if his speech is directed at some rebellious men who are hiding in the woods. The Intendant turns his back on the crowd and begins to walk inland. The terrain is steep and their goal is a hilltop in the distance.

Laure and the other girls find it hard to keep up, so the
Intendant slows his pace. "They're just a little tired from their
long journey," he says when some of the men start complaining
again about the girls. "You weren't much different when you
first arrived off the ship for your soldiering duties. They'll gain
strength quickly enough."

Although the girls had tried to clean off the worst of the
sea voyage back in Québec, they still look like a brigade of
beggars, their eyes too wide for their faces, spines bent like old
women. The assembly begins to move again. There is a long,
steep path that leads up to the hill, and their goal is a cross that
has been planted at the top. Laure catches her breath as she
tries to climb.

Along the way, a military officer indicates to the girls the
various stages of construction of the five or six settlers' homes
they pass. The men behind Laure chuckle at his grandiose
description of the shacks. When Laure turns back, one of the
men points at a tree and says, "There's my house right there,
just waiting for me to build it."

Laure realizes that the official's elaborate speech on the
shore was just an exaggeration meant to make the women feel
better. She wonders why he bothered trying to impress them,
since they have no way of fleeing back to France.

Once they reach the spot atop the hill where the cross is planted,
the Jesuit priest and one of the women from the Congrégation
Notre-Dame, the religious group that will house the *filles à
marier*, begin to sing the familiar *Te Deum*. Laure can't imagine
anyone other than a madwoman singing a *Te Deum* outdoors

in Paris. It is a hymn that belongs inside the heavy stone of
churches, a ritual song sung by girls confined in hospitals.
Cramped as they were for weeks onboard the ship, when the
passengers joined together to pray for a safe journey, it seemed
natural to use this song. But now it seems so strange to sing the
Te Deum while looking out from this hill in Ville-Marie, where
there is nothing but sunshine and a vast and empty country of
the darkest green below them. How can God even find them in
this place to hear their song?

*Te Martyrum candidatus laudat exercitus. Te per orbem
terrarum sancta confitetur Ecclesia.* The voices of the settlers of
Ville-Marie are strong and sound nothing like the feeble efforts
of the Salpêtrière *bons pauvres.* Despite the victorious way they
sing this miserable song, their voices are almost drowned out
by the twittering of the forest birds all around them.

The moment the ceremony is complete, Laure approaches
one of the men to ask where she can find the hospital. Later,
when she thinks back on this moment, Laure wishes she had
chosen someone else to ask. The man she approaches is pudgy,
with small eyes. He is dressed as badly as all the others. His
stout homeliness makes Laure think he is harmless. He is
standing talking with some men and looks surprised to see
Laure walking toward him. A look of importance comes across
his features as he excuses himself from the men. For a moment,
he stands beside Laure, his hands on his hips, surveying the
settlement below as if the whole scene belongs to him.

He introduces himself as Mathurin, a Carignan-Salières
soldier recently granted a tract of land beyond the settlement.
He says that he has built a fine house on his land. Laure ignores
this information and asks him where she can find the Hôtel-
Dieu. He tells her that he can bring her to it, but insists on

holding her arm. The sister of the congregation nods her head at him, indicating to Laure that he is trustworthy at least.

"Even for short distances a woman walking alone needs to be careful," he says as they head down the steep incline back to the water. "The Savages are faster than wolves and can capture you in the space of a breath."

"Faster than wolves?" Laure is growing tired of the way the men exaggerate to impress the women.

"Yes. They brought our regiment in all the way from France to fight them. One thousand men to protect the colony." He sticks out his chest as if he alone were responsible for all the guns and cannons of Old France.

"Well, I haven't yet seen a single one of these Iroquois enemies since I arrived, so you must be doing a fine job."

"*Was* doing a fine job. I'm a farming man now. That's the end of the soldiering for me. All I need now is a wife to work by my side." He turns his pink face to Laure and smiles. His teeth are as rotten as his words.

She wants to push his hand off her arm. Barely in Ville-Marie an hour and already she has her first suitor. She would rather have married sixteen-year-old Luc Aubin at the Salpêtrière than this man. Even the red-headed *quartier-marin* would have been a better choice.

The Hôtel-Dieu is the largest stone building near the water on rue Saint-Paul. Mathurin says that it is part of the original settlement from twenty years ago and one of the first places to be built in Ville-Marie. At the door, they are greeted by a young woman in a bright white habit. Laure feels her chest constrict. She forgets for a moment that she is in the middle of the forest. Instead she is standing in the sun on the *parvis* of Notre-Dame in Paris. She is surrounded by beggars and priests. She hears the ringing of bells. Women in white habits carry sheets from the river to replace the soiled ones on the rows of beds. The river is dirty and narrow enough to build footbridges across it. The ancient city centre is alive with the pleas of beggars and the horse hooves of the noblemen. The church at her back contains the souls of ancient spirits. Mireille is reaching for her with swollen fingers. It is too late.

Mathurin lifts his cap from his head when he sees the young girl at the door. Laure thanks him for the escort, assuring him that she will not need his company inside the hospital. She is relieved that Madeleine has been brought indoors. The Hôtel-Dieu in Ville-Marie actually looks like a hospital, not like the crowded Hôtel-Dieu of Paris, but a rudimentary and clean country hospital. Unlike the modest wooden houses of Ville-Marie, the Hôtel-Dieu is a sturdy stone construction.

Laure enquires as to Madeleine's whereabouts, and the young girl leads her into the cool entrance and up a spiral oak staircase. Laure smells herbs and tinctures as they pass the pharmacy. The room at the top of the stairs is large and bright. The windows are open and the air is gentle and soft. Madeleine is lying in her own bed. Two other girls from the crossing were also brought in exhausted by the sun and the arduous canoe journey. But, unlike Madeleine, they are sitting up chatting, restored by a few hours of rest and medicine. There are even several empty beds in the room. For the first time Laure feels hope that their lives will be favourable in the colony. Surely Madeleine will be healed in this room.

Laure walks over to where Madeleine lies. "Are you feeling better now that we're off the boat?"

Madeleine looks up. There is a puzzled frown on her face.

She is awake but doesn't seem to register her surroundings or recognize Laure. The nurses must have given her some medicine.

Laure sits on the edge of the bed and recounts to Madeleine the details of the welcome ceremony and the loud voice of the colonists as they sang the *Te Deum*. She also tells her about the hill with the cross from the early missionary days of the settlement. The men and women who established Ville-Marie planned to build a holy place. How all you can see are trees and fresh land from the top of the hill. Madeleine's face relaxes a little at the sound of Laure's voice. She falls asleep, and Laure continues to speak holding her hand.

After a few minutes, the Soeur hospitalière comes up behind Laure. "You will like it here, I am certain. The people of Ville-Marie live to help one another," she says.

The nurse is young. She tells Laure that she is from Paris and that when she was a girl she read about Jeanne Mance, one of the first women to tend the sick in Ville-Marie, and wanted to come to Canada. She said she saw the colony in her dreams. Laure thinks that this timid girl would have much in common with Madeleine.

Laure asks the young nurse if she had seen all the trees and the vast river in her vision. If there had been Savage Iroquois. Laure wonders how anyone in Old France could imagine this forlorn country.

The nurse replies that she didn't see the land at all but knew the name of the place. She saw only the hospital and the sick she was meant to care for.

"I got a sense of the helpful nature of Ville-Marie from my companion today," Laure says. "The man who brought me here," she adds.

The girl laughs. "There is no shortage of men looking to do favours for women here."

The girl is smiling at Laure the way a good officer would have done at the Salpêtrière. It is a look of charity. Laure is starting to think that there is nothing but piousness in this country. The nun on the ship was teaching the sailors and soldiers to leave behind their lewd ways; something about a baptism by sea. The Jesuit in the canoe insisted on the virtue of pushing forward to convert more Savages, and the Governor spoke on the hill about the worthy endeavour of pouring sweat and labour into the colony's forests to create a new French town.

Laure doesn't think she is good enough for the designs of these dreamers, especially without Madeleine to tell her when to hold her tongue.

Laure wrings out the wet cloth in the ceramic bowl beside the bed and places it on Madeleine's forehead. Hours have passed since the welcome ceremony and it is growing dark, but she cannot leave the hospital. What have I done to Madeleine by bringing her here? Laure wonders. Could I not have been content exchanging letters with her from here and hearing about the Salpêtrière as she became an officer? The Salpêtrière rules meant that the Superior would have to read Laure's letters before they reached Madeleine. But would that really have mattered so much?

Laure kneels beside the hospital bed and says a genuine prayer. It feels like the only thing to do in the empty, silent room. She cannot think of the appropriate Latin words repeated to her each day at the Salpêtrière, so she speaks in her French voice.

Laure first says to God that she hopes He really has followed them across the Atlantic to Canada. She prays that these priests and nuns are not deluded and being mocked in their Christian faith by some Savage deity with true dominion here. Laure asks for forgiveness that she urged Madeleine to leave the Salpêtrière. She has made Madeleine give up her dreams of being an officer, of reading from prayer books to the girls in the dormitories, only to be here, now, worn out from the long journey across the sea. Laure knows now that if she had prayed more, the way Madeleine did, she never would have written the letter to the King complaining about their food, nor would she have persuaded Madeleine to come with her. Being here with Madeleine so weak is worse than any fate she could have imagined in Paris. Laure makes the sign of the cross and touches Madeleine's hand.

As if her prayer had an instant effect, Madeleine awakens. Her eyes open and she tries to sit up. She begins to speak, and Laure smiles, elated to hear the familiar voice. But Madeleine doesn't ask about the hospital in Ville-Marie, or how she got there. She doesn't seem to be aware at all that they have crossed the sea and landed in the New World. Laure takes Madeleine's slight shoulders and lifts her so she is propped up and sitting.

Madeleine's eyes seem to be looking beyond the room around her into her past. She says that the Salpêtrière is the biggest building she has ever seen, greater even than the fort that looks out over the sea at La Rochelle. Some of the women inside the dormitories scream the entire day, but there is no need to be frightened. She says that Madame du Clos is kind and teaches her how to be deft with the sewing needle.

"She is so kind that she coaxes bright flowers of thread from our fingers," Madeleine says, her eyes growing wide. "You are my best friend and a tough girl. You expect more from this world than it intends to give you and cannot understand a quiet girl like me who does nothing but pray."

Laure is glad that Madeleine is speaking at last, but she fears she will expend too much effort and so pushes gently against her shoulders. But the small girl resists with remarkable strength.

"I like it when you talk to me during the dining hall prayers, about leaving the hospital, about making a place in the city. I am amazed by all the possibilities you come up with. *Let us be seamstresses*, you say, even though I don't have the hands for it. You tell me that we will find a small apartment and get hired out as servant girls just like you did as a child in the Enfant-Jésus."

Laure can see now how absurd it had been to dream of these things. After all, what chance did they ever really have of leaving the Salpêtrière except to be banished across the sea?

"We both know what happens to girls who can't find work as seamstresses or servant girls. You have watched the arrival of those fallen women and heard about the ones who end up chained in the basement of the hospital. But you don't worry about that fate. Instead you write a letter to the King, imploring him to give us a better life."

Finally Madeleine turns her head to look at Laure.

"Like Mary of Egypt, who crossed the Jordan to find glorious rest, I have also found peace across the water. I am happy you brought me here." Then Madeleine's eyes grow dull. They remain open but she is staring at the ceiling.

Laure needs for Madeleine to say something more. Even if only to request that they pray together.

Madeleine smiles, and Laure reaches in the air. She doesn't know how to hold back a soul in flight.

When Laure finally stands, her knees are red and sore from the hard wooden slats of the floor. The same young nurse re-enters the room and lights a candle. She tells Laure in a quiet voice that she will need to make her way over to Marguerite Bourgeoys' congregation before nightfall.

"The Iroquois wait for sunset and lurk close to our buildings, ready to pounce on us." She places her hand over Laure's and pulls the sheet over Madeleine's face.

The spell is broken. Laure begins to cry. She calls Madeleine's name over and over again.

14

In the middle of the night Laure hears someone drop the trunk in the attic room. She closes her eyes again, wanting only to sleep, to forget. But the calming effect of the laudanum is wearing off. Her stomach aches. She remembers screaming in the Hôtel-Dieu throughout the entire night until her throat could produce no more sounds. The following day two sisters came for her and brought her a long way across the trails to this room in the Congrégation Notre-Dame.

Laure feels her hands flutter up from her thighs like birds struggling to fly. She reaches beside her in the darkness for the trunk from Paris. Her fingers touch the sodden wood. She leaves her hand there and dozes again.

The next time Laure awakens, her third day in Ville-Marie is dawning. Girls outside the room are talking about a funeral. They are whispering about the strange girl from Paris who arrived at the congregation yesterday, crazed, from the hospital. Some of them remember Laure from the ship. She is the one who dances, the one who was baptized by the monster, they say. A few of the girls from la Pitié tell the others that in Paris Laure behaved even worse. Laure doesn't care about their lies.

There is enough dawn light to make out the shape of the trunk beside her on the floor. She gets out of bed and kneels beside it. When she opens the lid, the dank smell of mould rises up from it. The linen handkerchiefs Madame du Clos placed on top of Laure's belongings are moist and slimy. Laure removes them, along with the other contents from the top of the trunk, some of which have been damaged by sea water.

When she reaches what she is looking for, she is thankful that the paper is still dry. She lifts the heavy package onto the bed and removes from it the gown she carried from Paris. Laure runs her fingers across the fine yellow fabric and over the beadwork, feeling for any damage that might have occurred during the long voyage. She holds it up to the sun coming through the attic window. The dress has survived.

It seems like years have passed since this spring when Mireille died. So much has changed since then. Laure can hardly remember the times she spent working so hard to write a letter to the King, to adjust Mireille's gown to the latest fashion in the basement workshop of the hospital. Now she will wear the dress to Madeleine's funeral.

Laure can still smell the sea journey in her hair. She has not been able to cleanse herself of the long ocean crossing. She brings a strand to her mouth. There is still a taste of salt on it. Laure doesn't want to see the girls from the ship at the funeral. She barely spoke to them, staying most of the time below deck trying to coax Madeleine to eat, wiping her forehead in hopes that she would grow stronger. Neither did she talk to them much as they journeyed in canoes up the river to Ville-Marie. The ones they have sent to Ville-Marie, the farthest outpost of the colony, are homely country girls and gaunt Pitié residents. The best-looking and healthiest women were chosen to stay at Québec.

Laure will need to ask one of these girls, sleeping in the dormitory room outside the alcove, to tie the bodice of her gown for the funeral. For now, she climbs into the whalebone corset, lifting the heavy skirt to her hips and sliding her arms through the sleeves of the dress. She lies back down on the cot when this is complete. She can feel the sweat forming on her body from the congested warmth of the tiny attic room. She listens to the country accents of the girls in the dormitory and dozes a little, her arms laid across her chest like a corpse.

⚜

Laure enters the adjoining room in the congregation where the other girls have been sleeping. The room is smaller than the dormitory at the Salpêtrière, though each of the girls has her own bed. Laure has entered from the alcove room wearing the jewelled gown of bright yellow and red. Her hair is loose and hangs over her shoulders and down her back like a dark cape. The other girls still have on their thin grey nightshirts for sleeping. A few have already laid out on their beds tattered cotton frocks for the funeral.

The girl that Laure approaches to tie the dress makes a quick movement backward on her bed before agreeing with a nod to the task. With nervous fingers, she does her best to tighten the leather string around Laure's slight waist. When the dress is properly tied, Laure turns to the others and smiles. "I am here to marry an officer."

Laure removes from her bodice the small locket she took yesterday from Madeleine's trousseau. "This is the man I have come for. He will be my husband." She holds out the chain to them and they watch it swing back and forth. Laure doesn't let the three country girls, with their thick, dirty fingers, touch the locket. Instead she holds it open for them at such a distance that they have to strain their eyes, the way Laure once did, to make out Frédéric's features.

⚜

The funeral is held at the Ville-Marie cemetery near the river. The procession includes the Jesuit priest who travelled with them from Québec, a colony administrator several ranks below the Intendant who officiated at yesterday's ceremony, two soldiers from the Carignan-Salières regiment, including the one who walked Laure to the Hôtel-Dieu, the nurse present at Madeleine's death, some of the sisters from Marguerite Bourgeoys' congregation, and a few Algonquin Savages. The two Jesuit priests, including the young one who spent so much time talking with Madeleine, are holding the funeral ceremony. The younger priest keeps his eyes downcast as the rites begin.

The Algonquins have come to bury, alongside Madeleine, an elderly man of their nation who died of smallpox. He was a Savage converted by the Jesuits, which is why he will be buried in the Catholic cemetery. Two holes have been dug in the earth for the bodies. The Hospitalières have sewn Madeleine's body into a canvas sack, while the corpse of the Savage has been left exposed. His face and shirt have been painted red, which frightens the newly arrived girls. The other Ville-Marie residents seem accustomed to this tradition. An old woman takes the shovel offered to her by a soldier and begins to throw dirt over the body.

One of the younger Savage men looks past the assembly to Laure. He is standing at a distance, away from the priest and the other French settlers. He seems interested in Laure's bright dress but averts his eyes when she notices him staring.

Laure wonders if the other soldier is the officer Frédéric. She is wearing his locket around her neck. Looking around at the colonists, there doesn't seem to be anybody above the rank of shoe cobbler here. Laure wears the locket like an amulet to protect her from the brute she will soon be expected to marry. *Madeleine, there should be princes and dukes to honour you,* she thinks, gazing at the stark burlap sack with Madeleine's body inside. *What a small mark you have left in the world. Not one of these fools mumbling their incantations has ever heard you speak. What a gentle voice you had. And always such good words that came from you. Only the young Jesuit, shaking incense smoke over your body, has some idea what a fine and noble person you were. As pure as a saint.*

Laure wonders what the new priest feels to be uttering prayers over Madeleine's dead body. The older priest hurries through the incantations, accustomed to death. But perhaps the young one is touched by Madeleine's passing, heartbroken even. What will become of him, choosing to leave behind a soft childhood and a good education to be here among residents of the kingdom's poorhouses and merciless Savages? How long will it take before these vast woods swallow him too? A month? A year? Will he emerge like the bent man beside him with mutilated limbs, speaking words in Savage tongues, numb to death?

The priest keeps repeating what a shame it is that Madeleine's young life was wasted. That this girl, brought over at the King's expense, will never become a colony wife, will not live to raise any children. *If only this religious man could know that you preferred to die than to break the vow of chastity you made all by yourself without the support of any orders, without wearing the clothes of a holy woman.*

Only that ugly Savage sees that I have on my finest gown for you, Madeleine. You would probably tell me not to call him ugly. But even from a distance I can see that his face is scarred. Madeleine, you are the saint of nowhere now. How can you be laid to rest here, in this brutal forest? How will you know where you are? He is looking at me again, and I think it's sympathy in his black eyes, but I can't read the faces of Savage strangers.

Laure's shoulders begin to tremble and she sways on her feet. The young Algonquin notices and rushes over to her. "*Malade?*" he asks.

Laure shakes her head. His face is marked by the same disease that killed the old man. Laure has heard much about this disease that has claimed so many of the Savages living near the French, has even made some of them think that the Jesuit priests carry with them the curse of this disease. Unlike so many of his kind, though, he has survived. Mireille and Madeleine succumbed to their diseases. Now that he is beside her, Laure can smell the animal grease and hides that cover his body. It is already an odour she associates with Canada. She became familiar with it on the canoe journey, on the long, silent days spent cutting into the river with wooden oars and sleeping in the forest at night. The men laughed at Laure when she complained that they smelled of rotten flesh like butchers. That is the smell of Canada's silver, they said.

The Savage speaks in his strange language with some French words mixed in. He indicates the ceremony going on in front of them and begins counting something out on his fingers. Laure thinks he is lamenting how many people from his nation have died. He nods his chin toward the women from the Notre-Dame congregation, as if to suggest that Laure belongs with them and should be standing closer to them. She shakes her head. She wants him to go away, to leave her alone with her grief.

He tells her that his name is Deskaheh. He says that it is an Iroquois name but that he is an Algonquin. He waits for her to introduce herself. Instead, Laure points at the body and says, "Madeleine." Deskaheh does the same for the man painted in red. Laure doesn't understand what he utters as the old man's name.

She wants to tell this Savage that there was also Mireille, a girl in France who had died, that although she hadn't really liked her, she hadn't wanted her to die. Laure also feels like saying that she is still grieving for an old wealthy Madame who had been kind and taught her many things. And if she were to look even further down into her well of grief, she could tell him about her father and mother, who might both be dead by now as well. She could say that she still hears her father singing a song meant for a little girl and that it is a cruel trick of the mind to remember this melody after all this time. But she imagines this Savage could keep going with this game too. Laure doubts that this is his first funeral. She imagines that the scars on his face are just the beginning of his story.

Mathurin notices the Savage talking to Laure. He makes his way over to them, swaggering as he walks. Laure doesn't know which of these men disgusts her more. They both smell terrible, in different ways, and speak to her when they have no business doing so.

"She wasn't sent all the way here to spend her time talking with Savages," Mathurin says when he reaches them.

Judging by the puzzled look on Deskaheh's face, he doesn't understand all of Mathurin's words, but the tone is clear enough.

"*Malade!*" he exclaims, justifying why he has come over to Laure's side.

But Mathurin takes Deskaheh's word as an insult. His full cheeks fill with blood and he raises his shoulders, taking a step toward Deskaheh, who backs up.

Laure moves between the two. She doesn't want to attract the attention of the others at the funeral. But Mathurin has already raised his fist and is swinging it at Deskaheh in the direction of Laure's head.

Deskaheh pushes Laure hard to the side, and she falls onto her hands in the dirt, her dress spreading around her like a wave. The cry she makes on hitting the ground interrupts the funeral. She sees that the Algonquins look surprised to see that Deskaheh has thrown a French woman to the ground. Mathurin takes the opportunity to once again swing his fist at Deskaheh. This time his knuckles connect with Deskaheh's nose. Blood spurts from it. Laure scrambles back, away from the fighting men, but not before several bright spatters of Deskaheh's blood land on her skirt.

The nurse from the Hôtel-Dieu rushes away from the quieted priest and his followers. Laure wants to say something as the soldiers yank the two men to their feet, to explain what really happened. But before she can open her mouth, the nurse has given her a new dose of laudanum.

That evening, when Laure awakens back in the alcove of the Congrégation Notre-Dame, she asks for a candle and a paper and ink. It seems there is nothing these women won't do to protect her, with their kind words, the medicine and arms they extend to her. One of the sisters brings the requested items to Laure. The same woman also returns Laure's dress, saying they got most of the bloodstains out. Laure holds the skirt over the candlelight. The spatters are faded and brown.

"It's a lovely dress," the nun says. "You can hardly see that the stains are there. Nobody will look that closely."

That is a lie. Laure can see nothing but the traces of blood when she looks at the skirt. She runs her fingers over them.

There is a small desk in the room. The young sister who brought Laure the ink and paper says she cannot write herself. She asks if she can stay and watch while Laure composes the letter. Laure is at least glad that she has permission to write here. She doesn't have to hide, like she did at the Salpêtrière, waiting for a few minutes at the end of the sewing day to copy down the sentence she had been rehearsing for hours in her mind.

From what Laure has seen so far, Ville-Marie is a desperate enterprise of constant war against the Iroquois Savages, of soldiers being allocated pieces of the forest, of trading animal pelts for survival. The men's greedy fantasies of becoming wealthy are quickly replaced by an endless routine of chopping wood and fighting off insects. Most of the men give up and return to France. Only the crazed or truly desperate stay on. Laure hates it already and wants to leave. But for now she is glad that although she is only an orphan from the Hôpital Général de Paris, she has been given a candle and space on a desk to write.

Laure dips the pen in ink. She is still thinking of the funeral, of the Savage man who told her his name. She doesn't have anyone she can send a letter to, so she writes to Madeleine, who is dead but still Laure's best and only friend. Besides,

Laure has learned that it is probably better not to write a letter to a living person. In her experience words on paper are best kept secret.

July 1669

Dear Madeleine,

It is the day of your funeral. I have been given my own room. I suppose I am the Queen of the New World now. From the window I can see my dominion, a garden below and endless countryside beyond. Only my subjects are wild beasts, such as the raccoon, the beaver, the fox, the marten, and a countless number of forest birds. My prince is a soldier who looks like a pig. He defended my honour and saved me from a Savage who is Iroquois and Algonquin, both a friend and an enemy.

As it turns out, we were sent here for nothing. Most of the men want nothing to do with the women from the Salpêtrière. They are being forced into marriages when they are perfectly content to run through the forests in search of furs and Savage girls. They don't really want to settle down here and build homes and villages, towns in the forest. Most of them just want to leave, to return to Old France.

There is nothing I want more than to be able to blow out this candle and be back in the Sainte-Claire dormitory. To hear the morning bell, to see you kneeling at your cot, to eat what little there is. To know that nothing comes of complaining. To feel like you do, that a nourished body is nothing compared to a nourished soul. To be happy to wait. I am sorry for all that I have ruined. I am not worthy of your forgiveness.

> Your friend,
> Laure Beauséjour

Part Three

Ces filles de France purent s'apprivoiser au cheval et au canot; apprendre à préparer le pot-au-feu du pays, à faire la lessive à la rivière, à coudre ou à raccommoder, à filer et à tisser laine et lin, à tenir un ménage, à élever des enfants; surtout, s'habituer à vivre avec la peur des Indiens et à surmonter cette peur.

[These daughters of France became accustomed to the horse and the canoe; they learned to prepare stews with whatever meat was available, to do their laundry at the river, to sew and mend, to spin and weave wool and flax, to manage a household, to raise children; but mostly, they learned to live with the fear of the Indians and to overcome that fear.]

—MARIE-LOUISE BEAUDOIN,
LES PREMIÈRES ET LES FILLES DU ROI À VILLE-MARIE

15

Laure sits in the congregation's garden. She likes to spend her time here, away from the others. Ever since the funeral, she has been given permission to stay alone in the alcove, away from the dormitory where the other girls sleep. There is no denying the kindness of the Mère Bourgeoys and her two novices, Marie Raisin and Anne Hiou. Even Madame Crolo, who is called the "donkey of the house" because she works incessantly like the most brutish servant woman, is gentle enough. Although the congregation women are dedicated to housing the women from France and preparing them for husbands, their main occupation is teaching the Savage and French girls of the colony. Some of these young girls, orphaned perhaps, are boarding at the congregation. In addition, the building is used for signing marriage contracts, for teaching religion to old women on Sundays, and for laying out the bodies of the dead on the night before the funeral.

Laure meets the wealthy praying girl, Jeanne Le Ber, at the congregation. She is seven years old and already knows that she wants a life of prayer and mortification of the flesh. Although her dowry is valued at fifty thousand écus and she has suitors from Ville-Marie all the way down the river to Québec and across the sea to Old France, the little girl vows she will remain a virgin. Laure recognizes the stubborn set of Jeanne Le Ber's lips and knows that she will never marry, even though others tell her she is only a child and she has her whole life ahead and a fortune to manage.

Sometimes Jeanne sits with Laure and confesses the troubles in her heart. Some children are born into old age, is what Marguerite Bourgeoys says. The little girl tells Laure that she has only baby brothers and no sisters. She says that her parents do not like her spending so much time at Marguerite Bourgeoys' congregation and at the Hôtel-Dieu chapel, but these are the places she enjoys. Her father says that a young girl can't possibly spend the whole day praying like an old woman, but Jeanne says that she is content to do so. Her father plans to send her away to the Ursulines in Québec, where she will get away from these strange rituals and learn what is expected of her.

Besides her prayers, Jeanne enjoys learning needlework. Laure recognizes in the child the quick fingers, long and lean, of an expert seamstress. She stitches religious scenes onto fabric and gives her work to Marguerite Bourgeoys or to the Hospitalières at the Hôtel-Dieu. Laure cannot help but think that such talent and a fortune besides are wasted on this melancholic creature. Jeanne refuses to put on the dresses of fine material from France that her mother lays out for her each morning. Instead she wears a plain linen dress like the Salpêtrière uniform that Laure was so eager to shed.

Some days Jeanne's mother can be heard sobbing in the company of Marguerite Bourgeoys. "Ma petite fille, she whips her perfect white flesh until ugly welts appear. She refuses to eat and grows so thin. How can I watch my only daughter, the child I caressed and rubbed with ointment, that I handled with such careful hands, inflict wounds upon herself?"

Marguerite Bourgeoys is a practical woman who says that the best devotion comes through hard work and serving others, that scrubbing floors sends prayers straight to heaven. She doesn't know what to tell the family of Jeanne Le Ber. She can only do for this wealthy child what she does for all the girls under her care. She encourages Jeanne to grow humble through hard work, to carry pails of water, to light fires and to keep wood burning, to prepare the meats and vegetables for the daily meals. In this way eventually the little girl will be ready to marry someone and to manage a household. But Jeanne wants only to stare at walls, to kneel before the altar, to read her prayer book, and to stitch religious motifs. She is not interested in hard work.

Of course Jeanne is not like the other girls of the congregation, as she has with her at all times an attendant, her cousin Anna Barroy. This woman is boisterous and plump and concerned with practical affairs. She is the one who encourages Jeanne to eat and who coaxes her up from her knees when too many hours have passed.

The *filles à marier* think that Jeanne Le Ber is a foolish girl and they ignore her presence. It is only Laure who sees something familiar in her. For this little child has in her the piousness of Madeleine Fabrecque, the wealth and status of Mireille Langlois, and the same stubborn heart that beats in Laure's chest. She will become a saint, devoting her entire life to worship, just as she says, and nobody, not her parents, not even Marguerite Bourgeoys, will convince her otherwise.

Unlike most religious orders, the Filles de la Congrégation, as they are called, are free to travel about the countryside.

Laure wonders how these women could have left behind prosperous lives in Old France to come to this colony. Marie Raisin confessed to her that she misses the literature and music, as if Laure knew of these things at the Salpêtrière. She doesn't bother to tell Marie that she has eaten her first meat in several years here at the congregation.

So far Laure's circumstances have been more comfortable in the colony. It is the first time she has had her own room. How strange it feels to wake up alone in a bed and to look up at the sloping attic ceiling and out the tiny window streaming in light meant only for her eyes. During the day, Laure has also been excused from joining the other *filles à marier* in their lessons in the congregation's workshop. They are learning to do things Laure already knows, like how to knit wool socks and sew cotton shirts for their future husbands. Laure would rather be outside in the heat than inside listening to the congregation women go on about what great wives the peasant girls will make. The other girls don't really mind that Laure has special permission to be in the garden, as most of them spent their time in Old France outside in the fields and are happy now to be able to keep their skin away from the sun. They would prefer to learn to sew, as many of them were accustomed only to brute outdoor work. To excuse her absence, the nuns tell the others that Laure will soon be well enough to join them. She doesn't feel sick at all.

This is the first garden Laure has been in. In Paris, only wealthy women like the Superior at the Salpêtrière had gardens. Even Madame d'Aulnay didn't have her own garden. Laure sits on the soil between the rows of vegetables and herbs and lifts her face to the sun, imagining that she is back in France and that this plot of land is her very own. After a moment, she shakes herself out of her reverie and sets about her routine of looking after the crops the way Mère Bourgeoys instructed her.

She stands up to check the height of the cornstalks, then she walks through the rows of tomatoes and beans, making sure there is no evidence of an animal having slid under the fence in the night. Using both hands, Laure yanks the tough weeds from the soil between the plants and tosses them to the side. She crouches down at the strawberries and picks a few to eat.

When she looks up, Laure is surprised to see that Deskaheh is kneeling behind the fence with one of the other Savages from the funeral. She wonders how long they've been there watching her. They laugh when she notices them. Deskaheh's nose is bruised and swollen, which makes him look even uglier than before. But his grin is youthful and relaxed. He sticks his hand through the fence, and Laure jumps back. Both of the boys laugh.

The girls have been told not to give food directly to the Savages who beg outside the congregation. Donations first have to receive the approval of the Mère Bourgeoys. Laure knows that Deskaheh and his companion would be chased away by one of the nuns. They are troublemakers and not true beggars, who wear baggy white shirts like the French fur traders.

But Laure feels she needs to repay this Deskaheh who was kind to her at the funeral. After all, he was only concerned about her health. Mathurin should not have punched him. Laure picks two tomatoes from a stalk and hands one to each of them. Deskaheh looks at the fruit in his hand and exchanges a few words with his companion. They drop the tomatoes into their sacks. Deskaheh sticks his hand through the fence again. Laure walks down the rows of the garden, filling her hands first with strawberries, then with beans. Each time her arms are full, she brings what she has picked to the fence. She is careful not to touch the hands of the Savages when she passes the food to them. She even brings them a pile of lettuce leaves. Deskaheh's companion shakes his head at the offering and throws the leaves on the ground.

Laure makes a round of the entire garden, filling both their bags. When she has finished, Deskaheh sticks his hand through the fence once again. He is assessing her with the same look she received from the Duke and the Tailleur Brissault. He is still grinning. His friend pushes at the fence and motions for Laure to follow them. Together they speak in a Savage language, probably Algonquin, that Laure doesn't understand, even though she knows that Deskaheh can say some French words. They examine the different parts of her body and then discuss this among themselves. She takes a step back.

Laure sees that they both have knives at their waists, and although Deskaheh is taller, they are both as big as grown men even though they are probably only her age. The fence that separates her from them could easily be scaled. Laure turns away from Deskaheh and his companion and runs toward the house. She trips over her skirt and falls on her knees in the dirt of the garden. The sound of their laughter follows her into the cool entrance of the congregation.

❦

Laure doesn't tell anyone about the two Savages she saw outside. The other girls would think her mad for getting close to them. She is angry with herself for letting those boys see her fear. She should have been brave like when she left behind the hospital and walked to Paris to see Mireille. Like when the hospital director visited the workshop and said her dress was unholy, and she held her breath waiting for him to leave, pretending she was a wealthy young woman getting her gown adjusted by the poor residents of the hospital. What can she possibly have to fear in this colony?

※

Deskaheh returns to the garden the next day and again on the one after. He comes back with different boys. But none of these boys ever come back without Deskaheh. Each time, Laure fills their bags with corn, tomatoes, beans, raspberries, whatever is ready to be harvested. There is so much food growing in the garden that nobody notices the absence of what she gives them. Deskaheh continues to laugh at her, telling his friends about her in the Algonquin language, but she is no longer afraid.

※

One night, after Laure has been staying at the congregation for many weeks, she writes another letter to Madeleine.

Dear Madeleine,
 It is good that they still let me have my own room here. As a Queen should. Remember how you called me the Queen of the New World? The other girls behave worse than they did on the ship, as they are no longer afraid of catching their death at sea. They giggle and scheme all day long about which horrible peasant they

will marry. Some of them have been married before and they still dream that this time they will meet their prince. They are learning how to make curtains they will sew on their new shacks and how to darn socks for their future husbands. Their fingers are slow and thick, and Madame du Clos wouldn't tolerate their clumsiness in her workshop. I refuse to speak to any of them. Luckily they are afraid of me so they leave me in peace.

The nuns here are gentler with us than the officers of the Salpêtrière. They are desperate to do good work as they have left behind fortunate circumstances in Old France to teach girls in the colony. Like Marie de l'Incarnation in Québec, they prefer teaching catechism to the Savage girls more than they like teaching the girls from France how to knit socks. You would have liked these Savage girls. They are very pious, unlike the Pitié girls who came across with us on the ship.

At mealtimes there is plenty to eat. The stews are filled with meat from forest beasts. I spend my days in the garden watching the plants grow. I pretend to be working but really I am just sitting in the sun. My mind becomes so empty that I forget the whole day has passed until the light fades and I start to get cold.

The Savage from the funeral has been coming to the fence. I should tell one of the sisters about him. I have given him half the vegetables of the garden and he still laughs at me. He finds me just as ugly as I find him. When he speaks French, he sounds like a snake hissing

inside my ear. Still, listening to him is better than
being inside learning how to make socks.
     Soon I will have to get married. Then my life here
will really begin. I am dreading the day.
                              Your friend,
                              Laure Beauséjour

Laure blows out the candle and rests her head on her arms. Her dreams are strange in Canada. They are filled with the screams of the forest.

Laure's hair is long, and she sits in the congregation garden with it spread all around her. She has enough hair to fill the entire garden. The long black strands cover the vegetables. They grow over the pumpkins and the other strange things that emerge from the earth here. Her body is entangled with the garden. The soil is pulling her down by her hair. The fence keeps the forest away for now, but it is encroaching.

Deskaheh has come to see her. His ugliness makes her ache. She tears whatever she can from the earth to give to him. She hands the vegetables, still heavy with clumps of dirt, over to his waiting arms. But he reaches through the fence and grabs hold of her hair instead. He twists it around his fingers and laughs. She wants to make him stop laughing but doesn't know how to. He is pulling her, bringing her nearer to the fence. His eyes are full of hate.

When Laure awakens from this dream, there is only the forest outside and the moonlight on her tingling arms. She knows how to make him stop laughing. She picks up her comb and turns to the window. The Savages believe the dead roam through the trees at night, so they do not wander after dark. It is the safest time to walk through the forest for the French. Still, nobody does it.

Laure is tired of his mockery. She is wearing the grey dress from the hospital. She was still a child when they gave it to her; a new smock every two years for each resident. It has been almost two years since this dress was given to her. The linen has grown thin and patchy. She won't need a new hospital dress here. She grasps the material in her hands, digging her nails into it. The old gown tears easily down the front. She waits to hear something from the forest. There are only the voices inside her head reprimanding her.

Laure wonders what it feels like to run through the woods at night. To trip on stumps and branches, to get cut, bitten by insects, and attacked by animals. What it would be like to get lost in a world of trees. She wonders how far she could get before succumbing to the vast wilderness.

Deskaheh calls the congregation nuns Manitou women. They give themselves to their God instead of to their husbands. He says that the Savage women only give themselves like that to Manitou when they are very old, after they have had children and grandchildren and have experienced all things in life. Only then can they counsel others on how to live. Laure tells him about the very young Savage girl she saw in Québec and how these girls prayed with more fervour than the French and were more devout. She doesn't think these girls are preparing themselves for husbands. He shrugs and says maybe such girls exist. It takes Laure and Deskaheh half an hour to convey an idea with gestures and the bit of French he speaks, but Laure says it doesn't matter about the languages because the spirit of a person can be known before they even utter a single sound. That was true of the Superior, of Madeleine, Madame du Clos, and even some of the sisters Laure has met here in Canada. Of course, she was wrong about Mireille Langlois and isn't certain about Deskaheh either.

He shouldn't watch her in the garden, shouldn't watch her as she sleeps. Laure isn't as blind or deaf as he thinks. He must have torn his legs on the bark and the pointed edges of the branches as he climbed the tree to look into her window. Did he see the bright eyes of animals in the woods on his way here? Did he wonder if Laure would be in the same body and hair at night, asleep like a living woman, or did he think she might be out wandering, hungry like the animals and spirits of the dead?

She had told Deskaheh which window was hers, pointed up at it with her chin from the garden. Her arms were full of corn. She told him she had her own room because she was a Queen. He disagreed and said Laure was alone because she had been bad to the Manitou women. But she hadn't expected him to remember where she slept at night, to store it in his mind. Tonight Laure will let Deskaheh know that she isn't as blind or

deaf as the other congregation women. That she knows he is
there.

He has climbed the tree to the perfect height and is close to
the window. Laure pulls the remains of her dress down her arms.
The cloth belongs to the grave. It is frail as spider web, falls off
her like dust. Undressing for Deskaheh is the same as offering
him vegetables. She wants to fill his arms with the contents of
the garden. So he can taste the wheat, grapes, and pears that
won't take to this land, along with his corn, pumpkins, and
berries. She wants to steal for him from the soil until the garden
is empty and nothing more will grow.

❦

Laure takes her comb and begins to run it through her hair.
Once she has covered her shoulders and breasts, she puts it
down. She picks up her pen and dips it in the little ink pot. She
doesn't know what else to do.

She writes with a trembling hand: *The Savage from the
funeral is here. Deskaheh. At night and right up to my window.
He must think that I'm blind because he just sits there a few inches
from the pane, staring right in. A Savage man is in my dreams
now. He climbed a tree to come and see me. There are no vegetables
here so I know he has come just for me. I should probably be afraid
of him like the other girls are. They run when they see these men
on the street. Even the ones who are supposed to be our allies. The
Savages, like most things here, are the business of the men. His
scarred face is really the only thing that interests me in Canada.
Everyone else here thinks I'm odd, and I think even less of them.*

*Just as I expected, he enjoys it. He isn't laughing tonight.
Wait, I'll show him a bit more of what he wants to see. I think he*

likes this black hair of mine that is a curse because it repels all the
men of stature. The look on his face when I part it makes me want
to reach out the window and pull him through it.

But it's too late.

The game is over and for now I have won.

Laure waits until Deskaheh leaves before she gets into bed. She
hugs the remains of the old dress against her naked chest and
runs her fingers along her stomach. A new ache has entered her
life. It is joyful and sad and shrouds all the others. She was able
to make Deskaheh stop laughing. She gave him what he wanted
more than vegetables. Laure tightens her legs remembering how
serious his eyes were. She can't help but shudder at the vastness
of the new country, wondering how much further her body still
has to go. But, just like with all the other tender moments in
her life, Laure is already saying goodbye. She knows that this
new fire must be extinguished. If her life in Canada is to have
any meaning at all, if the Laure who is a seamstress, former
Bijou of the largest poorhouse in all of the French empire and
even beyond, is to continue, then she must put an end to this
unholy friendship.

16

Laure finally agrees to marry Mathurin in October. It is the only thing she can possibly do, as all the other *filles à marier* staying at the congregation have been married and are now living with their new husbands. It is why hundreds of women have been sent to Canada at great expense to the royal coffer. A few of the girls were happy to take the first man who came to Mère Bourgeoys seeking a wife from among her charges. Others, especially those marrying for a second time, were shrewder about their choice, enquiring about the material conditions of their new life. Would there be a cabin for them to go to? What furniture, what fortune, did their future husband already possess?

Like at Québec, those women who had brought with them some livres of their own did not wish to see these squandered on a man who possessed nothing. Strong women of proper child-bearing age, not too old or young, were able to be more selective about their matches. News of several pregnancies has already reached the congregation. But, like at Québec, two marriages have been annulled here as well. Both of these occurred when the new wife discovered that her husband had lied about the state of his fortune. But many of the women, even from previous years, have not been heard from since they left the congregation with their new husbands and are presumed to be happy.

Laure put off her inevitable fate for as long as she could. Her attempts to meet with Frédéric, the young officer promised in marriage to Mireille, were thwarted; she learned that he had already married a girl from the 1668 shipload of women from France, one of the *filles de bonne naissance* sent especially to marry the officers. It is good, thinks Laure, that Mireille did not make it all the way to the colony only to discover that she was one year too late. Mireille, with her good manners and careful words, would have been forced to marry a peasant the way some of the high-born women had done at Québec. Laure thinks that sometimes it is better to die than to live out what life has in store for you.

As for Deskaheh, how can Laure explain to him her decision to marry Mathurin? Does she need to? What difference does it make to the Savages what the congregation women do so long as they sometimes offer food and other goods at the door? Still, Laure whispered the news of her upcoming marriage to Deskaheh through the garden fence, over the fall wind, with all the vegetable stalks turned brown and withered at her feet. Deskaheh nodded along as Laure spoke, but she wasn't sure if he understood, since he usually nodded at the things she said to him.

Deskaheh didn't return to see her any more at their usual time in the afternoon, but Laure wasn't sure if it was because the night frost had put an end to the garden or if he understood that she was soon to be married and he should therefore stay away.

Laure's wedding will be a quick affair. Like for the other girls, the legal ceremony will be held in the entrance of the Congrégation Notre-Dame. The two witnesses who will sign Laure's marriage contract are the Superior, Marguerite Bourgeoys, and a lower-ranked sister. Laure has been around for a number of these ceremonies since her arrival in Ville-Marie last summer.

Throughout the early fall, Laure met several times with Mathurin before agreeing to the match. These meetings in the congregation's parlour weren't really necessary, since Laure knew all there was to know about her future husband on the day she first met him, at the welcome ceremony on the hill. Mathurin is more than eager to please her. He has an inflated sense of his accomplishments in Ville-Marie, which should at least give him the enthusiasm needed to survive here. Laure doesn't expect any pleasant surprises from her marriage to Mathurin and hopefully no unpleasant ones either.

Mathurin had been a poor man in France. Although Laure's future husband had been better off than those languishing in the men's division of the General Hospital in Paris, he was only one misfortune away from joining them. Mathurin had come to Canada, been a soldier for three years, and was now a free man with a wooded plot of land and a bride with a chest of supplies from Paris and a promise from the King of a fifty-livres dowry. He claimed that the hundreds of soldiers who returned to France, refusing the royal offer of free land, had been fools. That it is better to look toward the future than back at the past.

Mathurin's arms are as thick as his cheeks and neck. He is thirty-two and says that it is his first marriage. This was not the case for some of the other suitors who had shown an interest in Laure, including a fifty-three-year-old widower, a criminal from the King's galleys, proud that he had been released from his prison sentence in France because he had agreed to come to the colony. Mère Bourgeoys had scolded Marie Raisin for setting up that particular meeting. Another of Laure's suitors had been a sixteen-year-old *Canadien* accompanied by his father.

Each time Laure descended the congregation stairs to meet with Mathurin, he had been polite enough, perhaps overly so. He tells her that his cabin is fully constructed and is larger and sturdier than the houses of most settlers. A completed cabin is the most important thing the women look for in a husband. The two girls who had returned to the congregation seeking annulments had discovered that they would be sleeping in tents in the woods because their new husbands had not yet constructed their cabins. Given Laure's options, marrying Mathurin made the most sense. Once they have a few children, there is a chance that he will leave Laure to her own devices. She might still have the opportunity to become a seamstress.

❦

Laure wears Mireille's gown on her wedding day. It is still stained with Deskaheh's blood, although she has since fixed the seam of the bodice where it tore when he pushed her to the ground. Laure is happy to see that after several months of eating the congregation's more ample food, the dress now fits her better. She even had to let out a few inches to accommodate her new shape. Since it is her wedding day, Laure decides to pin her hair loosely on her head. She leaves the alcove and the now empty dormitory and walks down to the parlour. The sisters who helped her change follow Laure downstairs.

It looks like Mathurin has also tried to dress impressively for the occasion. He has traded his forest breeches for a cleaner pair and has on a coat trimmed with rabbit fur, although it looks tatty and a little rotted. His hair has been greased back with animal fat, giving prominence to his bright cheeks. He appears to be sweating despite the cold.

Ville-Marie is already colder in October than Paris in January. The sisters are concerned that Laure won't have enough time to adjust to her new household tasks before the hardest months of winter hit the colony. Mathurin has brought with him a list of his belongings, written up by the notary. Laure's coffer contains all that she owns. One of the hired boys of the congregation carries it down for the ceremony.

Mathurin is grinning at her. Seeing her bridegroom, Laure remembers the words from the Intendant's speech on her first day in the colony. He had said that the newly arrived women would be like biblical helpmates to the colony's men. The work ahead of them here was far more than was expected of wives in Old France. Laure had only half listened at the time, concerned as she had been about Madeleine and exhausted from the months-long journey, but now the words return to her. Laure managed to ward off men on the ship and suitors who came to the house only to finally settle for Mathurin. She thinks of the girls who requested annulments after their first marriages, trying a second time in hopes of a better match. But Laure has heard that some of these second attempts end up worse than the first. She is resigned to a life with Mathurin. After all, what other hope is there for her now that she has left Paris and her companion and best friend has died?

The notary arrives with the legal documents and to list the couple's goods. Along with the witnesses, the newly married pair signs the marriage contract. Mathurin makes his mark, a jagged cross, on the document that contains the date and place of their union as well as the places of their birth and the names of his parents. Laure is understood to be an orphan. She doesn't bother to correct them. The ceremony takes only a few minutes, and then they move on to the chapel of the Hôtel-Dieu on rue Saint-Paul for the Mass.

Afterwards, they return to the congregation house. Mathurin tells her that he has brought a cart in which to carry her to his cabin. He has in mind that he will pull her through the branches and fallen leaves of the forest path all the way to Pointe-aux-Trembles, the settlement where he has built his cabin on the land given to him by the King.

Laure sees that Deskaheh is standing by the entrance to the congregation. Does he know she has been married today? Word must travel quickly throughout the settlement. Deskaheh is wearing a fur jacket and the pants of a French man. He looks first at Laure, then at Mathurin. Laure can detect a hint of mockery in the tilt of Deskaheh's head.

Mathurin frowns at the way this Savage is looking at his new wife. Laure wonders if Mathurin recognizes Deskaheh from Madeleine's funeral. And if Deskaheh remembers being punched by Mathurin, what must he think to see them together now? Although Deskaheh is ugly, he is less so than the man she has just married. Perhaps somewhere deep in the forest he has a home that is more comfortable than the one she is being taken to. And he might not carry her to it in a ridiculous cart like a chicken. These thoughts are of little use, though, as no French woman has ever married a Savage.

Her new husband has stopped fidgeting with the cart's wheel and is now standing next to it waiting for Laure to get inside.

"Didn't I tell you about the Savages? How dangerous they are? Even the ones that seem friendly can't be trusted." Mathurin waves his hand at Deskaheh as if he is a pesky dog. "That one was captured too late by the Algonquins. He doesn't know where he belongs. Those are the most dangerous ones."

Laure remains quiet as they set off on the jostling ride to Pointe-aux-Trembles. She wonders how far the forest extends ahead of them.

Before long she tires of Mathurin's grunting and panting as he struggles to pull the cart over the uneven terrain. At this rate they won't arrive at their destination before nightfall. She orders him to stop and clambers out. She comes up beside her new husband and walks with him for the rest of the journey. She even helps him push the cart over the worst stretches of the path.

After they have been walking for a few hours, Laure feels as if her toes and fingertips are on fire. Mathurin drops the cart and takes her fingers in his hands. They are so red, she thinks they will start to bleed. He releases her hand and tells her that she is fine so long as her fingertips don't turn white. But he says it isn't cold enough yet for that. Laure can't imagine colder weather, but Mathurin says the worst of it will come in January and February. He says she will get used to the winters in Canada. When all things are considered, this is a healthier place to live than Old France. The distances between settlements and the air that is frozen for half the year prevent diseases from spreading. Not to mention that she must be eating better by the looks of things. She ignores this comment.

The healthy air is turning Laure's lungs to ice much like the puddles they pass that are beginning to freeze over.

"This is nothing. Wait until you see how high the snow piles up in the winter." Mathurin sticks his toe in one of the puddles, cracking the thin layer of ice over the mud. "This path will be covered in it. We'll have to send men to Ville-Marie to get supplies before the bad weather comes."

Laure gazes through the bare trees. She feels her mind looking for something she knows isn't there. A street in Paris, maybe. The bustling river road from the hospital into the city.

She doesn't speak the whole afternoon except to ask questions about the cold, about how much farther they still have to go. Mathurin talks non-stop.

Each time they come across a new type of tree, he points it out to her. He caresses the thick bark of the oaks and maples with his stout fingers. As the afternoon wears, on they begin to see the thin trunks of aspens along the trail. The new settlement has been named after this tree. Laure thinks they look like spears sprouting from the forest floor. Mathurin tells her that in the summer, the wind from the river makes the aspens come to life, that from spring to fall they will hear nothing but the leaves shimmering around them. They are silent only on the hottest days of summer.

"It will take us ten years to become self-sufficient," he says and laughs.

Laure's mind tries to move through ten years with this man, but sees only trees and snow. Ten years ago Laure was standing in the city with her father singing country songs for coins. She hadn't yet been taken by archers to the Salpêtrière, she hadn't learned to sew and make lace and chant prayers in Latin, nor had she met Madeleine. Ten years ago Mireille Langlois was still alive, living in a comfortable home with her father; Madeleine was hiding under the table while her mother was a prostitute to the sailors at La Rochelle; Madame d'Aulnay was still alive. "Ten years is a very long time," Laure says.

Mathurin continues talking, telling Laure about the plans to build a church at Pointe-aux-Trembles. It will be the first stone building of the settlement. His energy seems to increase as he tells her about the men who travel out west for furs. These are the other Carignan-Salières soldiers who have been granted plots of land in Pointe-aux-Trembles. They leave their wives for the winter. He says they are only trading furs until they have cleared enough land for farming.

"For the next ten years, you mean?" Laure asks.

Mathurin talks on and on. Laure can tell this is a great day for him. He has found a wife to make his forest life a little easier. While her new husband is getting excited about the future, Laure is searching the frozen landscape for signs of the past. But there is no trace of her existence along this trail. Once again, she is moving away from the familiar contours of her life.

By the time they reach the settlement, it is dusk. Across the river from Pointe-aux-Trembles, two rounded mountains block the view of the horizon. The charred remains of trees surround the settlers' cabins. Laure can smell the smoke of the chimneys. The whole scene is grey and squalid, as if an army has just passed through this stretch of the forest. Laure is hungry enough to eat whatever is available. But first Mathurin must show her his cabin among the smoking huts.

Mathurin explains that they are still waiting for a seigneurial home to be built in Pointe-aux-Trembles and that next summer they will construct the windmill. For now the *habitants*, as the residents are called, must pay their rents in Ville-Marie. On the Fête Saint-Martin on the eleventh of November, each *habitant* must bring to the seigneurial domain a bushel of French wheat, two live capons, and four deniers in money. Laure wonders how they will come up with this payment, but Mathurin assures her that this year they don't have to pay as there hasn't been much of a harvest. He is certain that next year, if they get started early in the spring, they will produce more.

"The King will take care of us this year, my wife."

Laure has less faith than her new husband in the generosity of the King.

When they arrive outside Mathurin's cabin, a priest is waiting to greet them. He has been staying with another family, the Tardifs, awaiting the arrival of the new couple so he can bless their conjugal bed. The cabin is much smaller than Laure expected. The wooden boards used to make it are rougher even than the servants' quarters at the Salpêtrière. The house Mathurin built over the summer is just an extension of the trees he has talked about all afternoon. It is a forest hut.

There is only one room inside the cabin where Mathurin has been living alone. In one corner, there are several logs, a rude attempt at a dining table and chairs, made of the same wood as the walls. In the other corner is a bed. It is a proper *lit-cabane*, and Mathurin is proud of its construction. In the centre of the cabin is an open firepit. Laure smells smoke, and her eyes burn, even though the fire is not lit and the cabin is as cold as outside. Otherwise, the room smells of sour leather and rotten meat. Mathurin has hung animal pelts from various hooks on the wall. More are piled on the dirt floor near the door.

The priest walks over to the *lit-cabane* and says the following to Laure and Mathurin: "Remember that your nuptial bed will one day be your deathbed, from which place your souls will be raised and presented to the Tribunal of God. You will receive the terrible punishment of Sarah's seven husbands if you become like they were, slaves to their flesh and their passions." Laure wishes she could reassure this priest that he need not worry about any such passion between them.

The sisters of the congregation have imparted on Laure what a wife in Canada needs to do. First she must accept the man her husband is. Mère Bourgeoys told Laure that very few men in the colony could match her sharp thoughts and her high expectations. But that did not mean that they were not good and worthy men.

Since for the time being Laure cannot accept with any joy the man that Mathurin is, she considers the other duties the nuns spoke to her about. She has brought with her cloth from the congregation, and she has needles and thread in her coffer from the Salpêtrière, which she will use to make curtains and blankets. At least her efforts will bring some colour to the grey shadows of the hut. As for cooking, Laure cannot provide much. The girls from the countryside already know how to make bread, to salt fish and meats, and to prepare fruit preserves. Laure's only experience in a kitchen was during the short years she spent in the house of Madame d'Aulnay. But the fine delicacies of the old woman's apartment, the stone oven, carved tables, and silverware will never appear in the cabins of these settlers. Laure will have to satisfy Mathurin on the open hearth by cooking whatever his hands bring to her. She must rely on him to provide for her the way she once relied on the officers to ladle out the dormitory's rations.

And of course Laure must bear many children to please the King and the colony officials who need a large French population to defeat the Iroquois Savages who are still threatening the colony. At the congregation, Laure was given a prayer book so that when the children come, she can teach them about God. It might be the only schooling they receive, along with whatever lessons she can impart to her daughter about caring for a family in the forest. Mathurin will teach their sons to hunt and fish and how to trade with the Savages that dominate this new country.

❦

The *lit-cabane* is a terrifying thing. Laure remembers the words of the priest as Mathurin closes the door around her like a coffin on their first night together: This is the bed where she will die. The enclosed space does serve the purpose of keeping them warm. But Laure has a hard time breathing in the darkness that is so complete that she feels only short puffs of breath coming from her nose. Her eyes are wide and seek some way out. Beside her, Mathurin is already reaching his hand under her skirt. Laure remains still, hoping he will find the tangle of her skirt and legs and the fur cover too much to contend with tonight. But she is surprised at how quickly he moves. He is concentrating hard and it sounds like he is skinning an animal.

Laure clenches her teeth and bites the salty hide on his shoulder to keep from telling him to stop. But Mathurin takes this gesture as a sign of her enjoyment and thrusts into her. She gasps and digs her nails into his shoulders. Something must be wrong, Laure thinks, to feel this much pain. But Mathurin doesn't notice. She closes her eyes tight and turns her head, seeking air. After a few moments, it becomes a little less painful. When Mathurin finishes, he mumbles a few words into her chest and rolls onto his side. Laure stays on her back, her thighs trembling. She wonders when the baby will be born.

17

$\mathcal{L}$aure can open the door to Mathurin's hut just wide enough to peer outside. Snow has been falling almost every day for weeks. The cabins of Pointe-aux-Trembles are so covered by it that they are nothing more than white hills, if they can be seen at all. For the moment, the snow has abated, but the air on Laure's nose and cheek is sharp and freezing. She opens the door and sees that outside the cabin the snow is higher than her waist. Should she try to dig her way through it? There really isn't any point as Laure has no intention of venturing far beyond the doorstep. She has only a general idea where the trails through the settlement are buried. On sunny days, the landscape is bright white all around, as uniform as the sea had been on the journey over. Today there is no way to distinguish among the grey landscape between the rooftops of the *seigneurie*, the river they face, the mountains beyond, and the forest behind. It is only in her memory that Laure has some idea of where these places once were.

Since Mathurin left, Laure has been marking the wall beside the door with a knife. There is one scratch in the wood for each day he has been gone, fifty-seven in all. Some mornings, there are icicles hanging over the markings. Mathurin left Pointe-aux-Trembles late last fall, several weeks after they were married. A few other men of the *seigneurie*, dressed in heavy furs and carrying some trading provisions, headed west around the same time. The men planned to travel first to Ville-Marie and then on to the *pays sauvages* beyond. They say that the thickest furs, which sell for the highest prices, can be obtained by wintering with the Savage tribes. Each year since the men arrived in the colony as soldiers, they have spent the winter with the Algonquins or the Montagnais, or whichever group lets them travel with them in search of game. It is illegal for the men of Pointe-aux-Trembles to seek out furs, as the officials expect them to stay with their families to build the new settlements. These illegal fur traders, including Mathurin, are called *coureurs de bois*. The authorities mostly leave them alone so long as they stay away from the trapping lines of the *voyageurs*, the fur traders authorized by the King. Mathurin promised Laure that when he returned they would have enough currency to purchase an iron stove and some more livestock and growing seeds for spring.

Only two of the seven husbands have stayed behind in Pointe-aux-Trembles with their wives and children. These men have been assigned the role of protecting the *seigneurie* against the Iroquois who might decide to attack this winter. Laure thinks how lucky these women are to have married men who stay with their families.

At night, lying shivering in the *lit-cabane*, Laure sometimes thinks she hears the children of Pointe-aux-Trembles. But it is only the wind, entering through the cracks in the walls, wailing like a living thing.

Laure begged Mathurin to take her with him into the woods as he packed one of his muskets and the clothing and trading goods he would need for the journey. But he had laughed at her pleas and told her that the *pays sauvages* were not places for women. Trapping furs and dealing with the Savages was dangerous work. Laure wishes she had insisted nonetheless. Now that she has felt the cold of the past few months and seen the snow rise halfway up the outside of the cabin, she wonders if Mathurin just wanted somewhere warm to spend the coldest months of the year. Maybe he was afraid of spending his first winter at Pointe-aux-Trembles alone with his new wife from the Salpêtrière. After all, Laure knows even less about the frozen forest than he does. At least the Algonquin Savages must have ways to stay warm and know how to survive on their provisions until spring.

Laure closes the door to outside and goes over to the shelf on the wall where Mathurin keeps his belongings. The gun he left behind is there. She refused to let him teach her how to shoot it last fall.

"Suit yourself," he had said, "but this isn't your sewing room in Paris. Even women need to know how to use guns in Canada."

There are so many things to shoot: animals mostly—deer, porcupines, rabbits, moose, bears, wolves, beavers. Mostly they are killed for their fur and their meat. But sometimes it is necessary to fire at these creatures simply for protection. Unlike in Old France, the forest teems with animals, and it is not only the nobles who are entitled to hunt them.

Maybe Mathurin was right about the gun. It might be Laure's only way to survive here. Maybe she will die if she doesn't know how to use it. She touches the wood of the musket's handle, picks it up. It is heavy and she isn't sure how to hold it. Mathurin also left her a fishing rod. He explained to her how to cut a hole in the ice of the river and to stick the line in it to wait for a bite. But walking out onto the river in the winter, he told her, is very dangerous and should only be a last resort if she has exhausted her other provisions. Besides, she has nothing to use as bait for the fish under the frozen ice. Laure hardly even knows where the river is beyond the deep snow.

Laure has neither gone hunting nor fishing since Mathurin left. Instead she has relied on eating the rations given to them at their wedding at Ville-Marie last fall, which included two chickens and a pig. In the first month after Mathurin left, Laure found one of the chickens frozen to death in the pen outside the cabin. Seeing no hope for it, she had killed the second one and eaten well off the two for several weeks afterwards. As for the pig, she decided to bring it into the cabin to prevent it from freezing like the chicken. Against one wall, Laure constructed a makeshift pen out of some fallen tree branches that she gathered outside the cabin. Fortunately, she had done this before the snow had become knee and then waist deep. Ever since, the pig, with its snuffling and snorting, has been a companion of sorts. She named it Mathurin, and sometimes speaks to it throughout the day, saying it is a better husband than the one she had last fall.

Laure cannot imagine that spring will ever come. There is so much snow all around the settlement, and the outside air burns her skin, stinging her nostrils and making her eyes water. Laure returns the gun to the shelf and reaches for Mathurin's *culotte*. She slides the sheepskin over her legs and ties the strings around her waist. Over the *culotte*, she puts on his moose pants. They are heavy and hang from her hips like the skin of a sick animal. Mathurin has taken his overcoat with him, but she puts on one of his white shirts over her dress. On her head she puts a red woollen hat. In Paris, only beggars stumbling into the city from the farthest ramparts of the kingdom would wear such an outfit, and no woman would dare. But at least she feels a little warmer with these extra clothes on.

It is only early afternoon, but soon the pale daylight will be gone, leaving only several more hours for her sewing. Laure is saving the stub of the candle given to her by the Mère Bourgeoys as a wedding gift. She keeps it along with the parchment sheet and the pot of ink. To sew, Laure relies only on the dim rays of the sun during the day and the light from the fire at night. She pushes the heavy wooden chest from the hospital across the dirt floor toward the fire at the centre of the room. Most of the heat emitted from the flames in the open hearth is sucked up through the chimney, leaving only the smoke to fill the room, but still Laure feels warmer hearing it crackle.

At night Laure tries not to sleep too deeply in order to remain vigilant over the fire. She fears that she won't be able to relight it if the flame is extinguished. She often dreams that she has frozen to death in her bed. Only in the dream she is usually in her cot at the Salpêtrière, and freezing to death is a disease that is spreading through the dormitories. Laure usually wakes up then, shivering in the enclosed *lit-cabane*, and gets up to stir the embers of the fire and add another log to it. This winter, she has burned all but a small pile of the wood Mathurin chopped last fall and left at the entrance. She had thought him strange and overzealous as he filled an entire wall of the cabin with wood. Now she wishes she had asked him to cut more, at least another row. The axe he used to cut the wood was borrowed from the Tardifs. Laure would have to wade through hip-deep snow to get to their cabin to borrow it.

She crouches down and reaches into the chest for the new dress she is making. Once she removes her sewing, she closes the chest and sits on it. She holds her fingers over the flame until they feel warm enough to begin. Above her, where she has hung it from the ceiling, is Mireille's dress. On evenings when the wind is howling particularly hard, Laure watches the dress. It both frightens and comforts Laure to see the diaphanous yellow material swaying, suspended in air, above the frozen dirt floor of the cabin. It is as if a ghost is performing a gentle dance for her.

There are other women in the *seigneurie*, but Laure hasn't seen any of them since early winter, when the paths between their cabins could still be traversed. Madame Tardif had even invited Laure to spend the winter with her and her children, but Laure had refused. She had been worried about how Mathurin would react if she abandoned the cabin for the winter. If she left, the snow and freezing air would soon overtake the feeble construction and its contents. They would have to start all over again in the spring, chopping trees to repair it, building a new fireplace, another *lit-cabane*. All of Canada was dotted with these inchoate, abandoned attempts at settlement. Where would she go in the spring if she lost even this? Besides, there is no way she could have carried their possessions to the Tardifs'. There were no horses or oxen in the settlement.

Of course Laure couldn't have imagined that winter would be this bad. Now that she really needs the other women of Pointe-aux-Trembles and would be more than willing to give up the foolish venture of holding on to Mathurin's meagre hut, the snow has grown so deep, up to her waist, that she doesn't dare try to make it to one of the neighbouring cabins.

Besides, Laure is the only girl in Pointe-aux-Tremble from Paris. The others are *Canadiennes* and accustomed to the winters and to being left alone to endure them. They have their children and the knowledge they need to survive until spring. Last fall, Laure had tried to show Madame Tardif the dress she was working on. In response, the severe woman had simply asked her if she had finished the needlework the women had been assigned by the Congrégation Notre-Dame. The sewing they were asked to do was meant to be their work for the entire winter. In the spring they would receive payment, probably in seeds to plant their first garden. Laure had proudly shown Madame Tardif the folded pile of men's white shirts and the dozens of pairs of socks she had finished knitting. Laure had finished the winter's work in the first two weeks after Mathurin left. But she was supposed to have children to care for, or at the very least to be pregnant with her first one. There was no work as important as birthing babies for the new colony.

Even when she saw that all Laure's assigned work was done, Madame Tardif was still not interested in the dress she was making. "We don't need city dresses like that here. You'll soon learn not to waste time on your appearance."

This same woman also told Laure, when she had complained about Mathurin's leaving her alone for the winter, that a woman who refuses her husband is to blame if he goes elsewhere.

※

Laure isn't sewing the new dress for herself. When she chose the material from her coffer, she had been thinking of Madeleine. It was the pale blue serge given to her by Madame du Clos as a parting gift. Instead of lace, Laure sewed onto the bodice a trim of fox fur from the scraps left by Mathurin in a corner of the cabin. It wasn't a dress anyone would wear in Paris. But Laure thought Madeleine would like it. It suited the new country, would be perfect for a forest angel.

Laure hums a few bars of one of the hymns Madeleine used to sing as she pushes the needle through the fabric. She tries to remember Madeleine's exact measurements.

When the last of the dim day fades, Laure carefully cuts off the needle and thread and packs it back into the chest. She takes the dress into her arms and carries it with her to the *lit-cabane*. She lies down and closes the door, gazing into the black. The fox fur tickles her nose. When Laure hugs the material against her chest, it flattens and she can feel her own ribs and hips beneath it. What a fool she had been to complain about the crowded quarters of the Salpêtrière. What she wouldn't give to have someone else beside her now in this bed that feels so much like a coffin. Laure's fingers move across the fur at the bodice as if she is holding a rosary. The sound of the wind makes her forget even the basic prayers she learned at the hospital.

Laure is awakened by a loud rapping at the door. It is the middle of the night. Her first thought is that a branch has come loose from a tree and is being hurtled by the wind against the cabin. She then wonders if there is an animal outside, a bear or a wolf. She crawls out of the bed and tries to distinguish the shapes in the room by the dim light of the fire. The knocking is clearer this time. But who could have reached her across all the snow? The board that she carefully places across the door each night might not be strong enough to withstand the force of whoever is outside. Laure fumbles for Mathurin's gun and takes it from the shelf.

She puts her shoulder to the door. "What do you want from us?"

"It's Deskaheh."

The sound of his voice brings a surge of blood to Laure's chest. What is he doing here? What if Mathurin had been here? She unlatches the door and he enters in a snowy draft. She doesn't recognize him at first. He is covered in thick furs and has snowshoes on his feet. Only his nose and eyes are exposed. He notices the gun in her hand and the clothes she is wearing that belong to Mathurin. But he doesn't laugh at her.

"You can't come here." She whispers the words, as if her neighbours, who are each ensconced in a tomb of snow, might actually hear what is happening inside her cabin.

"I know your husband is gone for the winter. I saw him leave." He looks at Laure, making sure she has understood his French. Then he starts speaking in one of the Savage tongues.

"I don't speak your language," she says.

"He should have taught you." He shrugs and shakes the snow from his shoulders, then removes his snowshoes and leans them against the wall.

"My husband was also going to teach me how to shoot a gun. In case there were intruders while he was away." Laure takes a step back into the cabin, holding the musket against her chest.

Deskaheh smiles. His shadow on the wall expands as he moves. Covered this way in furs, and standing so close to her in the cabin, Laure thinks that he looks more like a beast than a man. He is much bigger than she is. She regrets that she spoke to him through the fence this summer. That she undressed for him at the window.

Most women would scream. She is sure of that. And yet Laure remains quiet and waits. She puts the gun back on the shelf. Even the company of this Savage, who might very well have come to kill her, is better than being alone.

Deskaheh pulls something from a pouch at his side. The frozen offering looks like the corn mush she ate when she first arrived in the colony. It has retained the shape of the pot it was cooked in. She takes it in her hands. He looks down at her stomach and touches his own. She steps back to let him further into the cabin. She has been hungry for weeks and even the corn mush is a welcome meal. He also has with him a sack of dried berries.

She takes the frozen soup over to the fire and drops it into the pot suspended over the embers. She gets another log from the pile and takes the time to stir the ashes with the poker until the flame grows strong enough to consume the wood.

When she turns back, Deskaheh is seated against the wall on the chest from the Salpêtrière. He has removed the outermost layers of his furs and now looks less like an animal and more like she remembers him. He still seems taller than he did last summer. And older. She can no longer see the boyishness in his face.

"That animal looks starved." Deskaheh points his chin toward the pig, lying on its side, but his eyes don't move from Laure's face.

Laure glances at her stand-in husband. Lying among the branches, Mathurin the pig barely looks alive. She hadn't really noticed the extent of the animal's decline.

"Either it eats or I do. We take turns." Laure had been surprised at how much the beast needed to be fed. There were the oats from last fall, which she had given generously at first, but now the sack is so close to being empty that the amount she feeds him each morning has to be rationed to a small handful.

At the start of winter, Laure had to fight to keep the pig within the confines of the pen she had devised, but in recent weeks, it barely moves, lying listless and still.

"Your husband is staying with us this winter." Deskaheh looks at Laure with a serious expression. "He explained to everyone where he built his cabin. That's how I knew how to get here." He laughs, and she catches a flicker of his face as it looked in the garden last summer.

Mathurin had told her that he was going to get furs at a three-week journey past Ville-Marie on the Outaouais River. But Laure doesn't know much about what goes on beyond the settlements. The sisters of the congregation said that the forests are where the French men who are without God go to live and that the illegal *coureurs* are the bane of the colony, hindering settlement efforts by leaving their homes, and interfering with the conversion of the Savages by bringing brandy to trade with them.

Over the months, Laure has also heard scraps of stories, mostly about the men who die, ambushed by the silent and deadly Iroquois, or less glorious tales of accidents: slipping on the rocks trying to cross a patch of rapids in the river, or getting in a fight over a bottle of brandy with one of the allied Savages.

"We are camped close to here." The place Deskaheh mentions doesn't sound familiar to Laure. There are so many names for the same lakes, rivers, streams, and woods of the colony, depending on who is speaking. Laure cannot distinguish between them.

She goes to the fire and stirs the pot of gruel. The steam rises from the bubbling soup and her stomach starts to growl. "Mathurin is nearby?" she asks.

"Yes. Nearby. Our hunters have gone all the way to the

Outaouais, to the people you call Cheveux-Relevés. But not your husband. He has stayed behind with the women and children."

"Behaving like a dog?" It is no secret to the women of the settlement that the *coureurs* take on Savage women when they head into the forest. Laure doesn't really mind. She is happy that someone else has to sleep with him.

"He's no different from the others. They prefer the *filles sauvages* over their own wives."

Laure wonders if he is mocking her. She wants to say that she doesn't care what Mathurin prefers. She pours the soup into a bowl and brings it to Deskaheh, and then pours some for herself. She stands beside the pot looking at him in the corner of the room. He takes the fur overcoat he was wearing and carries it over to the fire, indicating that they should sit on it.

"When I was a boy among the Haudenosaunee, some of our leaders used to say that we should kill every single French man."

Now that he is closer, she can see that his nose is still crooked from when Mathurin struck him. He looks up at the yellow dress hanging from the ceiling. She wonders if he remembers that she had been wearing it when they first met. They eat in silence. He eats more slowly than she does, and she feels him watching her as she devours the contents of her bowl. The corn soup is thick and fills her stomach with warmth. Her fear has turned into relief. He points at the red hat on Laure's head. She forgot she was wearing it and removes it. He takes it from her hand and tries it on. She laughs at the serious expression on his face as he looks to her for approval.

"So how do you know they won't have moved on without you by the time you get back to them?" she asks him.

"When I left them, they were so drunk off the brandy the *coureurs* brought that they couldn't have killed even a rabbit if it was lying right beside them in their tent."

She takes his bowl and piles it on top of hers. "Thanks for bringing me this soup." Laure imagines Mathurin being fed by the Algonquin women each day, having a great time while she is barely staying alive in his poorly built hut. Her only company is a pig.

"I was captured by the Algonquins in my thirteenth summer. I can't imagine staying with them for the rest of my life. I want to leave in the spring."

"Where will you go?"

"Back where I belong. To the Haudenosaunee."

"The Iroquois?"

Laure remembers Mathurin's words on their wedding day. How he had said that Deskaheh was actually an Iroquois captured by the Algonquins. She thought Mathurin had just been making that up to keep his new wife from talking to the Savage.

Deskaheh doesn't look any different from the other Savages that hang around Ville-Marie, the ones that are allied with the French. She expected the Iroquois to look more frightening, to have their heads shaven and their faces painted, and for them to think only of butchering the French and eating their ears and fingers and hearts.

"If you go back and live with the Iroquois, you'll be the enemy of the people of Ville-Marie."

"No, I'll still be a friend of the Christians. I know enough people here that I will still be able to trade. Besides, there are other Iroquois here, the French Iroquois. The ones who left the longhouse to come live like beggars with the French."

Laure wishes she could go back to the place where she wants to live her life. But there is more than a forest and some Savage tribes between her and Paris. Besides, there is nothing for her to go back to. The hospital is probably filled with new women, the lacemaking workshop taken over by younger girls with smaller fingers.

As if reading her mind, Deskaheh says: "Your husband will be back soon. We have almost reached the beginning of the bright month, and soon after, the snow will become water and flow back into the river. When this happens, your husband will return."

After a while, Deskaheh stands up. Laure feels like a child. There is so much she wants to say, but she can only think of simple things like crying, gratitude. She almost tells him not to go, but it's too late because he's standing and saying *demain*, for her to eat the leftover soup in the pot tomorrow. She stumbles to her feet and hands him his coat. She promises him she will eat the rest of it. She wants to give him something, but she knows that she has nothing to offer.

❦

The following morning Laure opens the door to the cabin. She gasps to see that the fresh snow is stained red with blood. There is a deer carcass at her door. She drags the frozen animal into the cabin. Was it there all along while they sat and talked last night? Or did Deskaheh kill the animal after he left her?

She takes Mathurin's knife from the shelf and sits for a moment considering how to skin the animal. She lifts the head and shoulders onto her lap and digs the blade into the chest. It doesn't penetrate the frozen skin. She drags the deer over to the fire and puts two fresh logs onto it. After half an hour or so, the flesh begins to soften a little. She lifts the deer's head and stabs the knife into the chest. She saws the flesh open and is rewarded when heavy drops of blood spill onto the dirt floor. She reaches inside the animal and pulls at the guts that have started to thaw. Mathurin the pig has risen onto shaky legs and is whining. Laure tosses some of the innards into the pen.

When Laure's hand reaches the deer's heart, she tightens her fingers around it. She closes her eyes, expecting to feel a warm pulse. She waits for the animal to tell her something about where it came from, about the man who killed it. She wants the deer heart to release its secret into her waiting hand. Around her, in the cabin, there is nothing but the animal sound of hunger.

❦

Weeks of the winter pass, and the scent of the corn soup fades from the cabin walls. A few stringy pieces of deer meat, more rotted than dried, hang beside the fire. Laure chews on these to calm the hunger that has become a screaming rage in her gut. She has received only one other guest since Deskaheh left that night, and it was a colony official, dressed also like a bear. He and several others had traversed the paths with sleds and snowshoes to bring Laure and the other women of Pointe-aux-Trembles a package of supplies—some cabbage, a little pork, a wool blanket, and a few candlesticks. In exchange Laure had given him the sewing and knitting she had done for the colony's bachelors.

Bolstered by the soup she made from the pork and cabbage and encouraged by the French man's promise of spring, Laure borrowed an axe from the Tardifs and stumbled through the snow to chop some more wood for the fire. She had returned to the cabin from this venture with little more than a few sticks and fingers and toes that burned.

Amidst all of this, there is still no sign of Mathurin. Instead, it is Deskaheh who returns to see Laure late one night. She hears him first at the window and opens the shutter to see him there. She can see that Deskaheh's face is a scowling shadow and she has an idea what he has returned for before she opens the door. By now Laure can recognize that look on a man. A sick wave builds in her chest. She wouldn't call the feeling fear, although it emanates from the same place in her body.

She slides the board away from the door and steps back to let Deskaheh in.

"Your husband is still gone?" he asks.

"He will come back any day." Laure wants to ask Deskaheh why he has returned, why he has fixated on her in this way after she told him to stay away from her last fall. It isn't convenient, sneaking through the winter forest to meet her like this. Surely there is a woman in his village that Deskaheh can marry. As for Laure's situation, there isn't much to be done about Mathurin. But Deskaheh here now with that resolute look in his eyes isn't going to help that matter either. She shouldn't have let him in.

He removes his coat and seems like a frozen bird spreading giant wings of fur. He looks around the cabin, at Laure's sewing lying out on the table where they ate the soup a few weeks earlier, at the fire emitting its weak heat, at the near-empty cupboard, over to the corner at the *lit-cabane* where she has been sleeping alone. Then his eyes turn to look at Laure.

She is wearing a wool shawl over her arms and shoulders and a heavy winter dress.

"You are thin, like the dogs in my village." His voice is concerned and soft, a sort of sad whisper. Laure thinks she must look as though she is dying. Maybe she has misinterpreted his intentions with her. Perhaps he has come like the official to bring her provisions. What a pathetic creature she is, buried in this winter tomb of a cabin, abandoned by the man who promised several months ago to protect her for a lifetime.

"Let me make you something to eat." Deskaheh starts to move toward the cupboard and the fire.

"I don't need food," Laure says, blocking his way. He steps back, a surprised look on his face.

For once, she has frightened him. She is angry that the man who is supposed to be helping her to survive the winter is not here and that in his place she is being offered scraps by a colony official and this Savage who should have disappeared from her life months ago. It is darker tonight than when he visited last, and she has a hard time reading his face. "Someone might think you're here to kill me."

He doesn't respond.

"Why do you come to see me?" She waits a moment, thinking he hasn't understood. She repeats the question, looking at his coat, at his clothing made of pelts, at the long hair, up at his scarred face. These are just the external things that make Deskaheh Savage. How can she possibly comprehend his mind, let alone his heart? Laure recalls her baptism at sea by the strange creature they called Bonhomme Terre-Neuve. How much she has been warned about the dangers of the Savages of Canada.

Deskaheh steps toward her without making a sound and twists her hair around his hand. Laure's head jerks back and she looks up to see his eyes glazed. She doesn't understand all the words, isn't even sure that he is talking to her, but she hears something like this: *I didn't choose to seek you out in the woods, where it is dangerous. You appear in my dreams. When dreams push you toward someone, toward a place you've never been, there is no use in fighting it. It will eventually find you and the dream will be realized.*

She can smell his musky skin. It is the scent of rotting leaves, of damp earth. She inhales the warm stench of his breath. It isn't sour like Mathurin's milky tongue, but is bitter from the herb teas the Savages drink. Deskaheh lifts Laure from the ground. She can feel how light she has become, more starved even than she was in the Salpêtrière. She lets him carry her. He places her through the door into the bed and kneels on the dirt floor in front of her. Laure closes her eyes and waits as he runs his hands over her ribs and stomach. He is still speaking as if to himself in his Savage tongue as he works to undo the strings of her dress.

Deskaheh lets out a short cry, and she feels the wet warmth of her blood spilling from her breast before she feels any pain. Deskaheh lowers his head to the wound. He begins to suck as if trying to remove the venom of a snakebite. After a time, when the blood slows, the awful pain of the cut creates an intensity that mirrors the cold of the cabin, the brutality of living amongst trees. He is an expert at this mutilation, Laure thinks, and knows that there will be no more pain.

Laure expects there will be something more now, something to take away the pain he has inflicted. But Deskaheh is pushing Laure away and covering her back up. She burns with humiliation.

Everything with Deskaheh is a ritual. At least it is better to think that way. That he at least knows where they are going. That there is some place for this sort of thing in the universe. That there is a god that watches with pleasure waiting to see them intertwined, becoming liquid together.

Laure thinks of Mathurin who is her actual destiny. The cabin he built with his thick hands in preparation for her or for some other, tougher country woman from across the sea. When Laure would awaken screaming, haunted by the sounds of the woods passing through their feeble home, Mathurin would say that he doesn't dream.

Deskaheh stumbles away from her, and she reaches on the bed for the knife he cut her with. It is some traded item being used against her. Maybe Mathurin gave it to him. The handle is carved into a Savage animal, a bird of some sort. Deskaheh no longer has any fire in his look. He is reaching for his coat. Laure stays on the bed in the corner of the room holding the knife in her hand. She considers throwing it at him, but doesn't want to hurt him. She is weak with adoration for him. What woman would feel this way? Why can't I feel limp, consumed like this when Mathurin touches me? The door closes without making a sound and he disappears into the cold.

She wonders how it would have felt if Deskaheh had cut her deeper, if the blood had continued to flow out of her.

18

$\mathcal{T}$he dress Laure completed for Madeleine over the winter, blue with fox-fur trim, hangs from the ceiling of the cabin alongside the yellow one that once belonged to Mireille. From the material in her chest, the extra pieces given to her at the Congrégation Notre-Dame, Laure has also made two more dresses. She has sewn into the linen and serge patches of animal skin, a little tree bark, whatever she could find to continue with the patterns in her mind.

It is spring, and despite the four gowns hanging from her ceiling, Laure has on a linen housedress and a grey woollen blanket that once belonged to Mathurin over her shoulders. He must have stolen it from the ship when he crossed over from Old France, or perhaps it had been handed out in the colony to the soldiers of his regiment. Although the sun of early spring has grown stronger and there are hints of green coming through the remaining snow, Laure is still afraid to put out the fire in the cabin. The pig, Mathurin, has long forgotten the meals of deer flesh that ran out almost a month ago. He is once again hungry and listless in his pen. Laure watches the beast from the middle of the room. She has been ready all winter to try and shoot the pig if he decides to attack, but he does not.

Laure is as thin as the dresses she has hung from the ceiling when Mathurin, fattened up by his stay with the Algonquins, enters the cabin. He gags and covers his nose when he walks through the door. Laure wonders how she could have grown accustomed to the smell in the room if it is really that bad. When Mathurin sees Laure sitting by the fire, he takes a startled step back. She isn't sure if it is her appearance that frightens him or the gun she is holding on her lap.

Laure glances up at her husband, her eyes trying to focus on his figure. She remembers having many dreams of his return from the cold confines of the *lit-cabane*. The reappearance of this man is Laure's prize for making it through her first winter in Canada. Her mouth opens and the sound that comes out is a cry and a question. *Where have you been?* Only no words form in her throat.

Laure wonders what Mathurin sees when he looks at her: Has her first winter in Canada turned her into a madwoman, a heretic, worthy of being imprisoned? "You have returned to your wife," she finally says in a low voice, keeping hold of the gun on her chest. There is no way Mathurin can see in her features that she spent two of the winter nights in the company of Deskaheh. Even Laure can barely remember his visits. They have melted from her mind like the heavy snow around the cabin. She is empty now, a shell welcoming back her husband.

Mathurin notices the dresses hanging from the ceiling and his eyes grow even wider. He walks over to them, touches the seams where Laure has sewn in the debris of the winter she spent without him. "It's the Salpêtrière," he says as if to himself. "The men who married women from there are all complaining." Laure wonders if perhaps she has become a ghost as transparent as the figures she has imagined wearing the gowns.

The dresses are impressive, varied in cut and style and well stitched. Although to make them Laure has used up in one winter the thread and material in her chest from Paris that were supposed to last her a lifetime in the colony.

Mathurin walks toward Laure and crouches beside her. "City women can't handle life here." His voice is gentle now. He releases his hand from over his nose and reaches for her matted hair. Laure strikes his wrist in a quick animal movement. He backs away from her.

Up close, Laure can see that Mathurin has painted his face to look like a Savage. Her pink-pig husband has red stripes on his glowing cheeks. She begins to laugh. Mathurin returned from the forest after being away for 126 days suddenly seems hilarious to her. "This is how I passed the time," she says, indicating the dresses. Her voice sounds frail and hoarse, as if this one winter has turned her into a very old woman.

"Why didn't you go stay with the others? There are other women here. The wives of Tardif and Lefebvre ..." Laure thinks that Mathurin is seeking some way to alleviate his guilt at the sight of his wife's winter-starved body and the horrible stench of the cabin. What a coward he seems to her.

Laure recites to him each of these women's reasons for leaving her alone all winter. "Madame Tardif is a *Canadienne*. Born here." This was the woman Laure had shown her needlework to, the colony wife who thought that ways from

Paris didn't belong in Canada. Madame Tardif already has three children and arms the size of the cabin's pillars. She had offered to house Laure, but with about the same amount of emotion that the Superior of the Salpêtrière felt about providing a bed for another poor girl from the countryside. It was to be Madame Tardif's third winter alone in Pointe-aux-Trembles and she was proud of her ability to endure it.

Then there was Madame Lefebvre, a nervous rat of a woman much younger than Madame Tardif. She had asked Laure back in November to help her nail a board across the door to her cabin, to keep out the hungry bears. Then she had scurried off through the forest, with a brother who looked just like her, back to her father's place in Ville-Marie. "How was I to know?" Laure's words are an accusation, and Mathurin looks at his feet. What a weak man she has married.

Mathurin comes forward and takes the gun from Laure's hand. She relinquishes it and slumps forward a little. She watches as Mathurin lifts the gun, opening and shutting the chambers, clicking it into working order. She wonders for a brief moment if he is planning to shoot her. Perhaps the winter has left her unworthy of further life, like a horse who has outlived its legs. But Mathurin turns away from Laure and walks over to the pen. Mathurin the pig looks up with tired eyes. By the time Laure realizes what her husband is about to do, it is too late. The cabin resounds with the shot he fires. The pig lets out a disappointed sigh.

"Let me prepare you a feast to celebrate the end of our first winter in Pointe-aux-Trembles," Mathurin says. Laure watches

the dresses swaying around her husband, feeling as if another
ghost has entered her life.

Mathurin has insisted that they eat outside. Although it is still
chilly, much of the snow has melted. He has lit a fire between
two tree stumps. The damp air quickly fills with smoke. Laure
sits on one of the stumps and watches her husband roast
the flesh of his pig self. He carries the meat over to her in a
bowl, but she refuses to eat any of it. Mathurin devours the
contents of his bowl, his fingers and mouth becoming greasy.
Laure stands up, her knees wobbly, and returns to the cabin
with careful steps. She wonders if it would have been better if
Deskaheh had let her starve. She wouldn't be sinking her weak
legs into the muddy holes of her life with Mathurin if only the
winter had swallowed her whole.

Shortly after Mathurin's return from the *pays sauvages*, green
buds begin appearing on the dry branches of the aspen trees.
The snow around the settlement melts into little streams
that gather strength as they flow toward the river. Even after
a few weeks, Laure's body still feels weak, as grey as the mud
the melted snow has exposed. But it won't be long before
the long, cold months are behind her. The silence of winter
has passed, and she feels herself gaining strength each day.
Squirrels and birds dash in and out of the trees searching
for supplies to build their nests. Laure sees a robin outside
the cabin, its red breast an infusion of life. Despite herself,

she turns her face to the warmth of the sun and waits to
come back to life.

✲

Throughout the months of April and May, Laure and Mathurin
work, along with the other settlers of Pointe-aux-Trembles, at
preparing the settlement for summer. The men cut wood to
repair the cabins, patching up the places the women tell them
let in the cold. The roof of the Lefebvre cabin collapsed in the
winter from the weight of the snow. It is good that the woman
abandoned it early to go live with her family in Ville-Marie.
Her husband has decided to stay on with the Savages, so the
remains of their hut sit like a skeleton, a gloomy memory of
winter amidst the optimism of spring.

The settlers also look for open spaces among the trees, for
spots to plant gardens from the seeds they have received from
the Intendant. In the largest clearing they plant wheat, a little
barley and oat. In the smaller patches they plant cabbage, turnips,
carrots, peas, and onions. But digging into the hard ground to
clear the soil using axes, stones, and whatever else they can find is
painful work that nobody can stand to do for very long. Even the
women take turns so the men can rest. It is a beastly endeavour
to pound and rip at soil that is thick with ancient life. The work of
fools is what Laure thinks as she attempts to make some progress
despite the weakness of her arms. In the end, the settlers cannot
clear enough land to plant all the seeds they have been given and
decide to save some for the following year.

✲

Inside their cabin, Mathurin has constructed a rudimentary table, two logs with a plank overtop. They sit at it, Laure on her chest and Mathurin on a stump he has turned into a chair, eating a fish the men caught from the river. The summer insects haven't yet emerged, but the worst of the cold is long behind them. Laure is at least comfortable if not happy in Mathurin's hut. He works, still mostly chopping at trees, fishing and hunting with the men throughout the day, while Laure and the other women weed the garden, prepare meals, and mend clothing. For the time being there is no talk of life beyond the settlement.

"You know that *la Course*'s wife is pregnant again. Their fourth," Mathurin says. They have resumed sleeping together in the *lit-cabane*.

Laure does not respond. When women of the settlement do speak to her, it is always about their children or about being pregnant. They tell her what signs to look for, missed monthly bleeding, sickness to the stomach, swollen breasts. Laure feels none of these things, but doesn't dare tell the other women that she is relieved.

"The King will give three hundred livres to each family that has ten children," Mathurin says.

"Legitimate children," she mumbles, thinking still of the winter he spent away. She would probably be pregnant by now if he hadn't gone off with the Algonquins seeking money in furs.

"You're only eighteen. Ten children should be easy enough to produce."

Mathurin is always thinking of the future, in decades, whereas Laure cannot foresee the next week with him. She also cannot imagine being pregnant even once, let alone falling into the rhythm of having a new baby every two years the way the colony's women generally do.

When they finish eating, Mathurin nods his head toward the *lit-cabane*. Laure gets up and carries the dishes outside to clean them in the bucket of river water by the door. She takes her time to dry them and place them back on the shelf. When she has finished with the dishes, she makes her way over to the bed and crawls in beside Mathurin. He grabs right away for the bottom of her dress to lift it over her hips. Weeks ago Mathurin had noticed the cut on her chest. He had recoiled at the sight of it. Laure had told him that she inflicted the wound on herself, a form of bloodletting she had learned in the hospital. It was meant to give her strength to get through the winter. She told him she did it when she felt most weak. Mathurin had believed her.

Laure is tired of his advances, of his attempts to make her pregnant. "If you really want that money from the King," she says to him, "you should gather up all the Savage children you have running wild through the forest and send them straight to Paris. Maybe he'll give you more than three hundred livres."

Mathurin sucks in his breath. After a moment, he strokes her hair, laughing a little. They have been married for almost eight months and still there is no sign of a baby.

Laure says, "Unless you are also incapable of getting those Savage women pregnant."

Mathurin pulls his hand away from her. "With all the trouble you give me, I should have married an *Algonquienne*, brought her into the settlement. She would have been given a hundred and fifty livres to marry me and we'd already have two babies by now."

Laure snorts at this. "You know as well as I do how the

Governor gives out money. Lots of promises, then the amount gets reduced by half, and when it comes time to pay, suddenly there are no circulating coins. Your *sauvagesse* would have received the same pig and chickens that I got for marrying you."

"Do you know what I've been hearing all through the Ville-Marie settlements?" Mathurin's eyes have turned mean, his face shiny. "That the women from the General Hospital are diseased. That's why they can't have children."

The next morning Mathurin is packing his things when Laure wakes up. He is dressed again like a Savage, with a knife at his waist and a gun strapped over his shoulder.

"Where are you going?" she asks, her memories of the winter flooding back in a moment of panic.

"To collect more furs before the August trade fair at Ville-Marie."

He is probably going to a woman who will have him, will flatter him and need him. Laure is better off without Mathurin and is glad to see him go. She has survived the winter. Surely the spring and summer, now that she can visit her neighbours and walk through the settlement, will be easier to endure alone. But before Mathurin leaves this time, she asks him to teach her how to use the gun.

Part Four

Les filles envoyées l'an passé sont mariées, et presque touttes ou sont grosses ou ont eu des enfants, marque de la fécondité de ce pays.

[The girls sent last year are married and almost all of them either are pregnant or have had children, a sign of the fruitfulness of this country.]

—JEAN TALON, INTENDANT OF CANADA,
TO JEAN-BAPTISTE COLBERT,
MINISTER TO THE KING OF FRANCE, 1670

19

The shore of the river at Ville-Marie is lined with Savage canoes. Animal pelts are piled high on the fur-trading barges. A few uniformed French officers patrol the scene on the horses recently arrived in the colony. The smoke rising from the fires lit by the various Savage groups is so thick that it makes Laure cough. A few French women have come to the fair, mostly the wives of settlers. Some are selling goods at wooden booths along the river's edge; others are back in the settlement serving beer and brandy at the taverns.

The finest pelts of the fair have been brought in by Savages from the far north. Laure has heard about the soft fur of mink and ermine, the latter destined only for the King. The Savages are outfitted in elaborate regalia and have carried their canoes to the shore. Laure can hear numerous languages being spoken. Many of these groups Laure has never seen, including an old man with long hair as white as the strange pelts he carries slung across his arms. There are also in the crowd those born from the unions of French men with Savage women. These young men wear the attire—the bright weaves, long hair, painted faces—of the Savages but have lighter skin and eyes and even beards.

The Savage women Laure sees walk hunched over, carrying the weight of their half-grown children on their backs.

Laure is not worried that she will run into Mathurin. He is probably lying in a stupor in one of the many tents raised around the site, drinking and eating his fill and enjoying himself with the women. For trading, Laure has carried with her some tin cups, trousers made of flax that she has sewn, as well as some buttons. She also has a small pouch of Venetian glass beads that she took from Mathurin's stock. He told her that the Savages use these to make belts that they call wampum, a sort of prayer and recording method of theirs. The Savages will trade their best furs for these cheap Italian beads. Laure doesn't really expect to do any trading at the fair. It isn't why she has come, after all, but she plans to tell anyone who recognizes her that she is there to help Mathurin to earn a little more money. They will think her a generous and loyal wife for risking so much danger to be here.

It was easy enough for Laure to persuade the Tardifs of Pointe-aux-Trembles to let her travel with them to Ville-Marie for the fair. Even Madame Tardif had to admit that Mathurin should not have left Laure for the summer as well as the winter. She had disapproved of the small number of furs Mathurin had returned with in the spring compared with the rich supply her own husband had brought back.

❦

The girl sitting in front of Deskaheh at one of the Algonquin trading tents looks very young, maybe fifteen, although Laure cannot easily determine the age of the Savage girls. By the time they are twenty, they look like old women. It's because their

men make them work so hard is what Mathurin says. This girl
with Deskaheh still has the soft, chubby cheeks of a child and
impressive long, dark hair. They are seated together, their knees
touching. But what astonishes Laure the most is the girl's belly.
It is perfectly round, as if the moon has been taken from the sky
and placed beneath the dress she is wearing.

French men prefer the Savage girls over their own women.
These girls give their bodies freely and expect nothing in return.
The Savage girls call out to the men like sirens from their forest
homes. At least that is what Mathurin seems to think. Laure
hates all of these women. Their seductive presence makes her
life in Canada even more difficult. Although Deskaheh has his
back to Laure, she knows for certain it is him. She recognizes
his height, his shoulders, and the way his hair falls down his
back. But she doesn't want to admit that it's him. He is sitting
too close to the Savage girl, their hands almost touching, and
there is something protective and gentle about the curve of
his back. Laure knows for certain that the girl's baby belongs
to him. She has come upon them like a starved and scrawny
intruder, a beast that deserves to be shot. The girl's smile fades
when she notices Laure staring at them. She reaches across her
abdomen as if to protect herself.

What did the Savage girl see in Laure's eyes? Hatred? Envy?
Sadness? Could she read the thoughts passing through her
head? Deskaheh, wondering what the girl has seen to give her
such a scare, turns around and sees Laure standing there. He
looks surprised. Laure realizes she has made a terrible mistake
in coming to the fair. Even though she travelled all the way
from Pointe-aux-Trembles in the hopes of seeing Deskaheh,
she didn't really think he would be here. She tells herself now
that she had intended to make a little money, to buy some extra

winter supplies in case Mathurin didn't return at all. Of course she also planned to revisit the places where she had spoken with Deskaheh the previous summer: the cemetery where Madeleine was buried, the garden of the congregation, to stand beneath the attic window that she had looked out from. After all, hadn't he provided her with the only happiness she had found in this vast, miserable country? Still, she hadn't really expected to find more than his memory in Ville-Marie.

What a mistake Laure has made. The expression on Deskaheh's face turns from shock to anger at the sight of her standing before him. He must have felt, like Laure, that his visits to Mathurin's cabin in the middle of winter had been unreal. Some sort of frozen dream wherein he tracked a starving deer and dropped its warm, dead body at the doorstep of another hungry creature, as pathetic as the first. Had Deskaheh planned to cut through to her heart, but changed his mind because he knew that only the desires of a starving woman were buried in Laure's chest? What courage could she offer from the enclosed walls of her husband's cabin? After all, Deskaheh hadn't come back afterwards, even though the winter stretched on much longer. Perhaps he also found it hard to believe that Laure actually existed, that she could be standing in the flesh so near to him in Ville-Marie.

He looks so much older this year, Laure thinks. Deskaheh, the boy she amused herself with last summer and who saved her life this winter, is a Savage man with a pregnant wife, and Laure is a fool. She turns from the couple and hurries through the crowd at the shore back toward the auberge where she is staying with the Tardifs. She rushes past men from as far away as Rivière-du-Loup and Tadoussac. They begin bargaining with the Savages for pelts even before they are unloaded on the shore. The men's voices meld together, a collective language of trade sprinkled with Savage words and provincial dialects.

The fair is also the time for French men to chase the daughters of the trading Savages. Some of the girls are excited by the adventure, while others run screaming in terror as the men track them like game through the streets. The sounds of the crowd are like a beehive in Laure's head. The faces around her are even more blurred. She cannot distinguish any distinct form as the blood surges through her veins.

※

As Laure nears the auberge, she sees a fight break out between two men. She can't tell what mixture they are of French and Savage as she hurries to the inn. Before she can enter, Deskaheh grabs Laure by the arm and turns her toward him. His is the only clear face in the crowd. Her body is still. She looks behind him for the pregnant girl but he is alone.

"What did you think?" he tries to say, but it comes out as "What do you think?"

Laure cannot respond. Her voice disappeared at the sight of the young Savage girl, the perfect joy of the two of them sitting there, reflecting back to her the loneliness she has lived with for so long. There is nothing Laure can say to him. She has no right to accuse him of adultery like she did Mathurin. Deskaheh hasn't done anything wrong. It is her fault for thinking there was something more between them, for being foolish enough to come here looking for him.

"Are you well after the winter?" he asks her and looks down at her stomach the same way the colony men do. It seems that all the rest of Ville-Marie went into bloom after the hard winter.

Just as the Intendant predicted, most of the women now carry in their bellies the precious seeds of the King's dreams for New France: unborn wealth, military strength, a great and loyal population on the banks of a tremendous river. Whereas Laure is nothing but a tired version of what she was a year ago. Everyone agrees that women without children are useless and have no place in the colony.

Deskaheh asks Laure where she is staying for the fair. She points to the alley behind her and tells him the name of the inn. He releases her arm, as if he had forgotten that he was still holding on to it. Laure wonders what he wanted to tell her, why he left behind the pregnant girl to follow her through the fair, but he doesn't say anything more, and the next moment he has gone.

⚜

The innkeeper, the same Madame Rouillard, the midwife who travelled with them from Québec, makes an enormous profit on the debauchery at the annual fur-trade fair. She serves brandy, in barrelfuls as if it were water from the river, to the Algonquins and Montagnais and other Savages who come to trade. The only responsibility of the *Canadienne* is to keep the men from stabbing or shooting each other while drunk. For this she has the support of her brothers who live in Ville-Marie. The furs the Savages have brought with them from their forest homelands float out to the French at cheap prices on the stream of libations Madame Rouillard and the other innkeepers of Ville-Marie provide. For the duration of the fair, the authorities turn a blind eye to the illegal taverns that open up in the homes of Ville-Marie. The Sulpiciens, the Soeurs hospitalières, the

Jesuits, and all other *personnes religieuses* stay indoors and wait for the sinful summer orgy to pass. All of this Laure learns from Madame Rouillard, who never tires of speaking about the goings-on of the colony.

The fact that Laure, a woman staying alone, has been assigned her own room at the inn is proof of Madame Rouillard's indulgent eye. The authorities have bigger troubles to contend with at the fair than a married woman staying alone in an inn. Not that anyone dares to publicly announce the fact that Laure has her own room and is not accompanied by a man, not even Madame Rouillard, who comments on most everything else. The Tardifs have their own room next to hers and are out trading the goods they carried with them in exchange for pelts. Madame Tardif is quite proud that she was able to afford a maid of all work to look after her children while she accompanied her husband to the fair. Laure doesn't expect to see much of the couple until it is time to head back to the settlement next week.

At dusk Laure changes into the simple summer dress she has brought with her. She made it last winter from the cotton she had left over from sewing Mathurin's shirts. She cut the neckline of the dress in imitation of the déshabillé style that was fashionable in Paris when she left. She also trimmed the neckline in blue linen. The dresses Laure made throughout the winter, from the finest materials in her chest, still hang from a section of the cabin's ceiling in Pointe-aux-Trembles. She promised Mathurin she would try to sell these dresses over the summer to the notable women of the colony. The authorities would not allow the women of Pointe-aux-Trembles to dress in such finery. In fact Laure isn't ready to see the dresses go just yet. They are companions of sorts for her. In her imaginings they are worn by girls from the Paris hospital who understand the need for lacemaking and fine embroidery, for looking elegant even in forest cabins with crude men.

Laure ties her hair back from her face, letting her long tresses fall down her back. She has felt light and empty ever since she saw Deskaheh with the pregnant girl this afternoon. At least she is here at the inn, in the company of people, and far from Mathurin's hut. It is such a desolate place, even in summer, far worse than the Salpêtrière ever was. Laure smells fresh bread and spices and roasting meat emanating from the inn's kitchen and she hears voices speaking over the sounds of the clinking dishes. She locks the door to her room and walks downstairs.

Laure asks one of Madame Rouillard's brothers to keep the men in the dining area away from her table, and he assures her that he will. The brother calls her Madame Turcotte, the name she gave when she signed in. He brings her a meat-and-vegetable stew and some wine. Laure takes a few of Mathurin's coins from her purse to pay him for the food. There is a cheer to the room that Laure is not accustomed to feeling at mealtime.

Just as Laure is finishing her stew and about to return to her room, Deskaheh enters the inn. A few fur-trading men turn from the bar to look at the Savage who has just passed through the door. Deskaheh looks around the room and, spotting Laure sitting alone in the shadows, he walks toward her table. Madame Rouillard's second brother, older with a tough face, comes out from behind the counter, but Laure raises her hand to inform the brother that she knows Deskaheh and that it is acceptable for him to sit with her. The innkeeper retreats behind the counter, but continues to keep an eye on Laure's table.

"How is your husband?" Deskaheh asks, refusing Laure's offer of a seat.

"He is still the same dog," Laure replies, wondering why Deskaheh has come here to ask her about Mathurin. "He is gone most of the time. You probably see him more than I do."

Deskaheh considers her words for a moment. "Maybe you should have married someone else." He looks toward the men at the bar, as if one of them might make a good match for her.

Laure has been watching these *coureurs de bois* drink brandy while they exchange tales of their fur-trading adventures. "You have seen how all the dogs behave. They are all the same. I should have fought harder to stay in France."

Deskaheh nods. "Most of the French men go back where they came from after a few months here, sometimes a year or two. They stay long enough to get some pelts and go back when they grow tired of life here." Deskaheh's French has improved over the last year. "They complain about everything. The winter, the summer, the bugs, the food, the women." He laughs.

Deskaheh's eyes move to the neckline of Laure's simple dress. She feels ashamed. She put it on to feel clean and calm. It is nothing more than a garment for sleeping in.

"Where is your other dress?" he asks.

"I burned it," Laure responds right away, even though it isn't true.

Deskaheh nods as if he understands why she would have done that. "What do you think?" he asks her again. He means *What did you expect?* but his eyes are devoid of the anger and surprise she saw in them this afternoon. His face is wide and gentle. There is pity in his expression. It is the same look a kind man would give an old horse before shooting it. Or the sort of expression on the face of Madame du Clos and Madame Gage. Laure has learned to seek out kindness the way others search for food and water. Her survival has depended on it.

"I don't want to be with you," she says, even though he never asked her that at all.

"This cannot happen. There are things that … I … we … call it—" Deskaheh says.

"Don't talk to me as if I am stupid or a child. I know how foolish it is for us to be with each other. It serves no purpose at all. You have a family and I have learned to live with a pig."

"In one year we have both grown up." Deskaheh inhales through his mouth as if he is about to say something more, but doesn't.

"I know better than you do what the French King, Onontio as you call him, wants from us. He wants you to make Savage babies to serve him and for me to make babies with that dog to serve him as well." Laure reaches her hand across the table to Deskaheh's arm. "It looks like at least one of us is doing their duty for your new master." Laure feels vindicated when she sees his features tighten.

He sits down at the table. "The French King across the waters is not my master."

"He certainly is. Look at you, bringing him the thickest furs from deep within the forest where his men are too afraid to travel. And what do you get in exchange?" Laure reaches into her purse and extracts the pouch from it. She pours out the contents, and the beads she took from Mathurin, made of glass from Venice, come rolling out onto the table. Deskaheh scrambles to catch them as they bounce and roll across the hard wood. "In France these are worthless. Even a poor woman like me can have a bag full of them." Laure stands up.

Deskaheh tries to catch the beads in his hands, to save them from rolling off the table. He cannot grab them all before they hit the hard floor.

"You use these to write prayers to God?" Laure picks up one of the beads. "If yours is anything like my God, he won't hear you anyway. Wait here a bit and I will bring you another gift. This one means more to me."

Deskaheh looks stunned.

✤

Up in her room, Laure reaches in her sack for the knife she packed. It is the blade Mathurin left her for skinning animals and scaling fish, the same one she used to slice open the hide of the deer Deskaheh brought her. Laure's hands tremble as she raises the blade to her cheek. She must have known she would run into Deskaheh here. Only one summer has passed and everything is irrevocably changed. How innocent the two of them were, watching the fruits and vegetables of the congregation garden grow, seeking solace in their strange friendship for the losses of their youth.

It feels as if Laure has been preparing all along for this, for the inevitable severing.

She unties the ribbon that holds her hair back. The long tresses fall over her shoulders, a familiar weight. She raises the blade to her scalp. She thinks for a brief moment how much easier it all would be if she could start cutting at the forehead, slice straight across, the way Mathurin told her that the Iroquois do with their enemies. But she isn't that brave.

Instead, Laure grabs a fistful of the hair that has been with her since her years at the hospital. The strands contain the memory, the smells and the deprivations, of all the nights she spent in the crowded dormitory, the musky traces of Mireille and then Madeleine's funerals, of the sea salt and vomit of the crossing. Laure's hair has been with her throughout the brief, searing heat and interminable cold winter of the past year in Canada. But most of all, her hair is alive with the memory of meeting the Savage Deskaheh, the first man she offered herself to.

The sound of the knife slicing through the strands of hair makes Laure shiver. But she continues to cut, until it is all around her feet and a few shorn tresses cling to her shoulders. She has severed her hair from her scalp the way the male settlers chop at the trees to clear forests for their crude cabins. She gathers the mass into her arms and smoothes it out, tying around it the yellow ribbon given to her by Madame du Clos. Onto her head Laure fastens the bonnet she received at Marguerite Bourgeoys' congregation but has so far refused to wear. It is the badge of a peasant housewife.

When she goes back downstairs, Deskaheh is still sitting at the table. He must have picked up all the beads because they are no longer there.

Laure's hair covers her outstretched arms as if she is carrying an offering to an altar. "When I was still in France, I was warned that the Savages in the New World stole the hair of French women." She places the plaits of her hair over Deskaheh's arms.

His face fills with revulsion to see what she has done. Laure is satisfied, glad even, to see disgust in his eyes. It is what she has expected all along. She has wanted to prove to him that she is ugly. That they are both ugly and deserve to be alone in separate worlds.

In the alleyways of Ville-Marie, men meet to trade stories and occasionally to spill each other's blood. The French have given the streets Savage names like Michilimackinac and Outaouaise. Even during the day, women are cautioned against walking outside in Ville-Marie. At night it is unheard of to do so. The fur traders, both the *voyageurs* and the illicit *coureurs de bois*, as well as the colony's soldiers, emerge from the taverns with eyes turned glossy and red. There are even more men out drinking and causing trouble during the annual fur-trade fair.

Through the open window of her room at the inn, Laure can hear their voices, loud and slurred, echoing between the stone walls of the streets. It is against the law for innkeepers to serve spirits to any of the Savage men. But very few actually heed this rule, especially at this time. For the fur-trade fair, there are almost as many taverns as homes in Ville-Marie. There are enough establishments so that each Savage nation that has travelled to Ville-Marie can frequent its own tavern to avoid fights between rivals.

When the girls from France first arrived, they were warned by the sisters of the congregation about the dangers of the town. The religious orders blame the French for providing the brandy, the beer, and the cider that make the Savages do awful things like smash canoes, set fires, and destroy cabins. So long as they commit crimes under the influence of brandy, the Savages feel that they should be immune from punishment for their actions. The French men complain that no laws are enforced to punish the Savages for their violent acts because the furs they bring to be traded are so valuable to the authorities.

There is no question that New France is a lawless place compared to the rigid discipline Laure was accustomed to at the Salpêtrière in Paris. The King's arm cannot reach with the same authority across the sea and into the woods of Canada, although none would dare to say so in public. How else could Laure be staying by herself in a room above a tavern in a town filled with revelling drunkards? She was probably safer in the Parisian dormitory with the diseased and mad women, but how much more exciting that there is nobody to watch over her here.

After she offered him her shorn hair, Deskaheh asked Laure to meet him later behind the inn. She agreed to see him even though she was frightened by the idea of going out alone at night in Ville-Marie. Laure lies upstairs in her hot enclosed room waiting for the hours to pass. All the while she attempts to determine Deskaheh's intentions in asking her to meet him again. He seemed angry with Laure for cutting her hair and giving him the crude offering, so she is surprised that he still wants to see her. She is wearing the yellow dress from Paris, the one he saw her in last summer. She has covered her head in the shawl she wore to the funerals of Madame d'Aulnay and Mireille.

Laure invokes the memory of Madeleine. How she wishes her friend were here beside her so she could recount the events of the past day to her. Of course Laure knows that Madeleine would have little to say about Deskaheh. She would surely tell Laure not to meet him tonight. There is nothing to be gained for her soul in meeting a Savage on the sinful streets of this fur-trading town.

Once the final raucous cheers have faded downstairs and the last man has left the inn for the night, Laure gets out of bed and steps out into the hallway. She creeps past the closed doors of the other rooms and downstairs to the tavern. Madame Rouillard is still awake. She is behind the counter cleaning the glasses and dishes left over from the evening's debauchery. Madame Rouillard doesn't look surprised to see Laure standing on the stairs wearing a dress from Old France that is several ranks above her station. There must be very little that surprises a woman who is a midwife and runs an inn in a French colony.

The old woman takes a towel and wipes her hands. Although fleshy, Madame Rouillard's features are firm and unreadable. Only her eyes gleam with emotion. "You want me to open the door for you?" she asks, putting down the towel and crossing her arms over her bosom.

Laure cannot think of a lie and wouldn't dare utter one to this woman. She nods.

"You know that a girl out alone at night in this fur-crazed town is no safer than a fox or a rabbit." Madame Rouillard's eyes widen as they move down the length of Laure's dress. "Especially a young one like you. When you get to be my age, you know that trouble will find you soon enough. You don't have to go out looking for it."

Laure's face burns. What a fool she must seem in the eyes of this old innkeeper and midwife. She considers fleeing back upstairs to her room.

"Don't worry. I've kept plenty of secrets in my day. The lives of the women who live along the banks of this river are filled with them. I could recount stories of sin and heartbreak that would have a priest recanting his vows." Madame Rouillard laughs. "There's no doubt that some of these girls are enjoying their new freedom. Of course, the price we pay for freedom is that we have to live here." She laughs again. "Although I must say, and it does indeed surprise me, not many of the French women go for the Savage men. You see plenty of the other way around. But that's not to say it doesn't happen." Madame

Rouillard comes out from behind the counter, her ample hips making short strides toward the door of the inn. "Some people insist on making life more complicated than it needs to be."

Laure follows behind her. "Thank you," she says as Madame Rouillard opens the door onto the street.

"Don't thank me. Sometimes when God gives us what we pray for, it's actually a curse. Wait until morning before you come back here. That way I can get some sleep and the ones who are staying upstairs will think you just stepped out to get some bread."

Laure nods again.

"I know that one you're going to meet. He's actually a decent character compared to most of them."

The night is deep, and the blackness is lessened only by a single torch at the end of the alley. Laure uses her hands to guide herself around to the back of the wooden building. Deskaheh is already there, waiting for her. When he sees her, his expression is similar to that of Madame Rouillard. It is as if the Savage and the old midwife had known all along that Laure was capable of wanton behaviour, that it was only a matter of time before she became an adulterous woman.

The Salpêtrière teems with these women, their poverty and sins imprisoning them for perpetuity. Abortion is the only crime worse than adultery that a woman can commit in New France. Because women are still so much fewer than men in the colony, the laws about adultery are more lenient than in France. Some husbands decide to take their wife back, or to send her to a nunnery, so long as her dowry can cover the price, rather than to punish her according to the law. Abortion, however, is punishable by death, with the law enforced more strictly than in Paris, where there is an abundance of children filling the hospitals and workhouses at royal expense.

Laure wonders what Mathurin would do if he knew she had come to the fur-trade fair and parted ways with the Tardifs so she could meet the Iroquois Savage Deskaheh alone in an alley behind an inn. Would he free her from her prison sentence and bear the shame of her actions?

Laure and Deskaheh have already, in the few words they exchanged earlier on at the table, said all there is to say about their situation. Laure has married a pig and must spend the rest of her life in his forest cabin. Deskaheh will be staying in the tribe of the Algonquins with his new wife and the baby she is expecting. They have both abandoned their childish dreams for lives they cannot escape. What, then, can they hope to gain by this clandestine meeting?

Deskaheh grabs Laure by the arm as soon as he sees her as if she is a prisoner being taken by the police. He leads her to a street known as rue d'Enfer, Hell Street. It is the centre of the fur traders' nighttime revelry. French men sit with pistols guarding the pelts of moose, deer, fox, and otters, but also richer ones of wild cat, marten, sable, and bear. The objects of their trade with the Savages, kettles, pans, clothing, china, necklaces, litter the streets, abandoned by Savage men more enthralled by alcohol and firearms.

Deskaheh takes Laure into one of the buildings. She lowers her face, pulling the shawl over her forehead. She recognizes some of the men from Mathurin's trading party. Several candles burn in the room, and some men are singing *voyageurs* songs. There are other French women and a number of Savage girls as well. They seem to be as drunk as the men. The noise is a tremendous blend of songs and the pounding of feet and hands on the wooden floor and tables. Stories of adventure, exaggerated by drink, are interspersed with raucous laughter. This could be any tavern in Old France except that here there are also Savage men and women who eat flesh, driven out of their minds by brandy. The room is hot and the candlelight has turned everything red.

Although it is dark enough, Deskaheh knows better than to stay in the main area with Laure. He takes her through a door to the back of the building where curtains of animal hide divide the space into private rooms. Deskaheh has brought Laure where prostitutes gather to entertain men for money. All sorts of colony men mix here like in the bawdy houses of Paris. By day they have other lives, wives and children, business to tend to, contracts to sign, fortunes to chase after. But tonight they are drowning those worlds in one cupful after another of brandy, wine, and spruce beer. The new country will be made—trees chopped, stubborn land ploughed, crops tended, furs traded— tomorrow, in the fall, some time later. The bitter weather will come, but for now the air is warm, stifling even. Bowls are filled and refilled with meaty soups. Blood flows easily.

At this court, Laure can easily be a queen. But the silk screens of the prostitutes' quarters that Laure had imagined back in Paris are made of rotting animal flesh in Canada. The princes and dukes are bearded fur traders and Savage men. The enchanting women sing lyrics about forest romance in hoarse, drunken voices. Laure cannot even understand the serpentine movements of their Savage tongues.

There can be no mistaking why Deskaheh has brought her here, to this cubicle enclosed in hides. What must he think of her, a prostitute who gives herself away for free? Laure cannot determine if her pounding heart is filled with bliss or terror.

Deskaheh smells of soil, herbs. The Jesuit priests warned the women newly arrived from France all the way up the river and as they slept on its banks. *These men eat the flesh of their captives. They roast them alive and eat the morsels bit by bit. This, I have seen with my own eyes.* Laure feels sick with guilt. One of the priests who spoke to them was missing an ear. The Jesuits have all gone mad over the crimes they have witnessed, the desecration of their God by the Savages. Is this not Laure's God too?

But Deskaheh is gentle when he removes her dress, more skilful, more patient than her husband. Laure probably smells like sour milk, like Mathurin, like the diseased and crowded quarters of the Paris hospital. They both carry the story of their lives like ointment on their skin.

Laure is being dragged under the waves and it is so easy to let herself sink, to become one with the sea. The prayers she learned at the hospital are a distant litany, a thing of the past.

Questions fill Laure's mind as she lets Deskaheh consume her body, limb by limb. *Is this what torture feels like? Am I also on fire and being eaten alive? How does it feel to burn for all eternity? Will I become a hungry forest ghost? Am I sea water consumed by flame? What will remain when I have gone?*

❧

For days, Laure stays in this way, enclosed by furs, waiting for Deskaheh to return to her. She wears the same dress and is starting to smell like the hides around her. He returns at all hours to see her, but she does not know the difference between night and day in this place that is always filled with drinking and song and lovemaking. Deskaheh lies to the pregnant woman and to the others in his village so he can come and meet her. Laure is his dark and ugly secret. He devours her the way the other Savages consume the illicit firewater. Only she isn't sure which of them is being destroyed, who will emerge victorious when the trading is complete.

As with most everything in Canada, it is the weather that decides Laure's fate. It is late August, and the first wind of fall blows through the town on the last day of the fur-trade fair, when the inns are closing up and the fur racks are being dismantled. Laure stands on the street, feeling the breeze on her skin, as the men make their way to the canoes. She feels frail like an old woman facing the bright sun and fresh air. Deskaheh has already left for his village. There was no need to say goodbye. Every encounter with him was filled with parting. She makes her way back to Madame Rouillard, to the Tardif couple.

20

*I*t is October of her second year in the colony, and Laure is gathering the last of the garden's yield: some beets and onions that she tears with difficulty from the frozen soil. Her arms ache from struggling against the ferocious tenacity of the weeds and keeping them from overtaking the garden throughout the summer. There were the vermin, digging and chewing through the best of the crops at night, and then the worms burrowing their way into the corn when the stalks finally grew tall enough to offer up the cobs. Still, Laure managed to extract some sustenance from this beleaguered cultivation. The earliest crops had been the lettuce and cucumbers, then the beans, which seemed to grow better than the other vegetables and which she picked for weeks until her hands were raw and the beans themselves came to be filled with big purple seeds.

Fall signals the end of the fresh food supply in Canada, and it comes early. By October the earth has already turned hard and dry, ready to be shrouded in snow until spring. The trees have shed their leaves, and the brisk gusts of wind from the north offer an ominous sign of the winter ahead. The thick stalks of the final deep-rooted vegetables tear the palms of

Laure's roughened hands. But she is desperate to gather all the food she can, as if stores of dried vegetables and jars of preserves can protect her from the dark desolation of a second winter in the cabin.

❧

Laure is surprised to see Mathurin walking up the path one late-October day as she tends to the garden. He has been away for more than half of their first year of marriage, and she hadn't really expected him to come back at all until the following spring. Tardif, upon seeing Mathurin come along the trail, greets him as if he has been here all along. The other men and even their wives only speak to Laure to ask if she needs anything. As a resident of their burgeoning settlement, they want to make sure she survives, but beyond the basic formalities they have no interest in befriending her. The men are afraid of Laure, and the wives don't want their husbands speaking to her. She is from Paris, knows how to make lace, and refused for so long to cover her wild dark hair in the work bonnets all the other women wear. In fact it wasn't until Laure came back from the fur-trade fair, shorn like a prisoner, that she started to wear her bonnet and a rude dress to match it. Also, unlike the other women, Laure is childless and without any family in the settlement or in all of New France.

Mathurin's musket bounces on his belly as he walks up the trail to the cabin. He looks even more pink and fatter than when he left. Still like a baby pig well fed on grain. But unlike when he saw her last spring, this time Laure has also put on a little weight. The summer harvest throughout the colony and even in Pointe-aux-Trembles has been good. It would be easy to prepare for Mathurin a homecoming feast, except Laure knows what he has been up to and what she has done in his absence. There is very little to celebrate.

"Welcome back, my husband," she says. She stands up in the garden, wiping her torn hands on her apron.

"Look at this place. It's becoming a real village." He unslings his musket and sits it up against the house.

There is warmth to the settlement, a feeling of ease that was missing last year. The impression that this stretch of forest is a ransacked military encampment has somewhat dissipated. There are more curtains in the windows, greater food stores for the winter, fewer cracks in the cabin walls, the odd piece of furniture brought in from Ville-Marie, plans to build a church, and the foundations laid for a grand seigneurial home made of stone.

Laure is better prepared for this second winter. She has dried fruits and vegetables in the sun, purchased an extra barrel of smoked meat, and sealed up some of the biggest holes in the cabin. While inside, her stomach is satiated, her gut warmed by all the sunshine of summer and its foods, on the outside, her hands are cracked and her face and arms have been darkened by the sun. Laure's choices were either to remain a *citadine* and starve in this forest colony or to roll up her sleeves and yank from the earth whatever sustenance it had to offer.

In the cabin she prepares a soup of salted pork and cabbage while Mathurin grunts his pleasure at the sight of the curtains and the quilt she has made. He sets about making a fire from the light sticks Laure gathered over the past few weeks. She is glad Mathurin has returned, however temporarily, so he can cut a wood supply of heavy logs, larger than last year's, to fill the cabin wall. She learned last winter that it is the cabin's fire that will take her through to spring.

Unlike some of the more established Pointe-aux-Trembles families, Laure and Mathurin still don't have any more furniture than they did the previous year. The furniture that comes in from the ships is designated first for the nobles and religious houses of Québec, then for the wealthier settlers of Trois-Rivières, and finally what remains is transported to the nobles and religious of Ville-Marie. It will take years before the ordinary people will have furniture in their cabins, except for those who can make their own rudimentary versions or buy pieces from the few furniture makers in the town.

"Well, it looks like you have learned a thing or two in my absence. That smells good. I've been eating nothing but Savage stews for the past months. You know how foul those can be."

Laure nods. "Yes, day after day of eating that corn soup of theirs must be terrible." Does Mathurin think she knows nothing about the Algonquins and their ways?

Laure fills the two bowls with the broth and vegetables and carries them to the table. When she sets Mathurin's bowl in front of him, he reaches for her breast and gives it a hard squeeze. The swift movement and sharp pain makes her spill some of the hot broth from her bowl onto his lap. For the moment he doesn't try for anything more.

After finishing his soup, Mathurin leaves Laure sitting at the makeshift table and crawls into bed. Before long he is snoring and the sound fills every crack in the room's walls. Laure doesn't have an appetite for her soup. She is reminded of the trouble that has been gnawing away any reassurance that the bountiful crops could have brought. She rises from her coffer, opens the door to the cabin, and retches beside the entrance. Her stomach is empty, and so she heaves out only air and deep animal sounds.

Although it is still early, darkness is falling on the settlement and the air is sharp with the new cold. Looking out over the cabins, the most prosperous of which have lit extravagant early fires, and into the bare branches of the forest beyond, Laure can be fooled into believing that all is peaceful. The onset of the cold, already predictable and well prepared for, seems a trifling concern. Like death, winter is a certainty to be endured and ultimately surrendered to. Laure is accustomed to death, to the long trials of enclosement, to hunger, to the burying force of this country.

It is the new thing that she cannot accept, that is making her sick. Even now, bile is rising into her throat. She forces herself to put aside for the moment what cannot be ignored for long. When her stomach feels a little settled, she closes the door and comes into bed beside her husband.

In the morning she crawls out of the *lit-cabane* where Mathurin is still lying asleep and opens the cabin door again. The sickness is gone. Outside the sun has not yet risen and the air is cold and damp. The others in the *seigneurie* are still sleeping. With the crops all picked for the year, there isn't as much reason to wake up early any more. Besides, these days the sun barely rises until late morning. Soon there will be snow.

They say there are ways, even in New France, to procure the necessary herbs. If Laure were at the Salpêtrière, she could easily arrange to meet with one of these women by passing the message of her terrible dilemma from girl to girl. There has been rumour of a few abortionists practising their illicit trade in the colony. But these are only rumours. She certainly can't ask anyone in Pointe-aux-Trembles to help her find an abortionist. There is not a soul that Laure can trust with her secret.

For Laure, prayers are a last resort. Madeleine would tell her that she should turn to prayer first. Laure would answer that

God, like a good dormitory officer, would expect his children to exhaust all their own means of coming up with a solution before bothering him. Besides, Laure did pray last summer that no child would come of the nights she spent with Deskaheh in Ville-Marie. By late September, she knew for certain her prayer had not been answered. Ever since, she has struggled to think of a way to explain to the others in Pointe-aux-Trembles how she can be pregnant even though Mathurin has been away since April. Even heaven, Laure fears, will have no solution to offer. She must pay the consequences, however grave, for making such a terrible mistake. How easy it is to regret now what she could only surrender to in August.

Her prayer is simple. "Lord, there is a Savage baby growing within me. I ask only that you somehow take it from me and let me live. If you do this one thing for me, I will not disobey any of your commandments again."

❦

Laure doesn't know if the help comes from God or simply from her own mind turning over the problem for so long while Mathurin was away. Now that her husband has returned, there is one other option. It might not be too late. Babies often come early, after all. Of course this is only a temporary solution, for when the child is born, Mathurin will soon see that the baby does not belong to him. But many things could happen between now and then. Perhaps as Laure has been hoping for, there is still a chance that the beginnings of the child will fall out of her womb in a miscarriage, although with each passing week that becomes less likely. She has done vigorous work in the garden all fall to bring about this result. She has heard the French men say that it is the hard work of the Savage girls that keeps them from having so many children like the French women. But, even if the baby, which has so far seemed resistant to her efforts, is born after all, perhaps Mathurin won't see the Savage origins of the child immediately. It might take years for the features to appear. At least for now Laure can buy herself some time by lying with Mathurin and in a few weeks claiming the pregnancy as his. Laure boils pine branches for the occasion and pours the perfumed water into her hair and over her chest.

When Mathurin awakens, Laure is standing in front of him in her nightdress. She looks into his ruddy face and gives him her most seductive smile. He is surprised by this attention and pleased. At least the first part of her plan is easy enough to orchestrate.

"I've wanted so long for you to be my wife," he says, pulling her up against the soft weight of his body. "Laure, I've been waiting just for you." He looks like he might cry, such is his agitation at her willingness to have him.

She pats his back. She really wishes he wouldn't make this more difficult by lying to her about the Savage women. She winces as he enters her, but pretends to feel pleasure.

Two weeks later, Laure sits with Mathurin and announces to him that she is expecting his baby. By this time she is in fact three months pregnant and her stomach and breasts are so swelled that she can no longer wear her bodice.

⚜

To celebrate the pregnancy, Mathurin has killed two squirrels. He chased a rabbit for a few minutes, but couldn't shoot it. With her sickness now gone, Laure feels ravenous. Even Mathurin's squirrels—strung upon a stick—look delicious. It is as if she needs to eat for the whole winter ahead, for all the past weeks of sickness. There is not enough food in the cabin to satisfy her, but she adds what she can to Mathurin's catch. She prepares enough for six people. She boils one of the squirrels for several minutes, but can't wait to eat it. The smell of it cooking drives her mad. She pulls it from the pot and throws the hot carcass across the table. She sits on her chest and eats the entire animal, its soft flesh and salty blood satisfying her like no food ever has. Mathurin watches her, a contented look spread across his wide features.

21

Laure's fingers move along the stitches. She is embroidering a blanket. The baby will emerge naked into the cold of Canada and will need to be wrapped up, she tells herself. The child must be covered in something if it is to survive even an hour in this country. But does she really want the baby to live for an hour? Two hours? For a day? How long will Laure be able to hold the creature that has no future?

Madame Tardif sits on a wooden chair across from Laure. Although it is rustic, without any carving or a smooth surface, the chair is a luxurious item purchased by Madame Tardif's husband in Ville-Marie. Madame Tardif is a model colony mother, with children nearby as she works in the cabin. Her offspring are strong and her cabin is outfitted with the simple necessities. Heavy drapes cover the windows; there is a table and four chairs besides the one recently purchased by Monsieur Tardif. There are also cooking utensils and a wash basin. But it is the children, the beginning of a large family, that are the most obvious sign of Madame Tardif's success.

How much simpler it would be if Laure were having Mathurin's baby. But what would she feel for the offspring of her pig husband? It would be some other baby that she half reviled and not this child twisting in her gut filling her thoughts with Deskaheh, God, animals, and her own passions.

Mathurin stayed in the cabin with his pregnant wife until the middle of November, but grew more restless each day watching one fur-trade convoy after another being discussed, planned for, and departing Pointe-aux-Trembles. Finally, at the very last, Mathurin left, promising Laure that he would be back early in the spring, well before the baby was born.

Madame Tardif took Laure in with more affection than she had shown her in the past, if such a shrewd woman could ever be described as affectionate. Surely she was relieved that Laure was finally pregnant. Having Laure stay with Madame Tardif was a courteous agreement between neighbours that was arranged by Mathurin, at Laure's urging, before he left. Laure decided she could not face another winter alone with just the cabin's fire and this new baby within her.

Madame Tardif incorporated caring for Laure, the pregnant *citadine*, into her winter schedule. The *Canadienne* has three children in their two-room cabin, the youngest being barely weaned. She reassures Laure that having children is what a woman is meant to do. That they will come into the world less painfully than anticipated, unless of course you or the baby or the both of you die, but of course nothing can be done about that anyway, so there is no sense thinking about it. According to Madame Tardif, raising the children God gives you will be no harder than salting meat, darning socks, or weeding the garden. They are just another of the countless chores of colony life.

She preaches to Laure throughout the day as they tend to the fire, the cooking, the needlework, and the care of the children. The wisdom and preoccupations that govern Madame

Tardif's daily existence are of a practical nature: What rate are the commanding officers paying this winter to have their uniforms and socks mended? How can firewood be made to last longer by turning in early at night and keeping the door to the cabin closed, the curtains drawn, and the children indoors throughout the day? How much broth can be had from boiling salted meats and fish bones to make a stew nearly as watery as the Salpêtrière broth? Laure appreciates the practical lessons she gets from Madame Tardif on being an efficient and careful colony wife. She can see that a decade or two of such toil could lead to a slightly less encumbered life, but there is certainly no room in Madame Tardif's mind for dresses made of exquisite materials, for dreams of princes and royal courts, for letter-writing, for dangerous amorous relations with the Savages of this country.

Laure wishes she could trade for Madame Tardif's simple severity the vain curves of her creamy body, her gleaming eyes, the foolish thoughts in her head, and most of all, the sinful evidence of all her faults that now fills the space beneath her ribs.

"I don't know why you are spending your time making all those detailed designs," Madame Tardif says. "A baby is a dirty creature who doesn't have eyes for things such as embroidered flowers. You would do well enough to make a blanket using that grey wool I gave you."

Laure cannot imagine wrapping a new baby in such coarse material. She has taken apart one of the dresses she sewed last winter and is using the cotton to create a soft blanket for the baby.

"I don't know when you will finally understand that we are not in Paris, that Canada is nowhere near to the King's court, and that practicality and economy are much more useful here than flower designing and expensive fabrics."

Laure continues with her embroidering.

"You don't want to tell your child from the moment they are born that life is easy. What is the point of getting them accustomed to fineries at such a young age when that blanket will be the only luxury they will ever know?"

Better to have known something fine at least, to have tasted even for one moment that life is more than ugly coarse material and back-breaking hard work, Laure thinks, but she remains quiet. She is, after all, a guest in Madame Tardif's home, and the winter outside is vicious and cold.

"I do not possess the housekeeping skills that you do. Making fine clothing is all I know how to do."

When Laure has finished with the blanket for the day, she drapes it over the wooden box Madame Tardif gave her to use as a cradle. Laure cannot help but think that the box looks more like a coffin and that the blanket is like placing flowers on her baby's grave.

Madame Rouillard has come to the Tardif cabin to see Laure. It is February, and she is visiting Pointe-aux-Trembles as there are three pregnant women in the settlement. The Governor and Intendant are eager to hear her reports of all the pregnancies and births in the region of Ville-Marie so they can send the good news of the colony's fertility back to France.

Madame Rouillard is covered in furs and looks just like a *coureur de bois*. She removes her hat and overcoat and her cheeks are bright from the cold. She has travelled from Ville-Marie with an Algonquin convert named Louis and a young *Canadien*.

"You aren't paid very much to come with me, but I appreciate the company in those woods. Go back to the cabin we just came from and I'm sure they'll empty their brandy stores for you. Leave me to my women's business here and I'll get you when I've finished."

The young men close the door behind them, eager to escape the presence of yet another pregnant woman.

"You're not expecting again, are you?" the midwife asks Madame Tardif.

"No, it's not for me."

"That's a relief. I tell the women that nothing is more dangerous to mother and child than pregnancies spaced too closely together."

Madame Rouillard turns to look at Laure. She narrows her eyes as if trying to recollect where she has seen the face. "You're not her sister?"

Laure responds that she isn't. She tells the midwife that Madame Tardif has simply been kind enough to take her in while her husband is off in search of furs. Madame Tardif is pleased by Laure's words of praise, as they both know that news of her generosity will now travel to Ville-Marie.

"Now that I hear you speak, I remember you. You're one of those women who arrived from the Paris hospital. I was in the canoe with you from Québec, I think."

Laure nods. Madame Rouillard seems about to say more but instead reaches for the bag she's brought with her. Laure starts to tremble as Madame Rouillard walks toward her. She will be discovered in front of Madame Tardif when the midwife easily discerns that Laure is actually six, rather than four, months into her pregnancy. Laure can feel the midwife's eyes scrutinizing her face and body as if she knows her secret even before she touches her.

Madame Rouillard is silent as she kneels next to Laure and brings the candle near. She asks Laure to come and lie down on a pelt she has unrolled onto the floor. Laure stiffens as the midwife's hands slide over her belly. The older woman's eyes remain focused on a point in the distance as she feels for the limbs of the child through Laure's flesh. Laure fears that this woman will know so much about her just by touching her abdomen for a few moments. Finally Madame Rouillard puts an ear to Laure's stomach and listens for the baby's heart.

"Your baby is strong, Madame—?"

Laure tells her Mathurin's surname.

Madame Rouillard then asks Madame Tardif to fetch the boys at the neighbours'.

The midwife sits quietly for a few moments. They are enveloped in the silence, the deep slumber, of winter. Only Laure is wide awake, alert and ready to hear what Madame Rouillard has to say.

"You would be surprised to learn how many women have committed sins worse than your own."

Laure's eyes widen. Madame Rouillard does remember her leaving the inn to be with Deskaheh.

The midwife grows silent again.

Laure wishes she could tell her that she feels true regret for her actions. Of course her life would be much simpler if she were pregnant with Mathurin's child, or if there were no baby at all. But what could Laure hope for with such a life? She would grow swarthy and worn by work like Madame Tardif just the same. Only there would be no secret memories of Deskaheh, no Savage child within her. Laure would have tepid feelings, maybe even revulsion, toward her husband, her children, and her cabin in the woods of this rude country. How then can she feel any remorse for what she has done?

"The problem is that you were not sent across the sea at the King's expense to befriend Savage men."

"But the French men, including my own husband, are free to have relations with any woman they want."

"Yes, and that has only produced more Savage children and not a single French one. Only the women sent from France can give the King the French colony he wants to see in Canada. Besides, thinking about what the men do here isn't going to help you any."

Madame Rouillard appears pensive. "They cannot know what you have done. You need the respect of women like Madame Tardif if you are to survive in Ville-Marie. You are lucky because everyone is trying to believe good things about the women in Canada. As you know, it is a different story in Old France. Even though you spend your days imprisoned and watched over every minute in the General Hospital, lies will circulate about the lascivious things you are doing. Here women are worth much more."

Laure hears Madame Tardif outside the cabin. Her eyes grow wide.

"I will visit again soon with a plan for the baby. In the

meantime, take care of yourself. I am not looking to please people like Madame Tardif and your husband. I do this work to make sure that mothers and their babies survive. God knows I already face enough challenges from nature."

As the weeks go on, Laure cannot think of anything but the child growing within her. She is so exhausted that she can hardly remember when she was one person. The pregnancy is consuming her thoughts like a fire destroying all that came before. As she weakens, growing heavier and more tired each day, Laure can feel the baby's movements getting more powerful. Sometimes, lying awake at night, she can make out a hand or a knee protruding from her abdomen as if fighting against the containment. It is God's punishment to have filled her with such a healthy baby. The creature with no destiny has a strong will to live. But, worse than this, Laure has started to sing to the baby. She remembers her father and the safety she felt in his arms. Of course he had nothing to give her except those songs.

Before long, Madame Rouillard is back to examine Laure once again.

"Just remember that this child doesn't belong to you," she whispers to her this time.

Laure is entering her eighth month of pregnancy and is amazed that Madame Rouillard can say such a thing to her. After all, the baby is enveloped in the stretched flesh of her abdomen. There is no separating their two bodies from each other.

"You cannot keep the child. Your husband will know it is from another man. Even if he remains quiet about it, people like Madame Tardif will spread the gossip all the way to Ville-Marie. There will be consequences for you and for the child."

Laure attempts to follow Madame Rouillard's thoughts, but she cannot raise her eyes from her belly. She hasn't permitted herself to think about the outcome, the punishments that are levelled against adulterous women, including death. She has not dared to imagine what will happen when the child is born, a being separate from her and clearly not belonging to Mathurin. Like the skin of her midriff, Laure has let herself believe that this pregnancy will stretch on. That it has no end. That the half-remembered songs she sings are enough.

Laure doesn't want to hear what Madame Rouillard is suggesting. She wants to scream like a crazed woman at the Salpêtrière. To think that she will not keep this child, even though doing so could have her sentenced to death, makes Laure feel like she is losing her mind.

"Listen to me. It is better for everyone. For you, your husband, and especially for the child, if the Algonquin, the father, takes the baby."

Deskaheh? Laure hasn't seen him since the summer. Surely he doesn't even know she is pregnant.

"The authorities don't count the Savage children or question their origins the way they do for the French ones. Now, listen. I have been to see him beyond Ville-Marie toward the Outaouais River and he has agreed to take the baby. He was very concerned about you and wanted to come and see you, which I advised him not to do. He isn't bad, that one. A little foolish, but he has a kind heart. Misfortune usually chooses to strike fools with kind hearts."

Laure asks what Deskaheh will tell his village. How will he explain this particular misfortune to them?

"They have adopted children before. It is a war practice of theirs. Deskaheh was adopted himself. But try not to think about the outcome of the child's life. After all, it is better to be raised by Savages than to die."

Laure nods. The baby will live. Both she and the baby will survive, apart but alive. Laure has lain awake while the Tardif household slept and implored the grace of her dead friend Madeleine, the only divine angel she trusts to listen, for this very outcome. Her prayers have been answered.

"There is still much to do just to make sure that the child, once born, is brought to Deskaheh before your husband or Madame Tardif sees it. But don't worry about these things for now."

Her child will live. There will be a second chance for everyone. Laure imagines Madeleine's beatific face smiling. Laure is filled with gratitude.

22

Laure's second spring in Canada was the windiest any settler could remember. It was hard to sleep each night because they heard the wind whistling like a tormented being through the cracks of their small cabins. It was as if this year the winter was unwilling to relinquish its hold on the colony. Laure had many dreams. The sailor Ti-Jean who had crushed Madeleine's spirit rode the horses that came to wrench Laure from the arms of her father. In one dream, Ti-Jean was a monster dressed like the Bonhomme Terre-Neuve.

Laure lay on her side, unable to turn over from the weight of her belly, imagining the sounds of women screaming as Iroquois warriors raided the settlement, brandishing the long-haired, bloody scalps in victory. There were so many noises in the cabin, the Tardif children coughing and whimpering in their sleep. Madame Tardif slept through it all with roaring snores and awoke refreshed for her duties each day like a commanding soldier, whereas Laure began those spring mornings weary and drained, convinced that the demons of hell had visited her the previous night to chastise her for her sin.

If the baby inside her can hear any of it or feel the disquiet building in its mother, it shows no signs. It continues to grow through the beginning of April, kicking harder than before. By the end of the month, Laure is far bigger than any of the settlers have ever seen a pregnant woman who still has two months remaining to her pregnancy. She can no longer do much of anything other than lie in bed on her side. There is still no sign of Mathurin, and Madame Tardif has grown so tired of her unwanted guest that she comes in from her outside work just long enough to grudgingly prepare some broth for Laure and to sigh about how this winter has left her household economies in a dire state. In truth, Laure feels the woman is a bit afraid of Laure's unnatural size.

When May arrives, even though Mathurin has not returned with the other men from the fur country, Madame Tardif asks Laure to move back to her own cabin. She promises that she will bring Laure some soup and help as much as she can, given her own woeful circumstances, until Mathurin comes back.

Once Laure is in her own cabin, Madame Rouillard comes every few days to study her pregnant belly, to see if it is time to deliver, and also to prepare soup and bread and a little meat for her. The midwife feels Laure's stomach and assures her that the baby she is carrying is healthy, if the strength of its kicks is any sign. She offers to bleed Laure, to try to bring down some of the swelling in her arms and legs, but Laure doesn't see how any treatment other than getting the child out of her will do anything at all. She does take the herbs that are supposed to speed along the birth, because the midwife feels it is taking too long for the baby to be born.

At last, one night in the middle of May, the baby starts to come. At first Laure is uncertain whether the tightening of her abdomen and the pain that follows is any different from the signs of impending birth she has been feeling for weeks. But after a few hours, when she can no longer sleep, Laure gets out of bed and lays down some pelts on the floor of the cabin. She is unsure what force is guiding her actions, but somehow she is unafraid and purposeful. There is no room in her mind for thoughts or doubts as she prepares to give birth.

She doesn't know how long she stays like this, her face pressing into the furs, the smell of dead animal flesh rising into her nostrils. She attempts to doze between the spasms of pain. There is nothing to do but endure. She forgets all that has come before and what lies ahead. Hours pass like minutes and minutes become an eternity of agony.

⚜

Laure has been sleeping fitfully, caught between the world of dreams and the pain that keeps her awake. But in an instant the characters of her dream go cascading as if on a waterfall right out of her mind. She rises to her knees and feels a moment of terror. The months of swelling have deflated in a rush of warm liquid on the furs beneath her. The most excruciating pain Laure has ever felt replaces the bloated feeling. She releases into the settlement first one scream and then another.

Laure has opened the door to the cabin and is about to head outside, possibly into the forest, anywhere to escape the pain that is almost relentless now. But Madame Tardif is there, blocking her way. She pushes her back into the cabin and onto the pelts and tells her that she will send her husband to get the midwife. Laure can feel the baby thrashing inside her.

When Madame Rouillard arrives a few hours later, she dismisses Madame Tardif from her duties, saying she will call on her closer to the time when the baby is due to arrive. Laure hears Madame Rouillard say that it probably won't be before morning, that it takes a long time for a first baby to emerge.

The midwife helps Laure onto her elbow and lights the gas lamp she uses sparingly for the delivery of babies born at night. She lifts Laure's skirt and spreads wide her legs. Laure cannot feel Madame Rouillard's hands as she examines her, but she manages to calm herself a little by looking at the midwife's face.

"The baby is coming, but try to hold it back," she hears her say. "You haven't stretched enough to push it out." Laure feels her eyes rolling into the back of her head. It is impossible to heed the midwife's advice. She cannot stop the pressure of the baby's head against her spine. She is sure it will push through her back. The midwife comes close to Laure's face and tells her to forget the pain and to listen to her words. Then she works to stretch the opening between Laure's legs to let the head through.

Laure cannot concentrate on Madame Rouillard's voice or the room around her. She imagines a door opening in her mind and she passes through it. A bright fire burns in the room and she is back among the characters from the dreams that have been tormenting her all winter. She makes a snarling noise like a sick dog and resumes her screaming. The midwife tells Laure she is going to get a pail of water.

In bringing this overgrown child into the world of the living, Laure catches a glimpse of the world of the dead. She has been seeing it in her dreams all along as the baby grew through the long winter. But when the giant head tears its way out of her body and she begins to lose blood, Laure glimpses something else. It is as if she can no longer hear the noises in the cabin and there is only a deep and distant quiet.

This time she sees a stream as peaceful and inviting as a summer sky. The babbling sound is as gentle as birds playing in the branches. She doesn't feel pain and she is able to walk like she did when she first arrived in the New World. The heavy weight of the child is gone. Someone is there by the water. His hair is as long and black as hers and his arms are the colour of tree branches and just as strong. I didn't know Jesus would greet me like this to welcome me to heaven, Laure thinks. She recognizes him as he comes toward her. It has been a long time since Deskaheh has watched her.

This is your home, he says. She thinks he is referring to his arms, because she wants to run into them, to feel them around her slim body. But he smiles and extends his hand to indicate the great expanse where they are standing.

Laure wants to believe him, to shed the heavy clothes she is wearing, to drop the memories she has of stone buildings and men with stone hearts and the heavy, heavy stone she has been carrying in her stomach. She wants to bare her skin to the sky and let go of everything else. Stand with him in the cool, calm water. But there is too much distance between them and she cannot reach him. The peaceful river becomes the angry sea, and in an instant Laure is swept under.

Someone is smacking Laure's face and a new voice is crying in the room. Laure's stomach has turned to liquid, her body has been returned to her, a river without its banks. She is unable to move even a finger and cries without making a sound, or releasing another drop of water.

For the first time in months, Laure feels cold and thinks they must have moved her outside, the woman who hits her must have dropped her in the snow. Laure cannot sleep or stay awake. She prays to go back to the heavenly stream. Only there is a new animal life in the cabin. The midwife is putting the baby, a girl, to her breast. The creature that was so enormous and powerful inside her belly now seems so small.

Once the baby begins to suckle on Laure, Madame Rouillard busies herself preparing some food, from supplies she must have carried with her. "Some soup for the new mother," she says. "Giving birth is hard work."

Laure is hungry and eats first one bowl and then another of the soup filled with chunks of meat and root vegetables. Then Madame Rouillard says that she must leave. She has to rest after the long night, to travel the trails, to prepare for another birth. She promises to return in two days and advises Laure to stay in bed except to tend to the fire and to get more soup. "Keep the baby on your breast and against your skin so she stays warm, and get as much rest as you can to keep from bleeding too much.

"A fortunate birth," she says to Laure.

Laure spends the first day of her daughter's life in the cabin lying in bed, nursing the new creature. The baby is either sucking greedily or asleep. Laure strokes the fine tuft of black hair on the tiny head and marvels at the smooth pout of the baby's lips and the dark stains of colour on her cheeks. How could such a clandestine, impossible union have created this remarkable being so hungry for the next hours of her doomed life?

Laure is neither asleep nor completely awake in the hours following her daughter's birth. Instead she lets herself be carried on the soft waves of these new and tentative breaths. She feels she must remain awake, vigilant, so she can urge her baby forward, raising her with a mother's will, ever deeper out of the water, away from slumber and into the wakefulness of the world.

Laure tries to forget that they will soon be parted. In a few more days, she will be left alone, wounded and shapeless. What is the use of holding the baby to her breast and singing? Laure will soon belong to a time in her baby's life when being drowned was the same as being alive, a time before she knew the earth, this forest, the snow, her father and his people.

Later that day, Madame Tardif comes knocking on Laure's door. Laure considers not getting out of bed when she hears the loud, familiar voice outside. But she knows this will only elicit suspicion and might lead to a worse invasion later. Rising out of bed, Laure takes her baby and wraps her tightly in the blanket, covering the dark hair and face and nestling her against her breast. Then she stumbles, bent over and in pain, to open the door to the unwelcome guest.

Madame Tardif barely seems to notice the infant and Laure's weakened state as she pushes into the cabin. "Good, now that the baby has arrived, I need to talk to you."

Laure walks back to the bed. She needs to sit down. Madame Rouillard removed the wood cover of the *lit-cabane* to make it easier for Laure after the birth. She rests on the edge of the bed, holding her baby's head tightly against her chest.

"I wanted to tell you sooner but it was the midwife who asked me to wait. I don't think it should have been a secret at all." Madame Tardif crosses her arms over her chest.

What news can she possibly have for Laure? Whatever it is, it can't be good. Laure detects a note of smugness in the *Canadienne*. She is too tired to tell Madame Tardif that she doesn't want to know, that she has no desire to hear any bad news. That if Madame Rouillard, her trusted midwife, thought it could wait, then surely it can.

But the words are out of Madame Tardif's mouth before Laure can utter her protest.

"Your husband is dead."

For a brief moment, Laure is unsure who Madame Tardif is talking about. In a flash, she imagines that Deskaheh and Mathurin were engaged in a battle and that one of them has died. But which one? Mathurin has known all along about her relations with Deskaheh and now it has come to this. Perhaps they have both been killed and now Laure's secret is out. This baby, whom she already desires more than either of the men, will be wrenched from her chest.

"Mathurin fell through the ice and drowned on his way hurrying back to you and the child," Madame Tardif says. There is a note of accusation in her voice.

Laure feels relief even though her heart has already risen to her throat and is racing fast. Her secret is still safe. Mathurin, her pink pig fool of a husband, simply lost his footing and slid beneath the water, a greedy fur trader consumed by the cruel indifference of the landscape. But what face must Laure show to this woman, her shrewd neighbour? What new lie needs to be told? Surely Laure should appear sad, shocked, grieving. Mathurin is dead. But Laure is not really surprised. She has known all along that he would be swallowed whole by the force of her disdain.

"Our men are so brave," Madame Tardif says. "We are fortunate that they take such good care of us. We are safe here at the settlement while they risk their lives in the woods among Savage nations. Your husband had gone to winter with the Cheveux-Relevés along the Outaouais with some other men from here. They travelled further west than usual and had a good year acquiring plenty of pelts. But your husband left early, to get back to you of course. He travelled with some Savages, probably paid them in goods to take him across the dangerous terrain. But the ice was already beginning to thaw. You are now a widow." Madame Tardif utters the last word like it is bitter on her tongue.

All of Laure's past losses come flooding back to her. Gone are the protective arms of her father, the kindness and instruction of Madame d'Aulnay and Madame du Clos, Madeleine's friendship and prayers. How much more abandonment will she know? Only madwomen know the freedom that loneliness brings, what it means to let your life flow into and become one with the sea. Madame Tardif, with her husband returned from the fur country and her solid cabin filled with children, thinks she will escape her own drowning.

Madame Tardif casts her eye around the room. The expression on her face clearly shows that she thinks Laure is responsible for the squalor. If only she had been an industrious, practical wife, like Madame Tardif, Laure might also have some good pieces of wooden furniture by now, some iron pots and utensils in the kitchen, food supplies on the shelf, a warmer hearth. Of course Laure's husband would be alive as well.

"Well, you really don't have very much here. But whatever belongings you have, we will bring them to our place when you come with the baby." Madame Tardif is peering into each of the dark corners of the room, searching for anything of value. She runs her hand over the gun on the shelf and kneels before a pile of mangy pelts.

But when she goes to raise the lid on the chest from the Salpêtrière, Laure cries out with such force that Madame Tardif withdraws her hand as if burned. For inside the wooden box is all that Laure has preserved of herself. These things she will offer her daughter. The chest contains the physical reminders of Laure's life that will take the place of her mothering arms: Madeleine's prayer book, Mireille's yellow dress, and the letters Laure wrote to the ghost of her friend. Of course there may not be anyone among the Algonquins to teach the child to read, and the dress might be cut and refashioned into Savage garments, the letters used to start a fire, but these things are all that Laure can think to give.

"That belongs to me, from before I met Mathurin."

Madame Tardif raises an eyebrow. "We will bring this with the other things to my place tomorrow."

When Laure finds her voice it is lower, a growl. For has she not already become a beast, a demon? What is there in this life to make her human? She curses the home of the cruel, insipid woman standing before her. "I would rather be put in prison than to live with you."

Madame Tardif crosses her arms over her chest. "Don't be ridiculous," she says, but she takes a step back, away from Laure and the baby. "You will feel differently tomorrow."

But Laure knows that once she has given away her baby, she will have no use for this woman.

❦

As promised, Madame Rouillard returns to see Laure two days later. It is night. Laure just about throws herself into the midwife's arms when she enters the cabin.

"What is the matter?" she asks. "Is the baby thriving?"

"Yes, we are both fine, but Madame Tardif is trying to get us to move to her place."

Madame Rouillard nods. "Yes, I figured that would happen. I am sorry that I couldn't stay with you to keep her away, but it seems that every pregnant woman west of the sea has decided to have her baby this week. That is the way it is at certain times."

Madame Rouillard sometimes speaks of the particular beliefs and skills of her trade when she is with Laure. She was trained at the Hôtel-Dieu in Paris, the very place where Mireille died, under the tutelage of the famous midwife Louise Bourgeoys. There they studied drawings of the internal anatomy of a pregnant woman's body and learned the ways to quicken labour, to slow it, to deliver breech babies, to remove babies from their mother's wombs without severing limbs or causing hemorrhaging.

But today Madame Rouillard tells Laure how she also learned from priests how to administer the sacrament of baptism. That is what she has come to do today. Midwives are the only women Laure knows who are capable of officiating at a Catholic sacrament. Of course a midwife is only to baptize a child if it is expected to die. Laure's baby is not about to die. She is large, hungry, and has bright, alert eyes. When she entered the world, her cry travelled beyond the walls of the tiny cabin. Still, Madame Rouillard wants to perform the ceremony.

"A soul is an important thing to save. I have even on occasion baptized babies whose bodies were dead, impossible to save."

Although only living babies are meant to be baptized, it is known that parents and priests implore the saints and especially the Virgin Mary to return life to a dead child for a brief moment so that the sacrament can be administered. For many believe that an unbaptized child is a wandering ghost caught between the golden gates of heaven and the eternal fires of hell. Laure is relieved that Madame Rouillard wishes to administer the sacrament on her child.

First the midwife covers the table in a white cloth that looks like it belongs on a church altar. Then she removes from her bag a candle, which she lights, a wooden cross, and two vials, one which contains holy water, which she says comes from Venice, and the other oil. Madame Rouillard then fills a pewter bowl with some of the water she obtained from Madame Tardif on the night of the birth. She sprinkles a few drops of the holy water into the bowl as well.

Laure wraps the baby in white linen. She is relieved to be able to do this one thing for the child whose future is so uncertain. She will be raised in the forest by Savages. Who will teach her to be a Christian, to pray to Jesus and Mary and the angels and saints? Perhaps this one ritual, the blessing of the women who brought her into the world safe and healthy and strong, will be enough to make up for a lifetime of absence. Perhaps because of this one brief ceremony, the Holy Spirit, who is said to enter the souls of babies on their baptism day, will protect her daughter for the rest of her days. The unfortunate creature has no godparents to protect her on earth.

"What name have you chosen for her?" Madame Rouillard, who is so many things, has now taken on the voice of a priest.

"I would like to call her Luce." The name came to Laure as she lay last night between sleep and wakefulness in the darkness of the cabin. The name is Latin for light. The darkness that had threatened to envelop Laure so many times had been somewhat brightened when she held the tiny child against her chest these past nights. The soft form of her baby gave off a glow as strong and constant as the presence of the moon or the stars in the night sky. Besides, Madeleine had loved Sainte Luce. She had been a girl tortured to death in Syracuse during Roman times for refusing to give up her vow of perpetual virginity in the face of an eager suitor. It is fitting that on the feast day of Sainte Luce in December, the winter days begin to grow light again.

Madame Rouillard nods at the choice of her name. She anoints the baby in oil and asks Laure to lower her head into the bowl of water. "There are no godparents, as such, so we will implore Sainte Luce and Mary to watch over this child when we take her to her new life tomorrow." Laure also invokes the spirit of Madeleine to watch over her daughter. Already she is being cared for by ghosts.

When the ceremony is ended, Madame Rouillard puts away the contents of her makeshift altar. When she sees that Laure is frightened, she says to her, "You know, Luce's life among the Savages may be filled with happiness. I have baptized her more as an added blessing than anything else. In Alsace, where I am from, there are those who believe that there is a special heaven for children and no such thing as children being thrown into hell." Laure is grateful for Madame Rouillard's words. For why should her daughter be punished for sins committed by her mother?

Madame Rouillard is already gathering Laure's coat and the bag of keepsakes for the baby and placing moccasins on the floor in front of her. They must leave now if they are to make it back by morning.

By the time the sun rises in Pointe-aux-Trembles, Laure's baby will be dead. At least that is what they will tell Madame Tardif and the others. Madame Rouillard has promised to take

Laure with her to her inn in Ville-Marie. There she will help run the tavern, or assist Madame Rouillard with nearby births while she waits to be married again. Mathurin's cabin will be left, to be used up by the snow and rain, to be torn down for material, or to be inhabited by another young couple who will try their fortune in the settlement.

Laure dresses Luce in layers of clothing, taking care to be delicate with her tiny limbs. Then she takes the linen from the baptism and asks Madame Rouillard to use it to tie the baby to her chest. Laure implores any spirit who might be watching over this cabin tonight to forgive her for what she is about to do.

23

Madame Rouillard is practical and quick. She is placing the things Madame Tardif had deemed valuable from the cabin, the half-rotted pelts, the gun, a cooking pot, a few utensils, and Laure's chest, all together in a hasty pile in a corner of the room. She says they can return for these things once the baby is gone. "Best if we get going," she says, in a voice that is both gentle and firm.

When Laure holds the baby she once again recalls the tenderness she felt as a child for her father, who sang gentle songs to her in the Paris nights, the adoration she had for her kind old mistress Madame d'Aulnay, the ties of friendship she had with her friend Madeleine. But all of these feelings are as diluted as the Salpêtrière broth compared to how Laure feels for this new being. Even the summer nights she spent with Deskaheh seem sullied and violent in comparison to this new tenderness. The baby Luce is pure, still untouched by any of life's dirty stories.

Laure knows she cannot keep her baby. Madame Rouillard has told her so. It is the only way to save them both. But how can a mother hold her child for the last time? How can Laure tell her breasts to stop their libations? How can she dam up a body that has become liquid? What she is about to do has opened up all the wounds she has ever known. There is a deep and baffling emptiness within her gut.

When Laure was a child she saw a mother cat in the front of Madame d'Aulnay's apartment searching every crevice in plaintive tones for her kittens, all drowned. She wishes she could make that sound now.

It is a late-spring night. The earth is damp, even wet in parts. It is cold. The nights are always cold in this country, even in the summer when the days blaze hot. Laure would never dream of walking outside, along the trails beside the river in the dark. But Madame Rouillard is there up ahead, guiding the way with her torch and her sure feet. This was her idea, after all. Laure owes her life to this woman, but it is hard to muster any gratitude for the gift.

Laure sings to the baby tied tightly to her chest as they set out into the forest. She is desperate to give Luce the love she felt as a child from her father when he swung her high above his head while they hid from the police in the dirty alleys of Paris. But there is no artefact of her father's existence that Laure can pass on to her daughter. She has only fragments of the words of his songs, made indelible on her eight-year-old mind, filtered through the years that have passed since then. The words disperse through the chilly air, as insignificant in the forest expanse as the *Te Deum* she heard when she first arrived in Ville-Marie. Madame Rouillard places her hand on Laure's arm, calling for silence.

They enter the forest and the settlement is behind them. By morning Laure will be a childless widow in Pointe-aux-Trembles. The endless trees of Canada are swallowing all traces of her life.

After several hours of walking, the women reach the spot where they are to meet Deskaheh. It is a clearing on the forest path, a break in the trees. Traders frequently stop here to light a fire, to eat, to rest on their westward journeys to Ville-Marie and beyond.

Deskaheh is already there, sitting on one of the rocks beside the river. He has brought with him an Algonquin woman. Laure is grateful that it is not the pregnant Savage girl she saw last summer, but a slightly older woman with an unyielding, intelligent face. Madame Rouillard lowers her head and frowns as she appraises this woman. Deskaheh does not look at Laure and the baby, but greets Madame Rouillard in a subdued tone.

There isn't much to say in the way of small talk. Only Deskaheh knows how to speak both languages, but he remains quiet. It is important that they act quickly. French children have been kidnapped by Savages before. A few have even grown up among them and can no longer be fully trusted because of it. But Laure has never heard of a woman giving away her baby in this manner. Surely the Governor, and the King and his advisors, would rather she drowned Luce in the river than hand her, strong and healthy, to these people, even if they are allies and some have even learned to pray to the Christian God in their own way.

The Algonquin woman is the first to break the silence and begins to ask Deskaheh some questions about Laure, which he answers in a whisper. Seeming unimpressed by what the young man has to say, she walks over to Laure and circles around her. She rubs Laure's neck-length mess of hair between her fingers, looking disgusted all the while. But she seems satisfied with the width of Laure's shoulders and her straight spine. Laure's face she examines by placing her hands on each cheek. She pushes Laure's lip up to see her teeth. Laure holds the baby to her chest while the woman examines her.

When she has finished, she turns back to Deskaheh and says something to him in their language. Laure imagines the woman is telling him that he has created a child with a beast, a filthy and ugly creature. The Savage women mock the French women who are prisoners in their homes, giving birth to a dozen babies, isolated from the other settlers. The French authorities cannot understand why the Savage men must first confer with the women of their villages before they fight a battle, trade furs, or discuss the Christian religion.

Of course Laure doesn't even know what Deskaheh has recounted to this woman about the origins of the child. Perhaps he has said nothing to her about being the father. Maybe he doesn't even believe it himself. It is Madame Rouillard who has sought out Deskaheh through her contacts in Ville-Marie, who somehow persuaded him to come and get the child and to raise it among his people. "Don't worry," the midwife says now. "Luce will fit among the others. Babies are valued more than gold by the Savages. They tell me often that they love all children, not only those they give birth to."

Laure emits a sound between a snarl and a whimper when the woman indicates that she wants to take Luce from her arms. She has known that this moment was coming. Still, she could not be prepared. Laure's agony is sharper than any she has known. Not losing her father, not even Madeleine's death, could prepare her for this. Only a Jesuit priest about to have his heart ripped from his chest could understand how she feels.

Madame Rouillard unties the knot at Laure's back. The tie loosens and Laure takes the freed baby in her arms. Madame Rouillard steadies her as Laure extends the child to the woman, who waits with greedy curiosity. The Algonquin woman first looks at the baby, strips the blanket from her, holds her up to the moonlight, and gestures for Madame Rouillard to bring the torch closer. The Savage woman is dealing with the acquisition of the baby the way she would trade for beads or pots with the French. What kind of life will Luce have with these people?

It takes all of Laure's strength to keep from rushing over and covering the baby in the blanket. But she is powerless to protect the child from the cold or from any other unpleasant feelings the future holds. The infant wails and Laure's chest contracts. Deskaheh's eyes are tender when he looks at Laure, and even though he is powerless to prevent this older woman from poking and prodding at the child, he tries gently to get her to stop by walking over and touching the baby himself. He looks at Laure with the same eyes he did at Madeleine's funeral. She wraps her arms around her chest. There is no prayer, not even an animal scream, worth uttering. If God cannot stop this from happening, then who will emerge from the forest to help her?

The baby is crying loudly, which seems to please the woman, who nods her head at them, shifting her eyes over to Madame Rouillard, whom she obviously takes to be in charge of this exchange. She looks into the bag they have brought, taking out the book and the scrolls of paper. Then she tosses the objects back inside, hands the bag to Deskaheh, and returns to checking the baby. When the strange woman opens her jacket and places Luce on her breast, the baby stops crying. It is her first taste of the milk of her new family. Laure turns away.

Deskaheh says, "She wonders what you want in return. For the baby."

Laure has not expected this question. He is asking them what price they should pay for her daughter. She cannot say a word, such is her grief.

Madame Rouillard, who has told Laure that she is accustomed to babies entering and leaving the world in far worse situations than this one, is willing to bargain. She has seen the protective eyes of the father and assures Laure once again that this option is the only one they have. She tells Deskaheh that they want two pelts, one of fox, the other mink, and some tobacco as well, just as they agreed. Madame Rouillard tells Laure that she will give Laure these items when they leave. They will be the beginning of her new life.

New life? The words seem impossible.

Will Laure add this exchange, giving away her daughter, to her collection of losses and carry on?

Madame Rouillard nods. Yes, it will be possible. Tomorrow will dull even this agony.

Laure is a stone goddess carved by saltwater tears. She is a woman who has managed to cross the ocean without drowning. She has risen from the depths, intact, on new shores. When so many have not, when she has not even really wanted to, she has somehow survived. A living artefact of the absurd dreams of royal men who tear starving girls from their hospital beds and drop them in the frozen woods. Laure's body is the scroll upon which they write their plans: ten thousand people by 1680 and thousands more after that. The King is offering rewards to the husbands of women who give birth to ten, twelve children and more. More babies will be born here than anywhere else on earth. The villages will grow like cornstalks along the riverbank. The Savages, even the Iroquois, will kneel at the altar of the dozens of churches they will erect in this new world. The ships back to France will be filled with furs and tales of a prosperous new country. So much becomes possible now that French children are being born and raised in a country that for centuries did nothing but starve and mutilate the priests and traders that came down the river.

Except that Laure's daughter, the one being held up to the light of the moon, is not the one they want. She is worth less than a wolf skin. This baby brands Laure as a transgressor, a woman who spits in the face of the King's dreams. She is the one the sailors fear. The one they burn as a witch for fornicating with a Savage enemy, for killing her husband, for giving away her own flesh. Still, who can destroy her, when she is the one who guides the ships, when her gentle waves or foaming wrath decide who makes it to the other side? Whether the precious colony lives or dies.

Laure remains as long as she can, watching Deskaheh and the woman's swift retreat down the path. They walk close together, huddling over the baby between them. Finally, once the two are far up ahead, Laure and Madame Rouillard set out. They will go to Ville-Marie first. Madame Rouillard wants Laure to forget her life in Pointe-aux-Trembles. "You are still young," she says. "You still have time to settle."

Laure follows Madame Rouillard along the trail, her feet tripping on stones and stumps that were easy to avoid when Luce was pressed warm against her chest. The sun is rising behind them and they no longer need the torch to light the path. Laure wants to run ahead, to catch up with Deskaheh and the Algonquin woman, to take Luce back, or at least to see her one last time. But instead she comes up alongside the woman who delivered her of the baby, and will now take her to Ville-Marie. Together they will find a new suitor for Laure.

Soon Laure will be someone's wife, but for the moment she forgets about the river's shore and its burgeoning settlements. She remembers, instead, the place she came from. She lets herself return to the sea.

Historical Notes

The *filles du roi*, like most historical women, are largely figures of legend. Their story, at least its more legendary aspects, is very well known in French Canada. My impression as a child was that these founding mothers had been sent by Louis XIV, whom they had met at a grand send-off ball in Paris. When they disembarked in their elegant gowns at Québec, they would have been warmly welcomed. As the story went, in a feat of modest feminine heroics, they then went on to marry and have children with the brave pioneering men of the fur-trading rivers and forests. It wasn't until years later that I started to think again about these women sent from France to Canada. After having faced the challenges of living for several years in a foreign country myself and being half French Canadian, I wanted to know more about what the French counterparts of Susanna Moodie had really felt, arriving in Canada over a century before she wrote *Roughing It in the Bush*.

Between 1663 and 1673, approximately eight hundred women were sent from France to Canada to become the wives of men already in the colony, mostly fur traders and soldiers. But the historical record is sparse on details about the lives of the *filles du roi*. Most of what is known about them is contained in the comprehensive research of historian Yves Landry, based on marriage contracts and death certificates in Quebec's parish records. But to write a novel I needed to bring this demographic data to life. I wanted to know how the women got to Canada. Did they decide to go on their own? Were they forced onto the ships, as some historians have suggested? And most of all, what did they think of this new wilderness country and its inhabitants, both European and native, once they disembarked? Also, which of these women was going to be my protagonist? Surely each of them had a unique story worthy of being told.

Reading seventeenth-century accounts about the *filles du roi*, I realized that my childhood impressions of them as elegant ladies in ball gowns needed some revising. Marie de l'Incarnation, a seventeenth-century Ursuline nun in Québec, referred in her letters to the women sent from France as rude, troublemaking riff-raff. Of course the cloistered nun likely had very little interaction with the *filles du roi* and was probably commenting mostly on the appearance and low class of the women. Patricia Simpson, in her two-volume biography of Marguerite Bourgeoys, observes that this woman, herself a legend in French Canada, faced her own challenges as an uncloistered nun, and as such welcomed the *filles du roi*. She housed them at Ville-Marie upon their arrival, training them in the necessary housekeeping skills and presumably assisting with their matchmaking. It was also Marguerite Bourgeoys who gave the women the title of *filles du roi*. This had nothing to do with any royal connections, but was rather related to the seventeenth-century term *enfants du roi*, which referred to orphaned children being provided for from the king's coffer. The *filles du roi* were mostly poor, usually orphaned young women. But did they choose to come to Canada? Were they happy to leave behind their wretched conditions and sail across the Atlantic to find a husband as is commonly believed?

Historians, including Yves Landry, agree that at least one-third of the *filles du roi* came from the Salpêtrière in Paris. Michel Foucault considered the Salpêtrière to be one of the central institutions for the mass incarceration of the poor in Paris of the seventeenth century. Marthe Henry, a medical doctor writing in the 1920s, outlines the living conditions of the Salpêtrière: long work hours, a starvation diet, and days filled with Latin prayers and masses. Jean-Pierre Carrez's more recent work, *Femmes opprimées à la Salpêtrière de Paris (1656–1791)*, mentions women listed as thieves or prostitutes being sent to America, mostly to Louisiana, as a form of banishment. Although there are no surviving hospital records in France for the women sent to Canada, there is little reason to believe that their social status would have been much different. In France, the *filles du roi* would most likely have been women attempting to survive in desperate urban poverty, ending up at the Salpêtrière through petty crime or vagrancy and occasionally something more serious.

Off the beaten tourist track in Paris, you can still see the original structure of the Salpêtrière, a modern-day hospital, near the Gare d'Austerlitz. I visited the Salpêtrière several times during my stay in Paris. What a contrast it must have been to have this awesome stone structure with its magnificent dome chapel at the centre and thousands of impoverished women starving inside its walls. I was also struck by how it truly must have felt like taking a voyage into hell to leave behind Paris with its rituals, medicine, markets, horse-drawn carriages, and royalty to travel by night down the Seine with guards and to enter the hold of a wooden ship for a months-long journey across the sea. How there could have been any excitement or hope in such a dangerous and terrible venture is really beyond my imagining. I think we attribute a sense of heroism and purpose to our forebears because to really contemplate the challenges they faced, to think that maybe they didn't want to come at all and that they were miserable when they arrived, makes their lives seem unfair, even cruel.

The inspiration for my protagonist came from a brief biographical note in the records on Madeleine Fabrecque, a young woman who died, seemingly of exhaustion, shortly after reaching New France. I asked myself, Are these women valuable to us only as producers of a population? Did the choices they made and the unique contours of each of their lives matter? In the end, I decided to use a fictional, perhaps more mythological woman as the main character of my story. It was important that Laure survive, as most of the women in fact did, and that eventually she adjusted to life in the colony, although not necessarily as a wife and mother complicit in some grand design. Perhaps there were women among the *filles du roi* who were happy to "escape" the impoverished circumstances of their lives in France. Having the opportunity to marry, even a strange woodsman, would possibly have seemed like a once-in-a-lifetime opportunity. But through the character of Laure Beauséjour, I wanted to create a counterweight to this grand historical narrative of the *filles du roi* as founding mothers.

I would be proud to have Laure in my family tree, the sort of woman who thought about justice, who entertained possibilities—options—even when these were merely fantasy and served only to endanger her life. On some levels she is a selfish character, but how else in such circumstances, if not through wit and strength and even malice, could these women have survived and given birth to French North America?

Acknowledgments

This novel began as an M.A. thesis project at York University. I would like to thank my supervisors, Jane Couchman and Roberto Perin, and especially Susan Swan, who guided me to "stay light" and to find the creative in all the historical research I was undertaking. I am indebted to the valuable feedback and support of the group I met during the 2006 Humber School for Writers Summer Workshop: Hélène Montpetit, Rita Greer, Wayne Robbins, David Hughes, and Elizabeth Brooks. I am grateful to my mentor, Joseph Boyden, who provided encouragement and advised me to stick with the story for the "long haul."

I would like to thank my friend and agent, Samantha Haywood, whose enthusiasm for the novel spurred me on. At Penguin Canada, I would like to thank Nicole Winstanley, Sandra Tooze, Barbara Bower, and especially Adrienne Kerr for her brilliant insight, patience, and kind approach to editing, as well as freelance copy editor Shaun Oakey. I am indebted to staff at a number of archives in Toronto, Montreal, and Paris, with particular thanks owed to the archivists of the Assistance publique—Hôpitaux de Paris and to Patricia Simpson, who graciously met with me in the heart of a Montreal winter to discuss the life and times of Marguerite Bourgeoys.

For financial support during the researching and writing of the novel, I owe gratitude to the Social Sciences and Humanities Research Council of Canada, the Government of Ontario, York University, and the Humber School for Writers.

I am indebted to my family and friends who have indefatigably asked when this novel of mine was going to be available, especially my mom and dad, Joanne and Edmond Desrochers, who would have loved to see this story become a book, Joe and Cécile, Ross and Rose Dioso, and Cathy and Richard Nucci. I would like to extend a special thank-you to Anne and Dave Black, who first inspired me to seek out the history of French Canadians, who helped me to persevere in telling this story, and who provided some of my best critical feedback. But my greatest gratitude is due to my husband, Rod Dioso, whose love and encouragement have made my writing life possible.

Finally, I would like to thank Cynthia Varadan and Marlene Sagada at Toronto's Riverdale Community Midwives Clinic, for showing me what a woman can really do. Just three days after my manuscript was accepted for publication, I gave birth to a baby boy, who has filled my days ever since with endless inspiration, although very little time, for the telling of stories.

BRIDE OF
NEW FRANCE

Suzanne Desrochers

READING GROUP GUIDE

BRIDE OF NEW FRANCE

Suzanne Desrochers

AN INTERVIEW WITH SUZANNE DESROCHERS

Laure seems at times to be a dreamer, a rebel, and also a closed book. How do you see her character?

I see Laure as a slightly bitter young woman in the beginning. She felt shortchanged by her childhood and was not happy to be in the Salpêtrière. However, I think she comes to have a deeper understanding of human suffering as the novel wears on and she realizes that others have faced hardships as well.

Laure sees Madeleine as an angel figure. How did their friendship evolve over time?

These two characters complement each other. They represent on the one hand a steadfast engagement with the injustices of the world and on the other a strong focus on spiritual transcendence. Laure offers Madeleine a foothold on the earthly plane by talking about their future together as seamstresses and convincing her to board a ship for Canada, while Madeleine serves as a constant reminder to Laure that these aspirations are transient and that she must look deeper to find an inner peace.

Laure is desperate to pass something on to baby Luce. How do you view the links between material possessions, family history, and identity?

Laure has no material possession to help her recall her father, but instead clings to a few fading lyrics of a song he used to sing to her. She has little more than that to give her daughter, and Luce's only memory of her mother will be buried deep in her subconscious, since they were separated in the immediate postpartum period. These relationships and memories are in many ways a metaphor for doing research on marginalized groups who have not left behind a significant paper record. The depth of their feelings and the value of their lives are no less than those of their wealthier counterparts, but we need to rely on more intuitive tools to uncover their traces on the landscape.

Was this book equal parts historical research and creative fiction? How long did it take to finish?

Yes, I suppose it is part fact, based on the historical record, and part intuitive knowledge, which I suppose is what defines writing as "creative." It took about five years to research and write the novel. During that time I worked simultaneously on digging through the archives and learning the dates, the historical figures, and the factual details while imagining and writing the story.

Racism is woven deeply into the story and its characters as a subplot. Can you discuss the slave boat and the relationship between the colonists and the native people?

Colonialism was based on the premise of cultural superiority. Europeans used the people and the land they encountered to attempt to extract resources for material gain. Religion and social structures were imposed on the societies they encountered. These are the very foundations of contemporary Canadian society. We still study history, for the most part, as if the upper-class (mostly male) European players had it right, and we continue to replicate and live by the institutions they established.

Very few people saw anything wrong with colonialism during the period that I studied. In the novel, Laure observes the slave boat but does not have any strong sense of injustice toward what is happening onboard. She feels attracted to Deskaheh despite herself and views him through racist eyes even though he is her lover. But I think that because Laure has also been at least partly victimized by colonialism, she is more able to sympathize or at the very least to notice it is happening.

The history of the filles du roi *is fascinating and quite surprising. Did similar policies exist in what is now the United States?*

The concept of sending women from Paris to New France (Canada)—and also to Louisiana, as depicted in Abbé Prévost's *Manon Lescaut*—had an earlier parallel in England. Women were sent at the start of the seventeenth century from London's prisons and poorhouses to America. When colonial demand for women, either as wives or as laborers, needed to be met, colony administrators turned to urban institutions such as the Salpêtrière in Paris and Newgate Prison and the Bridewell in London. In particular, women were sent to Virginia to labor in the tobacco fields. Many of them perished. For the most part, the "New World" was not a popular destination for seventeenth-century Europeans.

Near the end of the novel (page 283), you write, "The endless trees of Canada are swallowing all traces of [Laure's] life." Can you explain this? Do you see this as a positive turn of events for Laure?

Only in the sense that there is a certain degree of freedom when your life becomes a tabula rasa. However, at that particular moment, when Laure is experiencing the beginning of her marriage to a man she is repulsed by, in the middle of a forest already turning colder than anything she has ever felt, her feeling is one of deep despair.

Why did you choose the ending you did?

So much historical emphasis on the *filles du roi* has centered on their collective reproductive achievement—that is, giving birth to a new nation. I wanted to explore the value and historical contribution of these women from within the contours of an individual life. There surely would not have been any reward for women who transgressed beyond the boundaries that were laid out for them by royal authority. Laure had to suffer tremendously for her rebellious nature.

Were you thinking about the concept of destiny when writing this novel? If so, how did it alter the plot lines?

I think for the France component I thought more about

destiny in terms of how Laure's life was being controlled and negotiated by hospital and royal authorities. However, once she reaches the New World, where many of these social structures are less rigidly adhered to, she begins to experience a more spiritual destiny. Her life choices are not easier in Canada, but the possibilities for her future become vastly open.

Can you tell us what you are writing now?
I am in the process of completing a PhD thesis at the University of London that compares the migration of French and English women to North America in the seventeenth century. However, I also have a few ideas brewing for a new novel that focuses on what happens to Deskaheh, Luce, and Laure as the French overpower the Iroquois in the succeeding decades.

DISCUSSION QUESTIONS

1. Laure's disdain for Mireille is so deep, she won't even speak to her. Why? Discuss how Mireille's life and death affected Laure's own character.

2. When Laure learns of Madeleine's childhood problems, she thinks that "so many times [she] had thought Madeleine would not be so kind and soft-spoken to everyone if she had encountered misfortune. But could it be that her devotion and simple, gentle heart were formed out of the suffering of her childhood?" (page 111). Do you feel that compassion is borne of suffering? Was this true for Laure? Does this tie into Laure's relationship with gratitude?

3. Discuss Madame Bourdon's comment, "Canada is obviously no place for women." Do you agree?

4. Do you see Mathurin as weak and cowardly? If so, why? If not, how do you see him?

5. Laure makes reference to herself as a madwoman at several points

in the story. Do you believe this to be true? How did you perceive her mental state as the story progressed?

6. Laure and Deskaheh both long to go "home." In what other ways are they similar?

7. How does the concept of destiny affect the story's plotline?

SELECTED NORTON BOOKS WITH READING GROUP GUIDES AVAILABLE

For a complete list of Norton's works with reading group guides, please go to www.wwnorton.com/books/reading-guides.

Diana Abu-Jaber	*Birds of Paradise*
Diane Ackerman	*One Hundred Names for Love*
Alice Albinia	*Leela's Book*
Andrea Barrett	*Ship Fever*
Bonnie Jo Campbell	*Once Upon a River*
Lan Samantha Chang	*Inheritance*
Anne Cherian	*A Good Indian Wife*
Amanda Coe	*What They Do in the Dark*
Michael Cox	*The Meaning of Night*
Jared Diamond	*Guns, Germs, and Steel*
Andre Dubus III	*Townie*
John Dufresne	*Requiem, Mass.*
Anne Enright	*The Forgotten Waltz*
Jennifer Cody Epstein	*The Painter from Shanghai*
Betty Friedan	*The Feminine Mystique*
Stephen Greenblatt	*The Swerve*
Lawrence Hill	*Someone Knows My Name*
Ann Hood	*The Red Thread*
Dara Horn	*All Other Nights*
Pam Houston	*Contents May Have Shifted*
Mette Jakobsen	*The Vanishing Act**
N. M. Kelby	*White Truffles in Winter*
Nicole Krauss	*The History of Love**
Scott Lasser	*Say Nice Things About Detroit*
Don Lee	*The Collective**
Maaza Mengiste	*Beneath the Lion's Gaze*
Daniyal Mueenuddin	*In Other Rooms, Other Wonders*
Liz Moore	*Heft*
Jean Rhys	*Wide Sargasso Sea*
Mary Roach	*Packing for Mars*
Johanna Skibsrud	*The Sentimentalists*
Jessica Shattuck	*Perfect Life*
Joan Silber	*The Size of the World*
Mary Helen Stefaniak	*The Cailiffs of Baghdad, Georgia*

Manil Suri   *The Age of Shiva*
Brady Udall   *The Lonely Polygamist*
Barry Unsworth   *Sacred Hunger*
Alexei Zentner   *Touch*

*Available only on the Norton Web site